A Personal Bounty

Markus Matthews

Tellwell Talent
www.tellwell.ca

ISBN
978-0-2288-1727-7 (Hardcover)
978-0-2288-1726-0 (Paperback)
978-0-2288-1728-4 (eBook)

To my mom for being a great role model, and to my dad, for teaching me that you need to take risks...

Chapter 1

Tuesday, April 29

The panicked chorus of *BAA*s pulled my attention away from the darkened woods I'd been intently staring at. I sighed and used my Air powers to lift my Werepanther companion back to us and away from the flock of sheep she had been creeping towards. Bree let out a soft surprised growl as she floated back to us.

I placed her sleek, muscular form down on the ground and gave her a disapproving look. She glanced up at me with her ice blue cat's eyes and then lowered her furry head in shame. A low growl, which meant *sorry*, followed. Bree could only growl in her beast forms, but through different tones, volume, and body language she could make her meaning clear. I shook my head. "You should be sorry; you are supposed to be the responsible one. We are here on a job and not so you can grab a snack! Focus—the Hellhound could be here at any moment!"

The lethal 300-pound panther beside me bobbed her head and turned her attention to the woods to the east again. That lasted for about five seconds before she turned her head towards the cowering sheep, her pink tongue hanging out in anticipation. I cleared my throat and Bree turned her attention back to the woods again.

"Damn it!" cursed Olivia, off to my left. "You so owe me a pair of shoes when this job is done! I keep stepping in sheep shit!"

"Then stop moving around. We are at a stakeout not a dance."

"Whatever. This is boring. We've been here like forever. Is this stupid Hell puppy going to show up soon?"

I ignored her question for the moment but could sympathize with her frustration. It was a mild spring night, but I was baking in the black knit balaclava I had on. It was a holdover from my hero days that I had used to protect my civilian identity. On nights like this one, I wondered why I bothered. I'd been bounty hunting now for over six years, and my hero days were long gone. On the other hand, I still was registered as a retired hero, and there were a lot of people out there from my Hamilton

Hurricane days who would like some payback. Maybe getting a bit hot and sweaty at times was worth it.

My discomfort might also have had something to do with the slight hangover I was nursing. Last night we'd had a team party with multiple bottles of champagne, celebrating the millions from the demon bounty that had just been deposited in our business bank account. That takedown had been one of the toughest of my career. It took us working with an oversized GRC13 team to bring down the demon. Fighting beside this country's premier Enhanced Individual Response team certainly had been a learning experience.

Stella and Blue stayed for a glass but then did the smart thing and headed up to bed, as they were off to an inventor's convention in Las Vegas in the morning. I stayed up and matched Liv and Bree glass for glass for a good chunk of the night. Trying to keep pace with a vampire and Were, both of whom had insanely high alcohol tolerances, was a very bad idea.

I glanced at my phone and worked out that we'd been in this field for less than an hour. To be fair, it was more like two hours, as it had taken an hour to drive out here. I was about to argue that with Liv, but I noticed Bree had started wandering back towards the sheep. "Bree!"

She growled unhappily at me but returned to her place on my right. I swear between the hungry Werepanther and the bored vampire, this was less bounty hunting and more like babysitting. The babysitting part brought up another concern, and I looked up at the sky. I was relieved to see Alteea's tiny rainbow aura doing leisurely circles above us. At least one of my three teammates was doing what she was supposed to be doing. It frightened me that the flighty pixie was the only one doing her job.

When Walter, my wizard friend, called me this afternoon and begged me to take this job, I figured it would be easy money. I would have preferred to do this with a full team though. With Blue's shadow-traveling ability, I could have had her and Stella here in an instant, but they both had been so excited about their trip to Vegas that I didn't have the heart to make them come with us. Hellhounds were dangerous, but Bree in her Werepanther form should be more than a match for it. Add in a vampire with a silver-edged sword and my Air elemental powers, and we should have more than enough firepower to take this thing down.

The job had seemed pretty sweet—well, other than having to stand around for hours in a smelly field waiting for the Hellhound to strike. The bounty was posted today and listed the reward as $10,000 US. The best part was we were double dipping. Walter needed belly scales from a Hellhound for a spell he was working on and would pay us $20,000 Canadian in cash for them. He also promised he'd owe me one. Between the extra cash and the favor, I accepted the job. I should have done more research though, as Walter had pulled one over on me. The lowest price I could find online for Hellhound belly scales was $30,000 US, so at the price he was paying, he was getting a heck of a deal. The bounty though, and him owing me a favor, took the sting out of it. Never trust wizards and mages—they were as tricky as fae to deal with.

Olivia spoke, pulling me from my thoughts. "Why don't we go out hunting for it?"

I was about to answer when I noted Bree was halfway to the sheep again. I pointed at Liv and said, "Your new job is keeping Bree from the sheep—go!"

Liv nodded. She took one step forward, made a face, lifted her sneaker, and cursed as she saw that she'd stepped in more sheep droppings. "I'm soooo burning these when we get home."

Before I could make a smartass comment, she blurred off using her vampire speed. I turned my attention back to the woods.

Despite Walter getting the better of me and the hangover, I was excited about this job. I'd never seen a Hellhound before, and the lore geek in me was pumped for the chance. I'd read about them and knew their capabilities. They weighed between 250 and 300 pounds and sort of looked like a large German Shepherd, except that they were covered in black scales, had glowing red eyes, razor-sharp claws and a mouthful of shark-like teeth. They weren't any smarter than an average dog, but there were three things that made them dangerous. First, they had glamor that made them invisible to the human eye. They only dropped that glamor just before they attacked or during an attack. Second, they were aggressive and mean. They preyed on livestock, but if a human interrupted, or if they were hungry enough, they'd happily go after a person instead. And finally, they healed quickly; not quite as fast as

3

Weres, but not far off. So, if you took a shot at them and didn't put the round in the center of the head or heart, you'd have a pissed off Hellhound coming for you.

Olivia returned with a growling Bree in tow and asked, "How do we know this thing is even going to show up?"

"We don't, but it has hit this field for a sheep three nights in a row. We just need to hope that pattern continues…"

Olivia frowned and was about to add something when Bree began moving closer to the sheep again. Liv blurred around her friend and intercepted her. She gave Bree a disapproving look. Bree let out a defeated growl and turned back towards me.

The moment Olivia and Bree returned, Liv said, "So, we could be standing out in this field all night for nothing?"

"Welcome to the glamorous world of bounty hunting…"

Liv was about to say something more, but Bree had started wandering off again, and she chased after her. I shook my head and smiled. *Nobody is going to mistake our team for Seal Team Six, that's for damn sure!*

My thoughts drifted back to the Hellhound and the bounty. Hellhounds were rare, and if the owner of the property hadn't caught pictures of it last night on the wireless cameras he'd put up to find out what was poaching his sheep, I wouldn't have believed it. Thankfully, that same owner was smart, and when he saw pictures of the creature on his computer screen, he called the cops. The owner was also a fan of mine from my hero days as the Hamilton Hurricane. He was overjoyed when I called him today to get permission to hunt this thing on his property and instantly agreed. Even better, he said that my team and I would be the only ones he would allow on his property for the next forty-eight hours. That meant we'd have an edge over any other bounty hunters going after this thing.

If the Hellhound would just show up, we were in pretty good shape to take it down. My ability to see the auras of any Enhanced Individual or supernatural creature and Alteea's fae ability to see through glamor meant that two out of the four of us would be able to see it. Liv and Bree with their enhanced senses would be able to track it by scent without issue as well.

Liv returned smiling with a growling Bree and said, "I thought with your lack of social life that I'd have to keep *you* away from the sheep more than Bree..."

I flipped her the bird and was about to send a verbal jab back at her when a small fireball lit up the night sky. It shot east towards the woods. This was our prearranged signal. When Alteea spotted the Hellhound, she would launch a fireball in its direction.

"Showtime! Let's go make some money!" I said.

"Finally!" exclaimed Liv as she drew her sword.

Bree growled excitedly in agreement.

I spotted a black, red, and purple aura leap over the fence between the woods and the field. It went for the nearest sheep like a guided missile. A few seconds later, it appeared in all its black-scaled glory as it took down the sheep.

Bree's eyes locked on to her prey, and she bounded off at top speed, heading directly for it. Liv started to blur after her friend but after a couple of steps, she let out a startled cry. Her feet went out from under her as she found yet another pile of sheep droppings, and she landed hard on her ass.

I snickered when she glared at me and yelled, "You now owe me a new pair of pants as well!"

I called my Air power to me and used it to lift myself into the air. I flew after Bree and started building up a charge for a lightning strike.

A series of angry growls erupted in the silent night as Bree's Werepanther form collided with the Hellhound. The two dark beasts rolled across the grassy pasture in a lethal embrace of snapping teeth and claws. Blood, fur, and scales flew as the two of them savagely went at one another. The bites and slashes were happening so quickly that I had trouble seeing who was winning.

The Hellhound let out a yelp of pain and sprang away from Bree. It bolted back towards the woods, and Bree shot after it. The Hellhound had engaged its glamor again, but it was a waste. Bree now had its scent and that visual camouflage wouldn't save it now.

I lashed out and sent a powerful blast of lightning at the fleeing Hellhound's aura. A split second before the lightning hit, it leapt up and over the fence, taking it out of the blast area.

I cursed at myself for missing. Not a moment later, Liv blurred under me and yelled, "Nice shooting, Zack. That grass won't be attacking anyone again!"

She laughed as she nimbly jumped the fence and disappeared into the woods in pursuit. Bree was just behind her and let out an amused growl at her friend's comment.

I rolled my eyes at them. While the trees were just starting to bud, the shear density of them would make it next to impossible to track the beast from the air, so I landed on the other side of the wire fence. I thickened the air around me as a precaution, in case the Hellhound doubled back and tried to attack me, and ran into the woods after my companions.

"Your sheep stealing days are over..." yelled Liv up ahead. Not a second later, she cursed loudly. As I closed in on her, I spotted her trying to remove her katana from the trunk of the walnut tree she'd wedged it into.

As I ran by her, I said, "The bounty is for a Hellhound, not a tree."

She flipped me the bird and then went back to trying to pull the blade from the trunk.

I laughed but kept my eyes locked on Bree's purple, red, and black aura as she darted between the trees, chasing after the fleeing Hellhound.

Bree went airborne for a moment as she pounced on the Hellhound. She crashed down on it and knocked it off its feet. Her momentum though had shot her past the prone Hellhound before she could latch on.

Before Bree could right herself, the hound jumped to its feet and came streaking back towards me.

Seeing 300 pounds of Hell's fury, with wicked teeth and claws charging straight for me, had my sphincter tightening so hard that it was up around my bellybutton at this point.

I jerked to a halt, raised my hands, and released another blast of lightning that briefly lit up darkened woods like daylight. To my relief, this time my aim was true. The hell beast let out a high-pitched yelp, shook like it was having a seizure, and slid in a heap towards me. It stopped a few feet from me with its mouth wide open, displaying its rows of deadly shark-like teeth.

Liv blurred by me, and a moment later, used her sword to separate the Hellhound's head from the rest of its body. Black blood spurted out for a moment and then began pooling on the forest floor in front of me.

She raised her sword and posed proudly for about half a second before her face bunched up and she gagged. "OH MY GOD! That stinks!"

On reflex I inhaled and wished I hadn't as the stench of sulfur, outhouse, and road tar hit me. I stepped back and tried to get upwind. I studied the decapitated hound for a few moments and was impressed at how lethal it looked, but the smell certainly was taking some of the joy out of scratching another exotic creature off my bucket list.

Liv darted over to me and said, "At least it's dead and I don't have to be near it…"

"Yeah, um, about that…" I said. Liv shot me a look and I added, "I need you to use your katana to cut off the belly for the scales Walter wants."

She planted her katana blade-first in the ground, crossed her arms, and said, "Nope. There's my sword, you can do it. I killed it, so I shouldn't have to skin it too."

"Technically, I killed it with the lightning, and you just beheaded it—" I was about to argue more but Bree came crashing out of the woods and stopped for a moment in front of us.

She looked down at the dead Hellhound, gave a nod of her furry head, and then took off back towards the sheep.

"Shit!" I said. "Liv, do this. Your share is $4,000 in cash. Think about how many shoes you can buy…"

She sighed, cursed, and picked up the katana.

"I'm going after Bree so she doesn't eat our bounty in sheep," I said.

I used my Air power to carefully lift myself between the budding tree branches and into the air. Once I was clear of the trees, I poured on the speed and flew back towards the field.

I was relieved to find my Werepanther chowing down on the sheep that the Hellhound had killed. *Waste not, want not,* I thought.

I touched down a few feet in front of her. Bree contently looked up with a bloody mouthful of sheep and then went back to eating.

"Okay, you can have this one, but once you are done, join Liv, alright?"

I got a muffled growl, as she was muzzle deep in sheep, which meant "yeah, yeah" if my growl translation was right. I took to the air again and headed for Bree's Toyota 4Runner to fetch the cooler filled with ice that we'd brought along to preserve the scales.

Two minutes later, I was back in the woods with Liv. She'd carved off the section we needed. I opened the cooler, and she dumped the bloody skin in it.

Liv glanced down at her formerly white top and shook her head. "I'm adding this top to the list of clothes the company owes me as well."

I nodded and closed the lid of the cooler.

I was just about to pick it up and carry it to our truck when my phone buzzed. I pulled it out from my pocket and saw 'A. Quinn' on the display. It was Annette, my buddy Rob's wife. I smiled for a second as it was always great talking to Annette, but then I grew concerned. She was just over eight months pregnant. I was the backup to get her to hospital if she went into labor, and if she couldn't get ahold of Rob. Rob was a Hamilton police officer, so there were times he was hard to reach.

"Please tell me you aren't in labor?" I asked in a light tone.

My stomach knotted as I heard the slight desperate hitch in her voice, "No. Rob's been hurt. I'm at the General and he is in surgery…"

"What happened?"

"I don't know much. He was responding to a call. There was an explosion. He had injuries and burns to his head, arms, and chest and was unconscious when they brought him in."

"Okay, hang in there. I'll be there soon."

I ended the call.

With her vampire hearing, Liv had overheard the entire conversation. "Go, Zack. Bree and I can deal with this."

I nodded. "Thanks. After you get the cooler back to the car, you need to call EIRT—"

"Not my first rodeo… go, we've got this. Take Alteea with you." The confusion must have shown on my face as Liv added, "If the doctors aren't telling you anything, you can use her to sneak in and find out what is going on."

At least one of us was thinking clearly. Alteea, with her small size and the glamor that made her invisible, could get in just about anywhere.

8

"Thanks," I said as I called my Air power to me. I searched the sky, found Alteea's rainbow aura, and headed for it.

Alteea dropped her glamor as I got close and held up her mini iPhone, "I got all of the fight recorded like you asked, Master."

The mini iPhone was a bit of a sore point with me. Liv, a couple of weeks ago, had gone behind my back and contacted Walter. She had him cast a spell on a regular-sized iPhone to shrink it down to about an inch in size. When Liv gave it to Alteea, I didn't think much of it at the time, but when Walter's $20,000 bill arrived in my inbox, I had much stronger feelings about it.

Liv and I got into a heated discussion about it that night at dinner. She argued that Alteea was a member of our team, and a smaller, lighter phone allowed Alteea to carry out her role as scout better, adding that she'd be able to film all encounters to strengthen our bounty claims. She finished by pointing out that the smaller phone allowed Alteea to cover it with glamor, so it wouldn't be seen, which she wasn't able to do with a regular sized one. The rest of the team sided with Liv, and it was agreed that Walter's bill would be expensed through the company funds.

I didn't disagree with any of her points. My issue was getting an unexpected large bill from Walter. Also, if Liv had gone through me, I would have been able to haggle a bit with Walter on the price. But that was in the past, and Rob was my main concern now. "We'll look at it later. Hold on to my collar; we need to get back to town quickly."

"What's up, Master?"

"Rob's been hurt and is in surgery at Hamilton General Hospital."

She nodded and flew behind me. The moment she gripped my collar, I launched into the night sky and headed for Hamilton.

Chapter 2

Tuesday, April 29

I made it to Hamilton General Hospital in just under sixteen minutes, which was impressive considering it had taken an hour by car to get out to the farm. I found a quiet, darkened area off to the side and landed. I took off my black balaclava. I was relieved to see Alteea's aura hovering in front of me; at the speed we'd been traveling, I had serious worries that I might have lost her at some point during the trip.

We walked. Well, I walked and Alteea fluttered beside me through the main emergency doors a minute later.

I had no idea where Annette was, but thankfully, there was a huge police presence, so I just followed the ever-growing line of officers. I turned a corner and exhaled in relief when I spotted the blonde pregnant lady I'd been searching for. Annette was talking to Dave Collins, his tall, lanky frame contrasting against her average height and rounded pregnant form.

I was glad to see Dave. He'd been a Hamilton cop for over ten years now and I'd gotten to know him quite well from Rob's monthly poker games.

"Zack!" said Annette as she saw me.

I ran over to her and gave her a cautious hug, avoiding undue pressure on her belly. She almost yanked me off my feet as she hugged me fiercely in return. Dave gave me a sharp nod and wandered off to join the group of officers further down the hallway.

"Thank God you are here," murmured Annette as she sobbed into my shoulder. I held her and gently stroked her hair. I felt awkward. I wished I knew the right things to say at times like these. I forced down the million questions I had and just focused on being there for Annette.

After a bit, Annette broke the hug and said, "Sorry."

"Don't be. Let's sit down for a moment and you can tell me what happened, okay?"

She nodded and fished a pack of tissues from her purse as we found two empty chairs nearby. Annette wiped her eyes and nose and turned her attention to me and said, "I don't know much; I was told he and another officer were responding to an alarm at some place in the industrial area. There was an explosion and Rob was hurt…"

"What about the other officer?" I asked.

Annette's mournful expression instantly told me the answer, and she just shook her head. That explained why there were so many cops here. Rob was popular, but no one was popular enough for this show of support. An officer killed in the line of duty though would certainly bring this many cops out.

"Any details on Rob's injuries?"

"They told me he had burns, a broken arm, ribs, and a serious head injury. He wasn't conscious when they brought him in. They have called in the healer the department has on retainer…"

I smiled at this and said, "Rob will be fine. There are some first-class healers in this city. I'm sure they will be able to fix him up."

Annette smiled and squeezed my hand firmly.

A moment later, Annette's name was being called out by an older lady who was heading for us at a determined pace. I recognized her a moment later as Annette's mom. The last time I'd seen her was a few years ago at Rob and Annette's wedding.

Annette looked up and said, "Mom!"

I got up and was about to help Annette to her feet when Helen said, "Don't get up."

Helen took over the seat I was in and wrapped her daughter in a hug.

From down the hall, Dave glanced over and gestured with his head in the direction of the cafeteria. I turned back to Annette and excused myself for a moment.

Coffee in hand, I found Dave sitting alone at a table off to the side. I sat down and said, "Sorry for your loss."

Dave nodded somberly. "Thanks, I arrived just before you did and didn't get a chance to talk to Annette—any news on Rob?"

"The department has called in a healer; they are looking at Rob now." Dave's face brightened at that piece of news, so I asked, "What happened?"

Dave glanced around and said, "The department is clamping down and keeping this one close to the vest. They don't want anyone outside to know what is going on, so this is just between you and me, okay? I'm only telling you because Rob and you are close, and this might be something you can help with."

Shit, I thought to myself. If he thought I could help, that meant there were Enhanced Individuals involved.

I nodded, and he continued, "Rob and Drew Davis were the first on scene. They were responding to an alarm call at a place called L-Tech in the north end."

"L-Tech," I said. "I've never heard of them."

Dave shrugged and said, "Yeah, they are some sort of small aerospace company. They make specialized parts for rockets or something like that."

Hamilton had been trying to attract non-steel related companies to the area with tax incentives and other goodies for the last couple of decades, trying to make the city less dependent on the declining steel industry. I knew they'd pulled in several medical research companies but had no idea that we had gotten anything aerospace related.

Dave continued, "Rob radioed in that they had spotted a number of costumed individuals and called for SWAT backup. Rob and Drew took cover behind their cruisers and were waiting for SWAT to arrive. Stacey was driving up in her cruiser and saw one of the perps throw something at Rob and Drew. She swore it looked like a smartphone. Whatever it was, it exploded, killing Drew and injuring Rob. The blast was strong enough that it cracked her windshield from eighty feet away. Stacey slammed on the brakes. She said that she saw four individuals in black armor, but then there was a bright glow and they just disappeared. Stacey then got out of her car and rushed over to help Rob and Drew."

Exploding smartphones, black armor, and disappearing people certainly sounded like something more than just normal human thieves.

Dave took a sip of his coffee and I said, "I don't think I'd ever met Drew before. Has he been to one of Rob's poker games?"

Dave shook his head. "Nah, he'd been working for the Toronto Police for a couple of years and only transferred to us about three months ago. I hadn't worked with him much, but he seemed solid."

Stacey's name triggered a memory for me, and I asked, "Stacey, brunette, about five foot eight or nine? Probably now in her mid-thirties? Tough as nails?"

Dave nodded. "You know her?"

"Yeah, back in my Hurricane days she helped get some civilians out when I was taking down a rogue Werewolf that went nuts in a bar in Hess Village."

Dave grinned. "Yeah, we still call her 'Full Moon' because of that."

The nickname made me smile. I felt a bit bad that she got stuck with 'Full Moon' but at least she earned that name saving lives that night, so hopefully she took it as a badge of pride. I focused back on the here and now. "Any news on the suspects or what was taken?"

"They seem to have disappeared into thin air. The owner has been contacted, but no news yet on what went missing. It was a break-in though. The lock on the front door was completely melted off. There was also a six-foot circular burn mark around the area where Stacey saw them disappear."

I pondered that. "Sounds like Enhanced Individuals. EIRT being called in?"

Dave shook his head. "Not at this point."

I wasn't surprised; with one of their own down, I knew they wouldn't be anxious to turn this over to the Feds, as EIRT would take the case over and lock them out of it. This was also why they were being so hush-hush about everything. I understood why Hamilton Police wanted to keep this in-house, but they were making a mistake. Their SWAT team was good, but none of their officers were Enhanced. All it would take was for one of the Enhanced Individuals to be a Tank, or something equally as powerful, and there wouldn't be anything SWAT could do to stop them. I got the impression Dave felt the same way and that was the main reason he was telling me everything he knew.

"We should check on Annette. Thanks for filling me in."

"No problem," Dave said and then in a serious tone added, "but this conversation didn't happen, understand?"

I winked and said, "What conversation?"

By the time we got back to the waiting area, it was jam-packed with cops and Annette's and Rob's families. It took me twenty minutes, but eventually I got a quick word with Annette alone.

"Look, there are lots of people here for you, and I'm sure Rob will be fine. If you don't mind, I'm going to take off and visit the crime scene."

"Sure, I will call you if anything changes. Thanks for coming, Zack," she said, a somber look in her eyes.

I gave her a hug and then said my goodbyes to her and Rob's parents. Alteea landed on my shoulder, and I was about to leave when I spotted a tired looking Marion quietly walk by. Marion was the healer I went to when I was injured. I had no idea she was the healer the police had on retainer. Though if I thought about it, I shouldn't have been surprised; there was only one other talented healer in Hamilton besides Marion, so the odds were pretty good she might be.

I pushed through the crowd and caught up to her. "Can I walk or fly you home?"

Marion looked at me in surprise and said, "What are you doing here?"

"Rob Quinn is my best friend."

She gave me a look of sympathy and said, "I have healed what I can, but he is still in a coma, so it is now up to him."

We walked out on to the street and I asked, "Will he be okay?"

Marion shrugged. "Head injuries are unpredictable; he could wake in a minute, an hour, or a day or…" She trailed off.

My stomach tightened at the unsaid 'never.' I told myself that Rob had to wake up; he had a baby on the way, a lovely wife who cared deeply for him, he was in good shape and was a fighter, so he had to pull through. I hated that feeling of helplessness; there was nothing I could do but cross my fingers and hope. My emotions were all over the place at the moment, and that feeling of helplessness was quickly turning into rage. I may not be able to do much for Rob right now, but I would nail whoever did this so no one else got hurt.

I nodded and asked, "Other than the coma, is he back to normal? It was reported that he had pretty extensive injuries and burns."

Marion gave me a half smile and said, "Those have been taken care of. If he wakes up, he'll have to take it easy for a couple of days but will be back to 100 percent. By the way, what do you have on your shoulder?"

I stumbled briefly when I realized that Marion had sensed Alteea, even though she was invisible with her glamor. I said, "Oh that's right, you don't know about the newest member of my team. Alteea, drop your glamor for a moment and say hi to Marion."

Marion's eyes always looked huge due to the magnification of her glasses, but now they went even bigger as Alteea appeared on my shoulder.

We turned a corner and there were a couple of people approaching us on the sidewalk. Alteea saw them and disappeared again.

Marion asked, "Is it just her or do you have a whole swarm of pixies living with you?"

I spent a couple of minutes explaining how Alteea came to live with us and then said, "I didn't know you were on police retainer."

"Tom is the primary healer on retainer. He is on vacation in Florida at the moment, so I cover for him when he is away, and he does the same for me."

We reached Marion's building and I thanked her for healing Rob and wished her a good night. Once she was safely inside her building, I slipped on my balaclava and took to the air again. I had no idea where L-Tech was but once I got a couple hundred feet up, it was easy to spot the mass of flashing police lights in the north end. It was time find out who hurt my friend and put a stop to them doing something like this again.

Chapter 3

Tuesday, April 29

L-Tech turned out to be a smaller company than I had been expecting. The building was a one-story job, and by its size, I'd be surprised if more than twenty-five people worked there. The entire front of the building was roped off with yellow police tape, the uniforms behind it keeping the sparse crowd back. There were cruisers at either end of the street blocking off vehicle traffic. There were two damaged and blackened cruisers parked in front of the place and I assumed they were Drew's and Rob's. A large blue tent had been erected on the street beside the two cruisers where Rob and Drew must have gone down. Flashes from under the seams of the tent lit the night as crime scene techs took pictures from within.

Further down the street was the SWAT van, two unmarked police cars, and several black and whites, all parked. I spotted two detectives talking to an older man in a golf shirt and khakis and assumed that must be the owner or manager of L-Tech.

I cursed, as I didn't recognize either of the detectives; I'd hoped to run into someone who knew me from my Hamilton Hurricane days, as they would be more likely to share information with me. I did, however, spot Sergeant Anders among the cops manning the perimeter. He had been a sergeant before I even started patrolling the Hamilton skies sixteen years ago as the Hurricane. He was gruff and outspoken, and the latter was probably why he'd be a career-long sergeant. I'd helped him out of a couple of tough scrapes during my hero days, and he had always been good to me.

I landed outside the police tape and talk of 'The Hurricane' rippled through the crowd as I did. The Sarge saw me and wandered closer. "Hurricane, it's been too long!" He held out his hand.

We shook hands and I said, "Condolences on Officer Davis. I just came from the General." I gave him a quick update on Rob. He nodded, and I continued, "Rumor has it that there were Enhanced Individuals involved in this, any chance I can speak to the detectives? Rob's a good friend and I want to help."

"They are keeping this one locked down, but I'll escort you over to the detectives. They can decide if they want your help or not."

He lifted the tape for me and just as I stepped under, a familiar voice yelled, "Sarge, why are you letting a civilian onto my crime scene?"

I groaned to myself at the sight of SWAT Sergeant Tim Murdock's short bulldog frame marching over towards us. If there was one person I didn't want to see tonight, it was Murdock. The two of us got along like oil and water. He hated me because he didn't like civilians playing in his sandbox, and I disliked him because he was a musclebound idiot. SWAT was called in when any Enhanced Individuals were involved in a crime. Therefore, it was his job to be knowledgeable about Enhanced Individuals and their lore; the problem was he wouldn't know the difference between an elf and vampire even if the vampire was biting him on the ass.

To be fair, more than 90 percent of the events SWAT were called out on were human-on-human crimes, so it wasn't the majority of their work. When Enhanced Individuals were involved, they were just a stopgap until a federal Enhance Individual Response Team (EIRT) arrived and took over.

Murdock's predecessor, Bobby Knight, was a shining example of what a SWAT sergeant should be. Bobby moved on a few years ago and was now on an EIRT team. Bobby's deep knowledge of monsters and lore was probably the biggest reason I disliked Murdock so much, as he didn't come close to meeting that same standard.

The Sarge came to my defense. "Relax, Murdock, the Hurricane is offering his services. I was just going to walk him over and let the detectives decide if they can use him or not."

"Yeah, that is not going to happen. You heard the Chief; this is to be an in-house investigation, which means just us. Have a good night, Hurricane," Murdock growled at me.

I forced myself to stay calm and said, "Sergeant Murdock, can I please have ten seconds of your time?"

He moved closer to me and said, "Ten seconds, and it starts now."

I kept my voice low, so this conversation was kept between the three of us and said, "Look, I know we don't always see eye to eye, but I know you like Rob and he's my best friend. We both want the same things here—to nail whoever did this. I also know that I have been useful to you on occasion. All I want to do is help. Please just let me speak with the detectives. I will sign an NDA and do whatever is asked of me, just let me help, okay?"

Murdock stood there for a moment and then said, "Time's up, you've said your piece, now get back on the other side of the tape and let us do our jobs."

God, he's such an asshole! In my anger, I had started to call on my powers, as I wanted nothing more than to fry the arrogant twit where he stood. Thankfully, Rob came to mind. He always chided me for busting Murdock's balls and out of respect for him, I brought my temper under control.

"I'm leaving because Rob wouldn't want me to start something with you. But, Murdock, one of these days, you and your team are going to run up against a monster that is too much for you to handle and I will get a call to come save your sorry ass; you make it real tempting for me to let that call go to voicemail…"

"Get out!" barked Murdock.

I flew up and over the police tape and flipped him the bird when I landed. He ignored it and went back to where the detectives were.

Thankfully the crowd could sense I was angry and stayed well back from me. In a low voice, I said, "Alteea, get over there and find out what the detectives are saying."

I smiled at the sight of her small rainbow aura darting towards the detectives. She ended up hovering a few feet above them and I had no doubt she'd pick up every word they were saying. Murdock could stop me from being part of the official investigation, but there was no way I wasn't getting involved in this.

Twenty minutes later, Murdock looked over at me standing behind the police tape and frowned. He turned and said something to the detectives and the owner of L-Tech. They nodded in response to whatever he said and disappeared inside the building with a small rainbow aura hot on their heels. I laughed when I realized that Murdock must have figured I was using my Air powers to listen in. *Close, my friend, but not close enough.*

While I waited, I texted Stella and Blue and filled them in on what was happening and asked if they could cut their trip short. Stella responded, saying they were heading into a two-hour seminar that they both wanted to see and asked if coming home after that was okay. I replied that I'd see them in a couple of hours.

The timing was good, as the detectives would be here at least that long, and Liv and Bree would still be tied up with EIRT and the Hellhound bounty. I wanted them all back so we could track down any leads Alteea found out about. I'd hoped the place had some CCTV cameras and we'd get some shots of the criminals who did this. So far all I knew was that they were four people in dark costumes and not much else.

Two hours and a couple of Timmies coffee runs later, the detectives were leaving, and Alteea came back to me.

She started to whisper in my ear what she found out, but I shook my head and said, "Not here; wait until we are home. Now hang on."

I felt her grip the collar of my jacket and took to the air, heading towards home.

Chapter 4

Wednesday, April 30

When Alteea and I got home, Stella and Blue were already waiting for us in the kitchen. To my surprise Stella gave me a hug and said, "Sorry to hear about Rob. Don't worry, I'm sure he'll pull through."

I tentatively hugged Stella back and after a few moments we broke apart. My eyes welled up a bit, and I almost lost it at Stella's gesture. She had been abused for years by her adopted father and as a result, was uncomfortable around men in general. For her to overcome her fears and give me a hug was a significant gesture on her part, and I was truly touched by it.

Blue was on her heels and simply said, "I will pray to Waatu, the healer, for your friend this evening."

On Blue's home world, they believed in multiple gods, like the ancient Romans and Greeks had. I had lost track at all the different ones she'd mentioned during the time I'd known her, but Waatu had come up a few times. I got the impression that it was one she prayed to quite regularly.

"Where are Liv and Bree?" asked Stella.

I explained about the Hellhound and that I'd left Bree and Olivia there to deal with EIRT and get a bounty claim number.

When I was finished explaining, I checked my phone. It was just coming up on 1:30 a.m. I did some quick math about how long it would take EIRT to send out an agent or team to the sheep farm, added in how long it would take EIRT to process the scene and for Bree and Liv to drive back, and figured they'd be home shortly.

The kettle started steaming and Stella said, "I was making us a cup of tea, would you like one?"

I shook my head and pulled a Coke from the fridge instead. A minute later, we all sat around the kitchen table and I brought them up to speed on everything I hadn't covered in my texts earlier.

Liv and Bree walked in from the garage and Bree immediately asked, "How's Rob?"

I filled them in as they both raided the fridge; Bree grabbing food and Liv taking out a pint glass of blood she'd stashed in there. Once I finished explaining Rob's condition and telling them what had happened so far, another thought hit me and I asked, "Where's the cooler with the belly scales?"

Liv placed her glass in the microwave to warm it up and said, "The stench box is in the garage. Oh, that reminds me—here."

She handed me the bounty claim ticket for the Hellhound.

I took it from her and pulled out my phone. I texted Walter to tell him that we had the scales and he could come by tomorrow morning at ten to pick them up.

We all gathered around the kitchen table, and Liv returned to the issue at hand. "If there were Enhanced Individuals at the crime scene, I'm assuming you want to go after them?"

"Nothing is going to stop me from bringing these animals down. They murdered a cop and injured my best friend. They need to be stopped or more people are going to be killed…"

I could tell from their nods and body language that they were in too, and I was touched. I was about to tell them that this wasn't a bounty case, and that this mission was strictly a volunteer one, but then it hit me that the case would, in fact, have a bounty.

With Hamilton Police keeping this under wraps, there wouldn't be a bounty posted to the UN bounty website, but any time a crime involved Enhanced Individuals there were set fees. The size of the fees depended on the crime and the powers of the Enhanced Individuals in question. As a police officer had been killed, this was a serious matter. We were looking at a minimum of $50,000 for each of the perpetrators, so with four of them the bounty would be at least $200,000 US. At least my teammates would get paid for their time if we took this group down.

In the lull, Alteea fluttered up and did an excited lap around the table and asked, "Can I share what I found out at the crime scene, Master?"

I nodded and she said, "They stole a prototype gyroscopic guidance system. The company announced it last month. They had managed to make it 50 percent smaller and lighter than anything currently out there. They already had a number of orders from Space X, Virgin Galactic, and some satellite companies, but they weren't going into production for six months."

I cursed to myself. This might just be a one-time highly specialized theft. It could have been paid for by a rival competitor, or one of the companies that didn't want to wait six months. If that were the case, then they'd be in the wind and we would never see them again.

I put those thoughts aside as Alteea continued, "They were quick; in and out in less than ten minutes. They disabled the alarm and the surveillance cameras, melted the lock off the front door, and burned open the safe where the prototype was stored."

Stella frowned and asked, "If they disabled the alarm, why were the police dispatched?"

"They disabled the alarm, but the alarm company got an alert that the system was offline. There hadn't been any power outages reported, so the alarm company called the police to go by and make sure everything was okay," explained Alteea.

"Interesting," I said. "By how quick they were, they sound like pros, but how they dealt with the alarm seems amateurish. You said they disabled the cameras. Any chance they screwed up there, too, and ended up on tape?"

"I took a picture of the video…" said Alteea. She buzzed down and grabbed her mini iPhone off the table. Her little pixie hands flew over the tiny screen and all our phones chimed a moment later. I opened up the new text message and it was a grainy picture of someone with their head down wearing what looked like black armor; they had shoulder-length dark hair and what looked like an 'A' logo on the sleeve of their armor.

As we examined the picture, Alteea added, "The detectives guessed the person was probably male but weren't 100 percent, due to the longer hair and the bulkiness of the suit. They estimated the person was between five seven and five nine."

The height range sucked, as it was a bit taller than the average woman and a bit shorter than the average man, which meant the person could be either. The forensics on the place would be crap too; the company probably had twenty-five employees, plus couriers, Canada Post workers, coffee suppliers, and water cooler deliveries, and Odin only knew what else going through, so even if the thieves left a stray hair or two, it would take months to sort through, if ever.

Blue asked, "Alteea, you mentioned the lock and the safe had been burned through, any details on that?"

"The detectives guessed they used an industrial torch to cut through both. Whatever they used, it was extremely hot and fast."

I caught where Blue was going with this and asked, "You're thinking it might be a Fire elemental or a super-class with some sort of fire ability?"

Blue nodded and added, "Or someone with a sword like my Keetiyatomi blade."

Blue could engulf her sword in flames, and when enflamed, that blade could cut through damn near anything. I wondered if flame guy could also be the same person who made the smartphone explode.

Stella interrupted my thoughts. "This officer, Stephanie—"

"Stacey," I corrected her.

She ignored me and continued, "You said she claims she saw a smartphone being thrown at Rob and the other officer. How confident are you that she is right?"

"Pretty confident. Stacey is a smart, no nonsense veteran cop, and if she said she saw a smartphone being tossed, then that probably is what it was."

Bree turned towards me and asked, "They disappeared after a bright glow, and there was a six-foot burn mark where they had been standing. Do they have someone like Blue with them? And have you ever heard of someone who teleports and leaves a mark like that?"

I shook my head and said, "Doesn't ring a bell. If they have a teleporter, that person isn't a shadow-traveler like Blue—the bright glow would disrupt the shadows. If this is a teleporter, then they are exceptionally powerful. Unlike Blue's power to open portals to anywhere, teleporters are usually limited in distance and mass. To teleport four armored individuals any distance would tax most of them greatly."

Blue said, "It might not be a person that is teleporting them; it might be a device. If the device had a self-destruct mechanism built-in, that would explain the burn mark."

Alteea fluttered her wings in agreement and added, "One of the detectives thought the same thing. He was going to have the techs take samples of the burned debris and analyze what it was made from."

Stella got a sour look on her face and said, "These people might not be Enhanced at all. This could all be high-tech equipment. They are wearing armored suits. They might be using a teleport device. The smartphone could just be a smartphone packed with explosives, and the burned door lock and safe might be another gadget they are using, rather than a power."

The whole table went silent at that. I couldn't argue with Stella's reasoning, but my gut was telling me that at least one of them was Enhanced. I didn't care if they were Enhanced or not; they killed a Hamilton cop and put my best friend in a coma—one way or another I was taking them down.

I wanted to keep things moving. "Okay, to sum things up, we have four people who might or might not be Enhanced. We don't know if they are male or female. They have access to high-tech goodies like the suits and possibly a teleport device. They are dangerous and seem to have no issues killing cops. Those details aren't that useful. I think we need to key in on the more unique features of this crime."

I got a few nods at this and continued, "They have stolen a prototype that would have a limited number of interested buyers; I'm guessing it is not a space exploration or satellite manufacturer that stole it. It is probably one of L-Tech's competitors. Blue, you and Stella find out who else makes gyroscopic guidance systems." I paused as they both nodded. "If this is corporate espionage, then whoever did it has some deep pockets. So, it will probably be one of the three biggest players in the markets. Find out who they are, and use the shadows to eavesdrop on their C-level executives. If we find out who bought it, we can visit them and find out who they hired to pull off this job."

Stella and Blue nodded, and I turned to Bree and said, "Bree, you and Liv research crimes involving exploding smartphones. There can't be too many, and if we find others, they may give us clues about who these people are. Alteea and I will research teleporting that leaves circular burn marks. This also can't be that common. Any questions?"

Liv broke the silence and said, "I need a quick shower first."

If I'd been in a better mood, I probably would have made a crack at how ripe she smelled thanks to our earlier Hellhound and sheep adventure but just nodded instead.

Two hours later, our results weren't good. Alteea and I struck out with the teleporting angle. We found a few sites that discussed rumors of Mad Scientists who had made teleporting devices, but most of these were sparse on details and didn't lead anywhere. Bree and Liv found tons on exploding smartphones, but these were due to bad batteries and not deliberate tampering. There were a few terrorist groups that modified iPads and laptops as bombs to try and bring down commercial planes, but none had tried with smartphones.

Blue and Stella found there were only two big players in the gyroscopic guidance systems development market. They found out the names of the main executives for both companies. Blue would begin spying on them from the shadows first thing tomorrow.

Stella suggested that this job might not be a one-time thing and set up a monitoring program that continually searched for any industrial break-ins in Ontario. It would text us if anything popped up. With Blue's shadow-traveling abilities, if we got an alert, we could respond in minutes.

With that, Blue, Stella, and I turned in for the night, and Bree, Liv, and Alteea retired to the living room to watch TV until the sun came up.

Chapter 5

Wednesday, April 30

A couple of hours later, I got up to use the bathroom. I was frustrated about not being able to sleep. I kept worrying about Rob, going over everything I'd learned so far about this case, and couldn't turn my mind off.

I squinted as I turned on the bathroom light and was blind for a moment as my eyes adjusted to the brightness. Before gaining my housemates, I wouldn't have bothered with turning on the light. I would have just had a quick pee and gone back to bed. Now, with five females in the house, I wasn't willing to risk missing the toilet bowl or, worse, not putting the seat back down—those were both crimes punishable by death in this house.

With my business done, I turned off the light and entered the pitch-black hallway. I couldn't see a damn thing, so I called my powers and started to create a small ball of electricity in my hand to use as a nightlight.

A voice to my left asked, "Couldn't sleep?"

I yelped and probably jumped a foot off the floor. A bolt of lightning surged from my hand and blasted the carpet. "BY ODIN'S HAIRY BEARD! How many times, Liv, have I asked you not to sneak up on me like that?"

A soft "Sorry" came from the darkness.

The stench of burnt acrylic caught my attention, and I fumbled around for the hallway light switch. I flipped it and groaned at the smoldering black spot on the carpet where the lightning had hit. I hastily stomped on it to put it out, which was a stupid thing to do in bare feet. Thankfully, the area wasn't too hot, and I escaped with no serious burns.

I glared at the smirking vampire and gruffly asked, "What?"

Liv's green eyes broke contact with mine and she stared at the floor for a moment. The earlier expression of amusement disappeared and was replaced with a serious one. My anger from being startled was still coursing through me, and I almost prompted her to get on with whatever she was here for, but I just managed to hold my tongue. I sensed she had something important to say.

She finally broke her silence, "I know you are worried about Rob, and I don't like seeing you like this. I came up here to cheer you up... I thought we might spend some time together in your room..."

My anger disappeared as I stood there completely staggered by her offer. Warmth instantly filled me at her kindness and caring about my well-being. It was times like this that I was glad I wasn't on my own anymore and had people around me who cared. I felt my eyes starting to well up a bit and realized that all the emotions from this day were starting to crash down on me. I fought them and regained control.

Her offer was tempting, especially as I noticed the lack of bra under the white crop-top, and the formfitting black booty shorts she was wearing had my imagination working overtime.

Rob popped into my thoughts and had me leaning towards declining her offer, as it wouldn't feel right enjoying myself like that while my best friend struggled to survive. Though a part of me argued that Rob's situation exemplified that life was short and anything could happen, so why not live for the moment?

I also just knew that if we did go to my room, we'd end up having sex. That would be a new level for our relationship. We'd been on a few flying dates and had a couple of nice moonlit walks on the beach. The nice thing about my touch of elemental Ice power and her being a vampire was that neither of us felt the cold, so we always had those icy beaches to ourselves. That was also why she was wearing so little clothing, even though it was April. I really cared for Liv, and the more I thought about it, the more I was convinced that now wasn't the right time.

"Liv, I'm very tempted, but with my best friend in a coma, it just doesn't feel like the right thing to do, you know?"

She gave me a nod and a small smile in response, and I knew she understood. She moved towards me and gave me a hug. I wrapped my arms around her and just enjoyed her being there for me. Strangely enough, that hug probably helped relieve my stress more than anything else in this world could have.

After a bit, she kissed me lightly on the cheek and said, "Get some sleep, okay?"

I nodded and released her.

I gave the carpet one last look to make sure it was out and turned out the light. Liv took my hand and led me back to my room. When we reached the threshold to my room, she let go of my hand. My night-vision had returned enough that I was able to watch her lovely form disappear back down the stairs. I knew I'd made the right choice, but a part of me certainly regretted turning down her offer.

***

The next morning, Walter arrived at ten on the dot. He gave me the cash, and I gave him the cooler with the scales. I told him he could keep the cooler, as I doubted we'd ever get the smell out.

Once he left, I headed up to my office and locked the $20,000 in the safe. I'd split the cash later with the team.

I yawned as I came back downstairs. Next order of business: coffee.

As I entered the kitchen, Stella announced her monitoring program had gotten some hits. "There have been two more break-ins."

"What? Where?" I asked in shock as I filled the kettle.

"A diamond heist in Antwerp and computer processors stolen from a factory in Seoul. At both scenes there were unexplained circular burn marks left behind by the thieves."

"I thought your program was searching for industrial break-ins in Ontario? How did it find these ones?"

Stella grinned. "The main monitoring program does that and will send us text alerts if anything pops up, but I added a couple of sub-routines; they search world-wide for any mention of exploding smartphones or circular burn marks. If they find any, the program stores links in the logs for me to check later. To be honest though, the diamond heist is front page news everywhere this morning."

I pulled out a mug from the cupboard while I waited for the kettle to boil and asked, "How much did they steal, and where's Blue this morning?"

"Two hundred million US in cut and uncut diamonds. Blue is up in her room, using the shadows to eavesdrop on the executives of the two gyro companies."

I whistled at the amount and shook my head. "How'd they pull it off?"

Stella sipped her tea. "They were quite brazen. They tunneled in from a construction site a block away. The interesting thing is they filled in the tunnel behind them as they went. Ten minutes after the vault was locked for the day at 9:00 p.m., they started cutting through the floor of the vault. Security noticed in less than a minute and called the police. The thieves had a hole cut in less than five minutes. At 9:15 p.m., a single person comes through the hole wearing a breathing mask, oxygen tank, and black armor. He sprayed paint on the lens of the camera and the feed went dark. The black armor had the same stylized 'A' on the sleeve that our thief had."

Stella was about to add more, but the kettle started whistling. Once I unplugged it, she said, "The police were on scene by this time, but there was nothing they could do. The vault is time-locked and doesn't open until 8:00 a.m. no matter what, and with the tunnel filled in, there was no way to reach the thieves. The authorities locked down the three surrounding blocks around the vault and let no one in or out without going through tight screening. This morning the vault opened, and it'd been cleaned out, nothing left behind but a circular burn mark on the floor."

I had to begrudgingly give them kudos for using the time-locked vault to their advantage. I made my coffee and joined Stella at the table.

Stella added, "The one thing I don't understand is how they managed to tunnel a block fast enough that they could do it on a single tank of air."

"An Earth elemental would be able shift the earth around almost effortlessly and probably could dig and fill the whole tunnel in less than fifteen minutes." She nodded, and I asked, "What about the Seoul job?"

"That one was more brute force than finesse. They cut the power to the entire plant. In the chaos that ensued, they ran in and grabbed the processors. A janitor saw a bright flare in the shipping area, and they were gone. When they restored power an hour later, a shipment of GPUs was gone and where they'd been stored there was a ten-foot circular burn on the floor. A security guard was hospitalized from being knocked out from a blow to the head. The only witness who saw anything was the janitor. He thinks he saw six people outlined in the bright flash but couldn't make out any details on what they looked like or what they were wearing."

It would have been nice if someone had seen the black armor or the 'A' logo to confirm, but the circular burn mark on the floor certainly made it seem like these were our guys. "No surveillance pictures?"

Stella shook her head and said, "None were reported. I'm assuming the cameras went down when the power did."

"How much did they take?"

"Two thousand GPUs used as components in high-end video cards."

A good video card ranged in price from seven- to twelve-hundred dollars, but they had just taken the processors meant for those cards. They were the main component, and I guessed they would probably be around three hundred each, so that amounted to about $600,000 in total. That was a small number compared to the diamonds. The prototype gyro they stole would also be worth a lot more than that. With the rise of Bitcoin and other crypto currencies, supplies had been tight on high-end video cards. Powerful video cards were the best way to mine the crypto algorithms to harvest the coins, so they may have grabbed them due to the lack of availability

The more disturbing thought was that our thieves had pulled off three large jobs in less than twenty-four hours on three different continents. This would make tracking them down or predicting where they were going to pop up next much harder. Thankfully, with Blue's shadow-traveling abilities we could go anywhere in the world in seconds, but the entire world was a big place, which meant this job just got a whole lot more complicated.

I shared my thoughts with Stella, and she said, "Good news on that; or maybe it's bad news. It has to be at least two different teams: the break-ins in Antwerp and Seoul happened at the same time."

"You sure?"

Stella nodded and said, "They have video from the vault in Antwerp of them cutting though the floor of the vault ten minutes after nine. They disrupted the power at the factory in Seoul at 5:00 a.m. local time.

There is an eight-hour time difference between the two locations, so both jobs happened at the same time."

If two different teams had pulled off these jobs, it was possible that a third had done the Hamilton theft. That would put one in North America, one in Asia, and one in Europe. The idea of three teams of possibly Enhanced Individuals with high-tech gear was a bit disturbing. This wasn't just a couple of people who teamed up; this was a major organization that had significant resources to pull this off. Heck, this could even be something government-sponsored by a rogue regime like North Korea or Iran. I doubted the government angle; they would be more likely to steal nuclear materials than diamonds or GPUs. The gyro guidance system, though, could be used in a missile.

I mentioned my third team theory to Stella, and she seemed to think it made sense. I added, "I also think that last night's job wasn't the end but is only the beginning. The diamonds were probably stolen for financial gain, but I doubt the gyro and GPUs were taken for financial reasons. There are much more lucrative targets like a mint, a gold storage facility, a Federal Reserve Bank. No, I think they are building something; I have no idea what they are making, but that is the only thing that makes sense. And if they are building something, I doubt GPUs and the gyro are enough to build it, so I suspect they are going to strike again soon."

***

Two hours later, I was at the Hamilton General Hospital again to check on Rob. I stopped dead at the sight of Annette in one of the two hospital beds. At first fear gripped me, and I worried the stress of Rob's ordeal had caused an issue with the baby, but I relaxed when I saw there were no IVs, monitoring equipment, or cables attached to her. I realized that they must have provided Annette with a place to sleep near Rob and that she hadn't been admitted. She was just sleeping peacefully.

Rob also looked like he was resting peacefully, but the various tubes, cables, and machines shattered that illusion. I was pleased that he physically seemed to be fine. Some of the skin on his neck and the left side of his face was a pinker shade than other parts. I assumed that must have been where he was burned, and the skin color was from Marion's healing work. I'd had similar injuries in the past that Marion had fixed and knew that in a couple of days the pinker shade would fade, and no one would be able to tell he'd suffered burns.

I didn't want to wake Annette, so I just stood there quietly for a few minutes. It was weird seeing Rob like this. I kept expecting him to wake and give me a hard time about something. I clenched my fists as I thought about the senseless attack. The thieves were wearing armor; Rob and Drew were using the cruisers as shelter and were waiting for SWAT, and I doubt they even considered engaging the thieves, so why toss an explosive at them? I could only assume the thieves panicked or were hardened criminals that hated cops.

I was angrier at the helplessness I felt. There was nothing I could do to bring Rob out of this coma. All I could do was hope and pray he would pull out of this and wake up. The sad thing was Rob was the lucky one; at least he had the possibility of recovery. I wondered if Drew had a wife or kids who would never see him again.

I let Annette rest, silently wished Rob to get better, and walked out of the room. I bumped into a tired and worn-looking Dave Collins at the end of the hall.

"You coming from Rob's room?"

I nodded and said, "Annette is sleeping, and Rob is still the same…"

"I'll visit them later then. Annette was up most of the night; she needs her sleep," said Dave. He then added, "An EIRT team has taken over the investigation."

"What? I thought the department was keeping this in-house. Why the change of heart?"

Dave sighed and said, "A picture of the circular burn mark hit the news. With the circular burn at the diamond heist being front-page news, the media speculated the cases might be connected. The rumor mill has it that the chief got an earful from the RCMP commissioner for breaking protocol and keeping the case under wraps."

"I hate to say it, but the chief made a mistake with this one. I understand that one of your own was killed, but this is looking like a global crime spree; it's going to need cooperation between all levels of law enforcement to stop it. If the thieves are Enhanced, you'd have needed EIRT to stop them anyways."

Dave nodded and said, "Yeah, I suspected this was bigger than us last night. That was why I let you know what happened. I just hope the feds don't shut us out completely."

***

I was barely in the front door when Stella said, "Looks like we weren't the only ones who think this is three separate teams. The UN bounty website added three new bounties twenty minutes ago; one for the Antwerp group, one for the Seoul group, and one for our group."

I hung up my jacket and asked, "How much?"

"Three million for the Antwerp, two hundred and fifty thousand for the Seoul group, and a half million for ours."

The three million for the diamond heist seemed high to me, but they were probably hoping that if the group was taken down that they could also recover the diamonds. The half million for our targets was a nice bonus; we were taking these guys down anyways, but if the UN wanted to give us money for it, too, I wasn't going to complain.

I told Stella about EIRT taking over for the Hamilton Police, and she didn't seem overly surprised. Blue came down the stairs, and we updated her about the new bounties and EIRT taking over the case.

Blue said, "No luck with the two gyro companies so far. I have been monitoring their people all morning. They heard about the theft of the prototype and both groups were surprised. I'm leaning towards neither group being involved, but I will keep monitoring them."

I pondered this and said, "Don't bother. It was a long-shot anyways and if one of them had grabbed the prototype, you would have gotten a hint this morning at the very least."

It would have been great if that hunch had paid out, as we could have gotten a lead to our mysterious group of thieves. With that track being a dead end, now all we could do was hope they struck again. Hopefully Stella's monitoring program would pick it up and we'd get a chance to confront them.

Chapter 6

Wednesday, April 30

Blue and Stella shadow traveled back to Vegas for the inventor's convention to attend another seminar. Blue returned around 6:30 p.m. to take Bree to her weekly Barrie pack meeting and then went back to Vegas again. When the sun went down, Liv and Alteea left to go shopping together. This meant I was on my own for most of the evening.

I was anxious and wanted to go after the thieves, but unless they made another appearance, there wasn't much I could do. In the end, I retreated to the basement and started working on a new model plane. I was sorely tempted to start the 1/72nd scale Lancaster I had on the shelf but that was a big project that would require a ton of patience and time, so I went with a 1/72nd Hawker Hurricane kit instead. A single engine fighter was a much easier project than a four-engine bomber. I started my forties music playlist and lost myself for a few hours.

By the time Bree, Blue, and Stella were home at just after nine, the model was fully assembled. I had most of the small detail work like the undercarriage, props, engine exhausts, and cockpit painted. All I had left to do was mask off the cockpit and paint the entire plane in a RAF camouflage pattern, decal it and it would be done.

As I cleaned up my brushes, there was a squeal of tires outside, which meant Liv and Alteea were back too. I turned off the music and the desk lamp and headed upstairs to join my teammates.

We ended up at the kitchen table. Bree was eating a sub with enough meat on it to feed an army. Liv and Alteea were sharing Liv's pint glass of blood, and Blue and Stella were having tea.

As soon as I entered the kitchen, Stella said, "We bought something in Vegas out of our own funds, but we'd like to have the company pay for it as an expense."

I started making myself a coffee and asked, "What is it, and how much did it cost?"

Stella squirmed a bit, and I suddenly got nervous; whatever they'd bought wasn't cheap. She nodded at Blue and said, "It would be easier to show you."

Blue pulled back the sleeve to her scale mail and exposed a two-inch wide gold bracelet. She tapped the band three times and disappeared. In her place was a tall, elderly gentleman who kind of looked like a chubby Einstein.

Alteea made an excited squeal and clapped her tiny hands; Liv simply said "wow," and Bree actually paused inhaling her sub. I just stood there open mouthed.

Blue's voice came from the old man, "It is hologram technology. A Mad Scientist created it for A-list celebrities so they could go out in public without being mobbed by fans."

Mad Scientists are Enhanced Individuals, though most of them would deny that and argue that they were creative geniuses. The problem with their argument was that if you took apart any of their creations and examined them, there was no way under the laws of physics they should work. That was why no one else could duplicate their inventions. I speculated that they infused each of their creations with magic, and that was what really made them work. I also knew they were Enhanced, as the couple of Mad Scientists I'd met all had auras around them.

Blue turned around, allowing us to check out the illusion from all angles. Gone was the well-armed blue-skinned alien with a tail, purple eyes and hair, and a mouthful of small shark-like teeth, and in its place was a harmless looking old man.

"I have to keep my tail close to my body—" she paused, and the last foot of her four foot long tail seemed to be hanging in the air unconnected to anything, "—and be aware of my personal space— the illusion is good enough to shake someone's hand or pass a business card or credit card to pay for something, but if someone came close enough to hug or kiss me, they would see through it."

The kettle whistled. I unplugged it and finished making my coffee.

Bree said, "It doesn't change your scent either. I can still tell it is you under that illusion. Why did you decide to become a man?"

Stella said, "With Blue being six foot three, if she stayed female, it would be more noticeable. By going male and elderly, we figured she'd blend in more."

Stella got up, took Blue's hand, and added, "If we are doing stakeouts, what is more unthreatening than a grandfather taking his granddaughter out for a stroll?"

Stella gave us all a cute little smile, playing up her youthful appearance. I had to admit they looked sweet together, and I wouldn't have given them a second glance if they walked by on the street. Our bounty targets wouldn't pay attention to a child and an old man walking by either.

In addition to it not hiding Blue's scent, I could still see her normal shimmering aura surrounding her, but as my power was unique as far as I knew, that likely wouldn't come into play during a hunt.

"How long can it run?" I asked.

Blue's elderly man face grinned and said, "Close to four hours on a full charge; it gives a soft warning beep when it only has fifteen minutes remaining. If I drain the battery completely, it takes sixteen hours to fully charge it again." Blue tapped her wrist and the illusion disappeared. "We also picked this up for personal reasons; it will allow Stella and I, or all of us, to go out in public without attracting as much attention."

I had always wondered why Blue and Stella were such homebodies. They usually spent most of their time either here at the house or at the secret lab in London, with occasional visits to the English vampire court. That always struck me as odd, considering Blue had the power to travel instantly anywhere in the world. I realized that Blue being a tall blue-skinned alien with a tail would make her stand out wherever she went. Blue was confident and self-assured, but constantly having people pointing, staring, and whispering must get annoying quickly.

I sat down at the table and Blue and Stella followed. I sipped my coffee and Stella said, "As for your original question, $200,000 US was the cost."

I coughed, choking on my mouthful of coffee. That was $280,000 Canadian. Liv leaned over and slapped me on the back to stop me from choking.

Stella said, "I know it is a lot of money, but this device will be helpful going forward and they only had a limited number of them. It also comes with a ten-year warranty. We are keeping it regardless of whether the company pays for it, but I do think this will allow us to use Blue in more roles than she currently has."

I exhaled and rubbed my chin. I knew we had just shy of a million in the company account at this moment, which meant we could afford it. It was still a big chunk, though. On the other hand, most of that million in the bank had come in during the three months we'd been working as a team. If we kept up that type of earning, by the end of the year the cost of the device would barely be a blip in our cash flow.

"Alright, I don't have a problem with the company picking this up, but in the future, it would be nice if we could discuss a major purchase like this first. Bree, Liv, you have any issues?"

Both said they were fine with the company paying for it. Stella and Blue smiled. As Stella was the one who managed the company finances, she'd deal with the details.

Blue smiled and said, "Now that has been settled and everyone is here, and it is still early enough, we can get in a training session. Nothing like a brisk run in the desert by moonlight to get the blood pumping."

I hated these forced marches with weighted packs, but I couldn't argue with the results. I hadn't been in this good of shape since I was a teenager.

Before I could bitch about it, all our phones started buzzing at once. I checked my iPhone and there was a text alert that a break-in was happening. Another text followed. The police were responding to an alarm at AAI Corp in Mississauga. I hadn't even finished reading that text when another one popped up adding that EIRT was also responding.

"Okay, folks," I said, "it looks like we might get a chance at our mystery thieves. Anyone know what the heck AAI Corp is or does?"

Liv, who with her vampire speed was quicker than any of us, looked at her screen and said, "Advanced Artificial Intelligence Corporation. Pioneers in AI technology."

Bree was already naked. Her body started to convulse as she changed into her Werepanther form.

"We are going to have a small window to nail these people. Peel Regional police will block off the access roads to AAI and will wait for EIRT to arrive. As the nearest branch is in downtown Toronto, it is going to take them at least twenty minutes to get there. I'm guessing the thieves will be gone before then, so we are getting there first and either taking them down or delaying them from teleporting until EIRT joins the fight." I paused for Bree to let out an angry growl as she settled into her hybrid standing form, and then I continued, "Remember these criminals have killed already, so keep on your toes and don't worry if you need to take them down hard—better them than us."

They all nodded, and I looked at Blue and said, "Can you find us a spot nearby?"

"Yes, there is a darkened area just off to the side of their front parking lot."

"Good. Open a portal. We go in using heavy formation."

We had been practicing different tactics and approaches, and heavy formation put Stella in the lead with Bree and Liv on her flanks and Blue and me behind them. The three of them could soak up more damage than Blue or I could.

Just as Blue was about to open a portal, Alteea asked, "What about me?"

I thought about it for a moment and said, "Come through last, go high and film everything on your phone—do not engage them, and make sure you're high enough that you are in no danger, okay?"

Alteea gave me a flutter of her wings, which I took as a 'yes,' and then Blue opened the shadow portal. Stella changed instantly into her Hyde form and stomped through with Bree on her heels and Liv just behind her. Once Liv was clear, I pulled on my balaclava and stepped into the shadows. Blue was right behind me.

I emerged from the shadows into a poorly lit parking lot. It was another mild night with the moon appearing and disappearing above in the overcast sky. The AAI Corp building was off to my right. The building was a modern looking three-story job with mirrored glass covering the entire front of the building. The AAI Corporation name was at the top of the building, lit up in large light blue LED letters. The front of the building and parking lot were well lit except for where we'd emerged. The streetlight above us was burnt out. There were police cars blocking the two entrances to the parking lot.

There was a large dark-skinned bald guy in black armor standing directly in front of the main entrance. "Boss, we got company!" he yelled as we stepped out of the darkness.

"They know we are here, folks, let's move!" I ordered.

Before we made it halfway to the front doors, seven more people came out of the building. Six of eight had auras, which put to rest the question of whether they were Enhanced or not. The good news was none of the auras were that large, which meant none of them were that powerful. The bad news was that the primary aura for all of them was orange, which meant they were part of the Super class, and I couldn't identify what most of their powers were.

The Super class was the newest of the seven classes of Enhanced Individuals. Charles Darwin created the original five classes to categorize Enhanced Individuals into similar groups. In the fifties, it was expanded to seven classes to add in the Super and Alien/Unknown classes. The Super class was comprised of people born after World War II that developed strange new powers when they hit puberty. It is commonly believed this was a direct result of a Ley line that was destroyed during the war. You dump that much magic into the world, and odd things are going to happen.

The wide range of powers that Super class individuals had meant that their auras could only give me clues about their abilities. Of the six I could see, the only one that I had the foggiest idea about was the large guy that had been standing guard. His aura was orange with red dots around it. Stella's aura was red and white dots but only around half her body, which reflected the dual nature of her normal appearance and her Hyde form. Since it was only red dots, I assumed that he could either take a lot of damage but wasn't any stronger than a normal human, or he could dish out some powerful blows but couldn't take any more damage than a normal human.

As we stepped over the curb to the front sidewalk, an older teen with long, dark greasy hair and bad acne said, "Who dares interrupt the Acolytes?"

The kid tried to sound authoritative, but he had a slight whine to his voice which lessened the effect. He looked like he was sixteen, but he might be a year or two older than that. Quickly looking at the people lined up in front of the door, I thought that most of them looked to be in their late teens. This whole encounter had taken me a bit off guard; I'd been expecting hardened professional criminals, not a bunch of nervous looking kids with minor powers. Why would teenagers steal gyros and advanced AIs?

Now was not the time to figure out the why. I focused on the dark-haired leader of the group. He had several smartphones tucked into his armor, which probably meant he was the one who tossed the exploding phone at Rob and Drew. In anger, I called on my powers but caught myself before I acted rashly. He may not be the one that tossed the phone, as all the other Acolytes also had a smartphone in holders by the waist of their armor. He was the only one with multiple phones though. I studied his aura; it was orange with black dots and dashes that made me think of binary numbers. I speculated his power had something to do with manipulating electronics, which would explain the exploding phones.

I stepped up between Stella and Bree and said, "I'm the Hamilton Hurricane, who are you?"

The dark-haired teen actually put his hands on his hips, lifted his chin, and announced, "I'm Terror-Byte, leader of the Acolytes!"

I couldn't help myself and laughed. Terror-Byte's face went dark red and he started reaching for one of his phones.

I instantly stopped laughing and in a commanding tone said, "Don't!"

He paused for a moment and looked apprehensively at me. Whether he was concerned about me or the symphony of sirens closing in, I wasn't sure, but I needed to end this soon.

"Okay, kids, play time is over. We have you outclassed in terms of power, and EIRT will be here soon. You have five seconds to get on the ground and surrender, or we will put you there."

All of them looked at Terror-Byte; their expressions were mostly nervous, but a few had determined looks that could be trouble. I quickly checked out the others that were part of his group. My attention went to the short, heavyset girl on Terror-Byte's right. She'd leaned over and said something to him and he nodded. The girl was the shortest of the bunch at barely over five feet. She was partially obscured by a large cloud of hornets that were flying around and crawling on her extremely pale skin. From her dark eye make-up, spiky jet-black hair, and enough facial piercings to set off a metal detector from ten feet away, she became 'Goth-girl' in my mind. By her aura and the cloud of hornets, I assumed her power was controlling insects.

I noticed that all the Acolytes were standing equal distance apart except for Goth-girl; she was standing much closer to Terror-Byte than to the blonde girl on her right. I wondered if it was because she and Terror-Byte had some sort of romantic relationship, or if Goth-girl disliked or feared the Barbie-looking blonde on her right.

The blonde girl, with her over hair sprayed hair, bright red lipstick, and large chest, looked like she would be more at home on a stripper pole than here. I probably also focused on her due to the two identical copies of her that were standing behind the main line of armored Enhanceds. The copies weren't in fancy armor and were just wearing black jackets, black jeans, and black combat boots. Stripper girl's aura was orange with an orange and tan checker-patterned outline. The two clones didn't have auras. I joked to myself that her power was giving someone their dream foursome.

The large half-Tank was on stripper girl's right and towered above her by a good nine inches. Beside him on the right end of the line was a tall, gaunt blonde guy who seemed a year or two older than the rest of them. He was good looking, but he gave off a seriously slimy vibe that instantly diminished the looks. His aura was orange with hazy neon colors around it. I didn't have the slightest clue what that meant.

The last person was on Terror-Byte's left and at the left end of the line. He was about the same height as Terror-Byte at around five foot eight and had short, bright red hair. He was holding a flaming knife in each hand, which must have been what they used to burn out the lock and cut into the safe on the L-Tech job.

Just as the five seconds was up, Terror-Byte pawed for one of his phones and clumsily tossed it at us. Before it even made it halfway, I called on my Air power and used it to shoot the phone way up into the sky. There was a dull boom as it exploded harmlessly way above us.

The hard way it is then. I arced out a powerful blast of chain lightning that hit all six of the armored teens in front of us, but it didn't reach the two stripper clones behind them. Goth-girl screamed out, "My babies!" as her cloud of hornets plopped lifelessly to the ground.

To my surprise, all six of them were still standing completely unharmed.

Terror-Byte looked at me and laughed. "Elemental-proof suits, dumbass!" Then he barked, "Hexadecimal, Meat-Shield, Bartender— deal with them while we finish the job."

Creepy blonde guy on the end started making funky hand gestures at us. The guy who looked like an NFL offensive lineman stepped closer, and I figured he must be Meat-Shield. His alias answered my earlier question about which half of a Tank's power he had, and I assumed he would be able to soak up damage but was missing the extreme strength that most Tanks possessed.

Stripper girl got a constipated look on her face and suddenly there were at least a dozen more of her in front of us. My eyes went wide at the new clones. They were all naked and barefaced, their blonde hair tangled in untamed rat's nests.

In her annoying, nasally voice, the original armored bimbo said, "Two through sixteen, deal with them as if they were last year's fashion trends!"

I sighed and all the naked clones and the two dressed ones screamed and charged at us with their long nails leading the way.

Liv warily eyed the girls coming at us and asked, "How sure are you that vampires can't get STDs?"

I laughed and said, "Pretty sure?"

"'K, it's Barbie whooping time!" yelled Liv as she blurred forward.

Bree leaped forward and came down on two of them in a flurry of claws and teeth and her targets exploded in a geyser of gore.

I glanced quickly at the original blonde, who didn't flinch or show any pain from the two clones being disemboweled by Bree. That meant there wasn't a physical connection between her and the clones. I was hoping there might be and that if the clones felt pain, she would too, as that would have taken her out of the fight, or at least slowed her down.

Stella lumbered forward and bowled over three more clones. One slipped between Stella and Liv, and Blue drew her sword, cutting the clone in half. I shot an arc of electricity at another one that emerged between Stella and Bree and had been heading my way. The clone screamed briefly and then shook violently as the electricity went through her. Her eyes rolled up in her head and she collapsed to the ground. To my surprise, the dead clone suddenly dissolved into a puddle of reddish goo.

Liv spat out a mouthful of blood and said, "Ewww, they don't taste right!" and then reached up and snapped the neck she had been biting seconds ago. The clone fell to the ground and started to liquefy.

Of the fifteen clones that were sent at us, we'd dropped eight. Then ten as Stella stomped two more into jelly. My teammates were going through the naked Barbies like lightning through a golfer, but then things started getting weird. Liv stumbled and giggled before engaging the next clone. Bree, too, staggered a bit as she moved forward and took out another two clones. Stella missed a swing at one of the few remaining clones but managed to kick it hard into the building, taking it out. Blue cried out and dropped her sword even though there wasn't anything near her.

I immediately went to her aid but tripped awkwardly over my feet. My lack of coordination was odd, but strangely enough, I felt amazing, almost like I had a good buzz going on. Olivia laughed as she took out one of the two original clothed clones. Bree let out a muted, half-hearted growl as she shredded the last remaining clone. It was almost like we were all drunk. I reached Blue, and she was on the sidewalk shivering, sweating, and curled up in a fetal position.

I had no idea what was going on. My mind was foggy, and everything seemed to be in slow motion. Through the haze, I came back to the word 'drunk' and vaguely remembered the Bartender. I looked up sharply at the building and blonde creepy guy was still making weird hand gestures at us.

Shit! We've been so caught up in dealing with the naked horde, we forgot about the others.

I raised my hand to aim a blast of wind at him but then everything started spinning. I collapsed on my knees and barely managed to lift the bottom of my balaclava before puking up a good portion of my dinner onto the sidewalk.

The ground shook a moment later, and after I retched again, I glanced over and saw Stella's Hyde form lying on its back snoring up a storm. I dry heaved a few more times. I could hear Liv laughing on the ground a good ten feet away. Bree's dark Were form gave another soft growl and then she too began to snore off to my right.

My whole team was down. I tried to stand up but got hit by the spins again and fell to my hands and knees, dry heaving. I'd only been this drunk one time in my life and that was at Rob's bachelor party—all I wanted to do was roll over and die.

After what felt like hours, but was probably only a couple of minutes, Terror-Byte yelled over, "Nice job on the 'world of hurt,' loser. So long, Hamilton Hangover!"

I moaned as I glanced over at him. He grabbed another phone, tossed it towards us, and went back into the building again with the Bartender, Hexadecimal, and Meat-Shield falling in behind him. *Oh crap.* I called on my Air power and barely managed to push the phone away a split second before it hit the ground. My control was terrible. I tried to shoot it up into the air again, but it hit one of the upper windows on the building. It exploded and shattered all the windows on the third floor, blew out half the AAI Corporation sign, and destroyed a good chunk of the second-story windows as well. I prayed Alteea was well away from the building and ducked my head a mere second before the glass and debris rained down on us.

The tinkling of glass on the pavement stopped after a few seconds. A bright white flare came from the lower part of the building. I looked up as it faded and realized that the Acolytes had teleported out. I'd also spotted a small rainbow aura flittering around in the sky above us. At least Alteea was okay. I rolled over on my back and groaned.

Chapter 7

Wednesday, April 30

"Hey, Hurricane, not your finest moment, eh?" said a familiar voice.

I blinked my eyes open as I lay on the glass and goo-covered ground. I hadn't been sleeping; I had just been lying there praying the world would stop spinning.

The voice belonged to Bobby Knight, and I had mixed feelings about him being here at this moment. He was a great guy, and I'd worked with him many times when he led the Hamilton SWAT team, but I was a wee bit embarrassed that a bunch of kids just handed me and my team our asses, and having a friend witness it sucked. On the other hand, it was probably better than an EIRT team I didn't know—with my luck they would have charged us with interfering with a police investigation.

"Hey, Bobby, at least we made it here before they left, unlike a certain well-funded government team that shall remain nameless."

Bobby laughed and said, "Yeah, yeah. Thanks to the construction on the highway, traffic was a bitch. That and some of us aren't lucky enough to have access to a shadow-traveler. Care to tell me how you knew they were here and what happened?"

I started to nod, but even that small motion made my stomach lurch again. I took a deep, calming breath and said, "As long as you don't mind me staying here perfectly still for a bit while I'll fill you in, sure."

"Damn, you really are in bad shape. Can I get you something?" he asked with concern in his voice.

"Gatorade," I managed to plead in a croaky voice.

He shook his head and said, "Sorry, how about water instead?"

"Please."

His heavy combat boots crunched glass as he walked away. I groaned as I realized I'd need to sit up to drink the water. I closed my eyes again and slowly shifted to a sitting position. I opened my eyes and immediately shut them again as the world shifted in unpleasant ways.

A giggle off to my left caught my attention and it was a followed by a "Whoa, I'm drunk," from Liv. At least one of my teammates was conscious.

"Are you okay, Zack?" asked Liv in a slurred tone.

"I'm alive, barely. Can you check on the others and see if they are alright?"

"Okey dokey."

Shortly after that, Bobby returned and put an open bottle of water in my hand. I took a small pull from it and almost sighed at how good the cool liquid felt going down my raw throat. My stomach didn't seem to mind it either, so I took another long pull.

I opened my eyes and the world stayed reasonably still. Bobby's large form was looking down at me in concern.

"Thanks. You asked earlier about how we knew they were here." He nodded, and I added, "Stella set up a program that scans social media, news sites, police bands, and Odin-only-knows what else for anything related to industrial break-ins in Ontario. As for your second question about what happened..." I took a deep breath and explained how the battle went.

Twenty minutes later, Bobby was done questioning me over the confrontation with the Acolytes, and I'd filled him in on some of the theories about them we'd been developing.

Bobby said, "I think you are right that there is someone behind this group. I find it hard to believe that a group of powered teens organized something like this."

I nodded and was pleased to note that the world didn't move. I looked around to make sure there wasn't anyone close by us and said, "Bobby, I want to make a deal."

He frowned and said, "What type of deal?"

"We may have filmed the entire battle, and the person who filmed it probably got close-ups of all of them. If this video exists, I will send you a copy, but on one condition."

"Withholding evidence is a crime," argued Bobby.

"Only if the video exists and you can prove we have it. Look, they hurt Rob and killed a Hamilton cop, and on top of that I owe them some payback for this evening. All I wanted is some cooperation. I'll turn over the film, but if EIRT identifies any of them, I want to know their names, okay?"

Bobby was quiet for a moment and then said, "I can't do it officially; there is no way my captain will agree to it. What I can do is let you know, unofficially, if I find out anything; that is the best I can do..."

I pondered that for a moment. Officially would have been better, as that way when any news popped up, EIRT would send it to us immediately. If it was just Bobby, we'd only get updates when he was on duty. Thankfully, the man was a workaholic, so it being just him wouldn't hamper the information flow too badly. "That is good enough for me. I will send you the video in a bit. Any idea what they took?"

Bobby shook his head and said, "Not yet. The CEO for AAI Corp is on his way and we'll know then."

***

A sleek black Mercedes sedan was waved through the Peel Police checkpoint at the end of one of the parking lot entrances. It coasted to a stop behind the second EIRT SUV. A man in his late fifties or early sixties got out. With the expensive looking suit, polished shoes, and distinguished silver hair styled within an inch of its life, I had no doubt that this was AAI's CEO.

While waiting for him to show up, I'd managed to get to my feet. I was as weak as a kitten and still a touch unsteady on my feet, but I was at least able to move around. Bree had also woken up and changed back to her human form. She was currently sitting in Bobby's SUV protecting her modesty with a blanket. Liv was sitting there as well, keeping her company. Blue and Stella, still in her Hyde form, were both asleep amid the debris.

I shadowed Bobby as he approached the Mercedes. He held out his hand and introduced himself. The CEO shook his hand and said, "Nigel Garett, CEO of AAI, sorry for the delay in getting here. I was at a charity dinner in north Toronto."

He had a slight English accent, but by how subtle it was, I guessed he'd been in Canada for a long time. His accent got me thinking back to Terror-Byte, Stripper Girl, and Meat-Shield. They all sounded Canadian. None of them seemed to have a Canadian maritime accent

47

or any hint of French Canadian either, so they were from Ontario or from Western Canada. I hoped that meant they were local. If they were, there was a chance we might find a news report of some of them using their powers in public when they were younger.

Bobby released Nigel's hand and said, "I'm afraid the thieves managed to break in, and we'd like your assistance in figuring out what they took. Your building took quite a bit of damage and we are waiting for city engineers to come by and let us know if it's safe to enter or not. They should be here shortly."

Nigel nodded and just stared at the building for a moment and said, "It looks like most of the damage is cosmetic. Any chance we could skip waiting for the engineers? I'm quite worried that they might have taken Lucifer."

"Lucifer?" asked Bobby.

"Sorry, AAI was founded by Dr. Noel Harding. He created two advanced AIs, Lucifer and Gabriel. Lucifer is much faster at solving problems than Gabriel due to not having any moral or ethical constraints in his programming. The problem is Lucifer's solutions to problems are sometimes unorthodox and unacceptable. Due to this, we keep Lucifer air-gapped from any outside connections to contain him."

I perked up at Dr. Noel Harding's name. The man was a legend and a genuine celebrity, like Musk or Jobs. A doctorate in computer science by eighteen, he made his first billion by twenty-five designing programs that were bought out by Facebook, Amazon, and Google. He then went into AI where his creations were generations ahead of anything out there. I remembered the news coverage from a few years ago. He announced he was bored of AI and turned his attention to autonomous vehicles. The media had been buzzing recently that he was about to debut his prototype self-driving car any day now. If he founded AAI, I'd assume that he left the code to his AIs here and let others carry on his work.

Bobby looked confused, so I said, "Sorry, Mr. Garett, if you'll allow me." I turned to Bobby and explained, "Lucifer is Skynet. Give it a problem like dealing with environmental issues, and his solution might be to eliminate all humans. And by 'air-gapped,' he means that Lucifer was kept isolated on his own computer and not connected to other computers or the Internet."

The only reason I knew what air-gapped meant was because one night Stella went on a rant about computer security after a major corporation had a data breach. Computers, like most things, were more her area of expertise than mine. Stella was one smart cookie.

Bobby's facial expression changed to one of understanding and Nigel said, "Precisely, Mister...?"

"Sorry," said Bobby, "Mr. Garett, allow me to introduce the Hamilton Hurricane."

To my surprise, Nigel Garett's face lit up at that and he said, "This is a pleasure. I have always wanted to thank you for stopping that zombie outbreak in Oakville. My home was quite close to the cemetery that necromancer was operating out of. It made for quite a tense night on the home front for my family and me. It is hard to believe that was at least ten years ago now; I still can vividly remember that night."

I hadn't been expecting a fan, and we shook hands. I decided to indulge my curiosity for a moment and asked, "I assume that when Noel Harding turned his focus to autonomous vehicles, he left his AIs and code with you and your employees to continue on with his work?" Nigel nodded and I asked, "Do you sell the AIs?"

He shook his head and said, "No, the AIs are the company's greatest asset. Our revenue comes from consulting. Companies have the AIs analyze their problems and pay us for the solutions they come up with."

That made sense. I was about to ask another question when Bobby's phone rang. He answered it and after a couple of 'Okays,' and an 'I understand,' he hung up.

He held up his phone and said, "That was one of the engineers. They have been delayed and are still assessing damage to a bridge. They hope to be out here in about an hour now. And to answer your earlier question about skipping waiting for the engineers, I'm afraid we have to wait."

Nigel's phone rang, and he answered it, and to my surprise put it on speakerphone.

A precise sounding male voice said, *"My apologies for disturbing you, Mr. Garett, but I have been unable to reach Mr. Sato."*

Nigel interrupted the voice and said, "Gabriel, please hold for a moment." He turned to us and said, "James Sato is our chief technology officer and first point of contact for Gabriel if he has any issues. He is currently on a flight to Tokyo to attend a conference. The Gabriel AI, besides analyzing problems for our clients, also answers and routes calls for us, monitors and adjusts the climate controls for the building, and greets and keeps a log of any people entering or exiting the building. If he is calling, then the thieves didn't take him, any of our client records, or source code, as all of those are on the same server cluster. If they didn't take any of those, then the only other thing of value in the building is Lucifer."

Nigel said, "Thank you for waiting, Gabriel, what is the reason for your call?"

"I no longer have audio or visual feeds for the building, and I am unable to maintain the prescribed eighteen degrees Celsius required for after-hours climate control. How shall I proceed?"

"Thank you for the update. The building has been damaged, and we will be getting it repaired shortly. For now, just do your best and we'll talk shortly."

"Thank you, Mr. Garett. I look forward to talking to you later."

Nigel put away his phone. "If Lucifer has been taken, I have to call Dr. Harding and make arrangements. Are you sure we must wait for the engineers? If Lucifer is out in the wild, then we need to deal with that as soon as possible."

Bobby shook his head, but I turned to Bobby and said, "What if just you, Nigel, Liv and I went in? If the building starts to collapse, I should be able to use my Air powers to hold it up long enough that Liv can get you and Nigel out."

Bobby studied me for a moment and said, "What about you? And are you up for this? You were in pretty rough shape earlier."

Honestly, I was still pretty woozy, and my suggestion might just have been drunken courage. I agreed with Nigel's assessment that the damage to the building was superficial and doubted it was in any danger of collapsing. The sooner we got in there, the sooner I could go home to bed. If the building did come down, I had enough power to deal with it; it wouldn't be pretty, and I'd probably use more power then I needed to, but I'd get the job done.

"I'm a little unsteady on my feet, but my power reserves are still high, so we should be fine."

Bobby went quiet as he considered it, so I added, "C'mon, Bobby, Nigel's right, most the damage is cosmetic; the risk is low."

Ten minutes later the four of us entered the building. I was a touch unsteady on my feet, but Liv had grabbed the back of my jeans to make sure I didn't fall. Bobby gave me a disapproving look, but I waved him off.

Nigel proceeded past the main lobby, which now had an eight-foot circle burned into its marble floors from where Terror-Byte and his crew teleported out. We went down a hallway and made a right.

"That isn't a good sign," said Nigel glancing at a solid looking steel fire door that was hanging open.

The door had its lock burned off, like the front door at L-Tech. We followed Nigel through the door and down a flight of stairs to the building's basement. We turned left at the bottom of the stairs and saw that another door to a climate-controlled room had been breached. We entered the room, and in the center was a large vault. Its main six-inch-thick door had also been burned open. The vault door was partially ajar.

"No, no, no," said Nigel as he ran to the vault.

He swung open the door and inside the dimly lit vault was an empty pedestal—Lucifer was gone.

Bobby insisted that we exit the building, and Nigel nodded in a slight daze. When we got back outside, I scanned the parking lot for my other teammates and exhaled, relieved. Blue was on her feet and standing by Stella's slumbering Hyde form, looking at her friend in concern. Nigel had regained his poise as well and excused himself to make some calls.

Once Nigel was back in his car, Bobby turned to me and said, "How dangerous do you think this Lucifer is? Are the machines really going to rise up and take over the world?"

"I doubt it. The thieves might be smart enough to keep Lucifer isolated and just use him to analyze their problems. Even if Lucifer gets on the Internet, I don't think he will be able to build an army of robots to take over the world; we aren't anywhere near that level of automation. Worst case scenario is the thieves force Lucifer to work on their behalf. Think about how many things are computer controlled. Lucifer could hack alarm companies and their systems, traffic and power grids, financial markets, and Odin-only-knows what else."

One of the members of Bobby's team called for him, and he left me with my thoughts. The more I pondered about Lucifer, the more I was convinced whoever was behind Terror-Byte and his crew wouldn't want to risk Lucifer getting out. If Lucifer managed to connect to the Internet, there was a good chance it would upload its program to the Cloud and use it to escape. No, it was more likely that they would keep Lucifer isolated and use it to analyze jobs and targets for break-ins, or assist in refining the design of whatever they were building.

Liv interrupted my thoughts. "I want to go keep Bree company, are you okay standing on your own?"

"Yeah, I'm feeling better and should be fine."

She blurred off, and I wandered over to Blue. I was overjoyed that she was up, as that meant I didn't have to fly everyone home.

I wandered over to Blue and asked, "Are you okay?"

Blue nodded and said, "Yes, my healing trance got rid of the poison."

Poison? I was confused for a moment and asked, "You mean alcohol?"

"My form cannot handle alcohol."

I frowned and said, "But that night the demon bounty came in, you had a glass of champagne."

Blue smiled and said, "I held a glass of champagne but didn't drink it. The ritual of celebration seemed important and I didn't wish to be impolite. I poured the contents into your glass when you were distracted."

I smiled at this and said, "You should have mentioned it; it would have been easy enough to get you something non-alcoholic."

She shrugged and turned to Stella's large sleeping form and said, "I was unaware her Hyde form could get drunk. How are we going to get her home?"

I wasn't sure I wanted to take her home in this state. If she woke up and wasn't in control of her drunken Hyde form, it could smash our house to pieces in seconds. Then I had an idea.

A few minutes later, Blue, Liv, and I were standing around Stella's Hyde form with a bucket of cold water in each of our hands. I'd convinced Bobby and his team and Nigel to move their vehicles out of the parking lot and onto the street in case this didn't go well. I prayed Stella would be in control when we woke her up. Liv had a big grin on her face like this was the greatest prank in the world, but Blue's somber expression matched mine.

"On three?" I asked and they both nodded.

I started the countdown and on three we all tossed our water. The water splashed over our Hyde and it let loose an angry roar and scrambled to its feet. Its bulbous eye looked around, as if searching for a target for its rage.

"Stella?" asked Blue, who was bravely standing less than ten feet in front of her.

Liv and I flanked Stella's Hyde form on either side, but we were a good fifteen feet back.

Stella's monstrous form seemed confused as it studied Blue. I began calling on my Air power, in case this went terribly wrong.

"Stella, it's me Blue," Blue said calmly, her tone soothing.

Hyde's large head bobbed up and down in a nod, and I exhaled in relief when a moment later it reverted to Stella's much less dangerous ten-year-old appearance.

Stella glanced around and asked, "What happened? Did I fall asleep?"

Blue nodded and we all moved closer to Stella. Blue examined Stella with concern and said, "How are you feeling now?"

"I'm perfectly fine." She paused, and a look of horror appeared on her face as she took in the damage around her. "Did Hyde do this?"

Blue shook her head and said, "No, the damage was from one of Terror-Byte's exploding phones. One of his henchmen has the ability to intoxicate people. He zapped all of us and you just passed out in your Hyde form."

Stella's body language relaxed, and she said, "I remember fighting with the blonde clones, but it gets hazy after that. Did they get away?"

Blue nodded and informed Stella what happened. I turned to Liv and told her to tell EIRT that it was safe to come back. She sped off. I was swaying on my feet and moved over to a concrete ledge and sat down.

Twenty minutes later, Bobby was done with us and I had Alteea send him the video she made of the battle. Blue opened a shadow portal. After a quick stop at the lab to use the Food-O-Tron to get Bree food and Liv blood, we were home. Everyone was going to watch the video, but I'd look at it tomorrow. I excused myself, stumbled upstairs, and fell into bed fully dressed and passed out.

Chapter 8

Thursday, May 1

Aloud crack of thunder woke me the next day. Normally, nothing put me in a better mood than a good thunderstorm. My whole body tingled and felt alive with all that electricity in the air. My power levels were humming nicely, but that was barely noticeable against the pounding in my head. The sounds of the raindrops hitting the roof were like tiny needles being driven into my brain. My mouth was like a toxic waste dump, and my throat was abused and raw. Starting another day with an epic hangover sucked. I wondered what the hell I drank before flashes from the previous night started flooding back to me.

I swore the next time we took on Terror-Byte and the rest of his teen terrors, I would fry the Bartender where he stood. I sighed as I remembered their fancy armor suits were lightning resistant and changed my vow to sending him into orbit using my Air powers instead.

My right butt cheek hurt, and I realized I'd slept with my iPhone in the back pocket of my jeans. I fished it out and was surprised to see the locked home screen covered in text messages. I unlocked the phone and had eighty-three new text messages waiting. Most of them were from Rob's cop poker buddies. They were all making comments and shots about the battle last night. The first three I read were from Hamilton police officers, so I assumed that EIRT had shared our video with other law enforcement agencies. The fourth text, though, was from Brent, a Were bear from the Barrie pack who had nothing to do with anything police related, and I wondered how he saw the battle. I texted Brent back and asked how he knew about it.

I browsed quickly over the remaining texts and all of them were related to the battle last night. My phone chimed as yet another message rolled in; it was a reply from Brent. It contained a YouTube link, so I clicked on it. I groaned as a video titled 'Hamilton Hurricane vs. Naked Amazons,' popped up. My headache got worse when I noticed it had over 1.5 million views. It opened with a shaky shot of us lined up facing

Terror-Byte and his crew in front of the AAI building. By the angle and the distance, some late night office worker or cleaning staff must have filmed us from an adjacent building.

I watched the video in silence; in part out of curiosity and in part hoping I might spot a clue to our opponents' identities or learn more information about their powers. My stomach lurched towards the end when the camera zoomed in and caught me tossing my dinner all over AAI's front sidewalk.

Really? I thought to myself in exasperation. The bulk of the video was done in a wide shot and yet the camera person just *had* to film that part in close-up. Somehow, I knew Rob's poker buddies would have that clip and be replaying it in slo-mo just to annoy me.

Poker had me thinking of Rob. I scrolled through the messages again to see if there was any update from Annette. Unfortunately, there wasn't anything, which likely meant there had been no change in his condition.

My own condition was still poor, and I badly needed my three cures for a hangover: caffeine, grease, and aspirin. Stella and Blue were in the kitchen and seemed annoying bright and cheerful.

I put on the kettle and said, "How are you two not hungover?"

Stella smiled and said, "Any condition that I have while as Hyde or myself goes away when I change between the two forms. That is why I don't get sick. If I feel a cold or sniffle coming on, I just change to Hyde and back and it's gone."

"My healing trance last night removed all the poison from my body," explained Blue. She paused and asked, "Why? Are you not well this morning?"

"Understatement of the year there. Any chance you could hit the Food-O-Tron and grab me a burger and fries?"

Blue nodded and left the kitchen. I finished making my coffee, swallowed a couple of aspirin, and joined Stella at the table.

"I got a ton of texts last night; it seems our battle was filmed and has gone viral."

Stella made a face and asked, "Why would that be popular?"

I laughed and said, "Are you kidding? Naked bimbos, superpowers. The only thing missing to make it the perfect YouTube click-bait would be a grumpy cat. Technically, with Bree in her Were form, we have the cat part so no wonder it went viral. Speaking of videos, how was Alteea's, and where is she this morning?"

Stella sipped her tea. "She did a wonderful job. Lots of close-ups on each of the Acolytes. She stayed up with Liv and Bree last night, so I assume she is still sleeping. We might have a lead on a couple of their identities."

I perked up at that, the caffeine working its way through my system helped, too, and asked, "Which ones?"

"The dark-haired girl with the insects and the Bartender," said Stella.

I smiled at the Bartender's name. Other than Terror-Byte himself, he was the one I wanted to nail the most.

"This morning we started doing searches on any incidents involving the powers they displayed and on their armor suits. Suits that can stop lightning, cold, and fire can't be that common. We haven't had any luck on the suits but got two good leads on the powers. About a year ago, a girl surrounded by bugs was arrested for vandalizing a bug-spray display at Home Depot in Kitchener. There was no name in the online article due her being sixteen at the time, so her identity was protected by the Young Offenders Act. I found her name on social media though—Carla Priest. Better yet, I found some pictures, and it looks to be the same girl. She was very active on Twitter and Instagram, but about nine months ago all her posts stopped. We are trying to find a home address for her but so far, no luck."

So at least one of them was local. I wondered how EIRT hadn't found her and if Bobby wasn't living up to his end of the bargain by giving me any names he found. He probably was at the end of his shift last night and hadn't had a chance to make a full report or investigate it any further.

Blue came back into the kitchen carrying a cast iron pan and put it down in front of me. I grabbed the cheeseburger and took a huge bite. A lot of people avoid heavy foods when hungover, but I wasn't one of them. I found nothing worked better for soaking up alcohol then a ton of grease.

As Blue sat back down, Stella continued, "As for the Bartender, we have a name, an outstanding arrest warrant, and bounty for him. He is Brandon Owens, twenty-one years old and wanted for two charges of manslaughter and three date rapes. A bounty of $100,000 for him has been out for almost a year on the UN site."

I swallowed another mouthful of burger and said, "Wait, I remember this one now. He was a DJ at an underground rave in Scarborough and used his powers to get everyone wasted, but a bunch of them already had drugs in their system and two of them overdosed and died. The date rapes were random pickups where he used his powers to get the girls blackout drunk and took advantage of them. I investigated him about seven months ago, but no one had seen him for a couple of months. With no leads, I let it go. Back then he had a neon green mohawk; that was why I didn't recognize him last night."

I took another bite of my burger and Blue gave me a disapproving look; probably for not recognizing Brandon Owens. In truth, I was pissed at myself too; looking for suspects with different hair was like bounty hunting 101.

I'd spent a week trying to track him down, studying him and his habits, and a mere hairstyle change shouldn't have been enough for me not to know it was him; I was usually better than that. In my defense, I hadn't really focused on him much during the battle, as I was more focused on Terror-Byte, not to mention the bunch of naked blondes attacking me.

It might have been, too, that after my week of trying to track him down, I came up completely blank. I had concluded either he was dead or had left the country and started a new life somewhere else in the world and promptly forgot about him.

There were a few things bothering me about our encounter last night. There was something obvious that I was missing about the Acolytes, but each time I tried to figure it out, my head throbbed. Where do a bunch of minor-powered teens get state-of-the-art high-tech combat suits? Brandon and Carla were both locals, and Terror-Byte and Hexadecimal didn't have accents, so they were probably local too. How do a bunch of Ontario kids get involved with an international crime ring? There had to be someone behind this financing and running it. This was too sophisticated for the group we took on last night. A bunch of teens would go after a bank or a liquor store, not a prototype gyro or an AI.

A mysterious shadow figure or figures running this operation made the most sense. The question was were these kids being forced into this or were they recruited? I had no doubt that Brandon would have jumped at the chance to be recruited and disappear with that bounty on him. Carla already had one minor criminal charge due to her Home Depot incident. Maybe there were other crimes she had done, and joining this organization was a chance to up her game. The more I thought about it, the more my recruitment theory made sense. How hard would it be to talk a bunch of disaffected teens into dumping their lives and joining an international gang? Power, money, and fame would sound a hell of a lot better than being that lonely freak kid that everyone makes fun of.

I finished another bite of my burger and shared my theory with Blue and Stella.

Blue nodded and said, "Stella and I were thinking along the same lines when we discussed this earlier. Even the name 'Acolytes' implies that they are serving someone else."

Stella piped up and said, "Brandon has been missing for eight months, and Carla vanished about nine months ago. They must have been recruited then, and whoever is running the operation kept them out of sight until now. Oh, I forgot, the thieves in Seoul struck again last night. They hit LG Chem and stole a shipment of prototype lithium batteries. Same MO as before; disrupted power to the plant and in the confusion, they snuck in, grabbed the shipment, and teleported out."

I mentally added the batteries to the list of goods the Acolytes had stolen so far and tried to figure out what they all had in common but came up blank.

My head throbbed again, and my thoughts went in a different direction. Something about last night's encounter was still bothering me, but I couldn't put my finger on it. Was there another member of their team that, like Brandon, I should recognize? I'd never seen Terror-Byte before last night. Bug Girl and Hexadecimal's cloning powers were unique enough that I would have remembered them. Meat-Shield, the half-tank, might be someone I'd run across before; his bouncer-type build was something I came across a lot in this line of work. The redhead with the flaming knives didn't ring any bells. Flaming knives weren't that common, and I would remember that.

No, it wasn't that. It was something else, something that just didn't feel right or make sense.

"Zack?" asked Stella.

"Sorry, lost in thought there. Good work by the way on Carla and Brandon."

A small smile appeared on Stella's normally serious face and she said, "Blue and I have gone over the video Alteea took a number of times, and we'll look at the one on YouTube, just in case it shows something the first video missed. Do you want to go over it after your lunch?"

I had taken another bite, so I just shook my head in response and winced as that motion caused another painful gong to go off in my head. I swallowed and said, "No, I'm going back to bed right after this to get rid of this hangover."

It would be a few hours before Bree got up and a good five hours before the sun set and Liv was awake, so me grabbing a couple hours of sleep wouldn't slow us down much. I was impressed that Stella and Blue had found out two identities already. The Bartender was a dead-end but maybe Bug Girl would give us a lead.

"Keep looking into Carla's past. See if you can find a home address, names of friends or anything from her pre-Acolyte life that might give us a clue about where she might be now." Stella nodded.

I finished eating my burger while Stella and Blue went back to their work.

***

I woke up a few hours later and my hangover had dulled to a manageable ache. I sat up and my eyes drifted to the far wall where there was a framed Hamilton Hurricane uniform. A warm feeling filled me as I looked at it. A replica of my old black and gold hero costume was mounted under glass and surrounded by signatures of local politicians, cops, fire personnel, and EMS workers. It was a thank-you gift from the mayor's office, given to me a few months after I retired.

As I studied my old mask, a light went on in my brain and it finally hit me what was bothering me from last night: none of them wore masks. Wearing a mask to intimidate opponents and to protect your identity was like Super-Villain 101, right up there with coming up with a clever name and a terrifying catch phase.

The only villains I could remember that eschewed a mask were Khaos, Death-dealer, and World Master. Khaos was insane, so nothing he did made sense. Death-dealer originally wore a mask, but after she escaped prison, she stopped, as everyone knew who she was anyways. Her power of being able to kill with a single touch was unique enough that even if she did wear a mask, it wouldn't have hidden anything. World Master didn't wear one probably due to ego; he planned to take over the world and wanted everyone to worship him as a god before he was taken down. Those three were also high-level villains, not a bunch of nervous kids with minor powers.

Why didn't they add helmets to those high-tech suits? The black suits with matching helmets and maybe just a glowing red strip for eyes would be intimidating as hell. By the Acolytes not covering their faces, in less than twenty-four hours, we already knew two of their identities, and between us and EIRT, we'd probably have the others figured out in the next couple of days. Why make things easier for us?

I found Stella and Blue in the upstairs office. They were hunched over the computer, still doing research. I asked for their opinion on why the Acolytes hadn't bothered wearing masks or helmets.

Blue frowned and said, "It is likely that whoever is behind this purposely left off the masks to bind them closer to him."

I puzzled over that for a bit. We'd already figured that there was someone or some group that was financing, equipping, and training these kids. Whoever was behind all of this wouldn't want them leaving after investing that type of time and money into them.

I said, "You're right. If their identities are known, they can't go back to their old lives, and they become even more dependent on the mastermind behind all of this."

Blue nodded and added, "Back on my home world, there was a death cult. To encourage loyalty to the cult, its members were given a large red dagger facial tattoo. This made anyone with the tattoo fanatical; the authorities executed anyone they found with a red dagger tattoo on sight, so they had nothing to lose."

They sounded like a fun bunch. Blue was usually fairly close-mouthed about her old world, but on occasion, she would share a tidbit of information. Between death cults, god-kings and vengeance vows, her old world sounded like a brutally tough place to live; it certainly explained how she could be so ruthlessly practical at times.

Stella's voice pulled me from my musings. "We found Carla's mom. Her name is Paula Priest, single mom. Carla is her only child. She filed a missing person's report with Kitchener police after Carla disappeared. The police investigated but didn't find Carla or even any leads. The case is still open. By how thin the file is, I don't think the police spent much time on it. They probably figured Carla just ran away and would turn up sooner or later."

"Had she run away before?" I asked.

"Yes, twice before, once for a few days and another time for two weeks," said Stella.

Hard to blame the cops for this one. A troubled teen with a history of running away; no wonder they didn't spend much time on it.

"Do we have an address for the mom?"

Stella nodded but Blue said, "We have an address. The mom is at home but is sleeping. She is a nurse and is on nights this week."

I was going to ask how Blue knew this but then figured she used the shadows to spy on her. Carla had been gone for nine months, so visiting her mother was probably a waste of time but we might get lucky.

I thought about it. "Good job, we'll wait until sundown and then you can transport Liv and me out to the house and we can pay her a visit."

Blue said, "I can come with you and field test the hologram device."

"Not this time; three people showing up unexpectedly on someone's doorstep is a bit much. This is something I would prefer to do solo; the only reason I'm bringing Liv is for her mind-control powers."

Blue nodded and we spent the rest of the afternoon doing more research.

Chapter 9

Thursday, May 1

"What's with the suit and tie? Tired of bounty hunting and you're getting a real job now?" asked Liv as she entered the kitchen in search of her breakfast.

I explained that the two of us were going to interview Bug Girl's mom and that people responded better when you showed up on their doorsteps well-dressed. I finished by giving her current outfit—a sleeveless white top, no bra, and black yoga pants that hugged her lovely form—a pointed glance.

"What?" she asked and then looked down at her outfit and added, "Oh right, I guess I need to change."

She pulled a pint mug of blood from the fridge and put it in the microwave to warm it up. While she was waiting for it to finish, an expression of almost pure joy appeared on her face. "I have the perfect outfit for this…"

Somehow those words made me nervous. I worried about what her idea of a perfect outfit would be and how long it would take her to get ready. Before I could respond, the microwave dinged. Liv took the glass out and I got a touch queasy as she drained the entire thing in one long pull.

In the blink of an eye, she dumped the glass in the sink and shot out of the kitchen.

"We don't have much time before it is too late to knock on someone's door!" I yelled after her.

"Yeah, yeah. I'll be super quick."

Thanks to her vampire speed, she was back in just under ten minutes. My jaw hit the floor at her new outfit. Her dark hair was up, and she was wearing elegant wire frame glasses that seemed to enhance her beautiful green eyes. The glasses were fake, as her vampire vision was perfect. She wore a nicely tailored dark gray business suit jacket over a white blouse with a matching knee-high skirt, skin-toned nylons, and a pair of shiny gray modest two-inch heels.

The awe I felt must have shown on my face as she said, "Really? You have seen me naked, in a bikini, in at least ten super cute outfits, and yet this gets that reaction. You are so weird at times…"

"You look amazing, but I'm not sure that outfit will work for interviewing people."

Liv put her hands on her hips and said, "Why not? It's perfect—it's conservative and non-threating. I couldn't be dressed more appropriate for this if I tried…"

"That isn't the problem. The problem is I want to just stay home and play with my sexy librarian…"

She smiled at this but rolled her eyes. Liv grabbed my arm and dragged me to the living room where the rest of the team was hanging out.

Bree laughed when she saw us and said, "No thanks, I have already found Jesus…"

"Shush, you," chided Stella. "They both look very smart and respectable."

Blue's tail moved in wide leisurely circles. She studied Olivia and said, "Yes, that outfit is superior to the usual garments you wear."

Liv thanked them but then frowned as she caught Blue's unintentional slight towards her normal fashion choices.

Bree stopped snickering long enough to add, "If you are 'playing with your sexy librarian' someone better find me some earplugs…"

I felt the heat rush to my cheeks and cursed Were hearing under my breath. Thankfully, Liv saved me by having Blue open a shadow portal, allowing us to flee before Bree could get in another shot.

We stepped out of the shadows into a townhouse complex in suburban Kitchener. By the peeling paint on the fence around the complex, the debris on the lawn, the faded look of the houses themselves, and the range of older worn-looking automobiles, I decided this wasn't the most luxurious part of town. There were some nicer houses further up the block, so maybe it was just this complex. I bet that at least half its residents were on some form of government assistance and the other half were single moms or low-income families that were just trying to get by.

Paula's unit was the third one on the left. As we walked up the short driveway, a few things stood out. Her front yard looked better than the others due to it being greener and lusher. There were also flowers and small bushes planted along the walkway. The other neighbors hadn't bothered. The car in her driveway was an older model Honda Civic, but for its age, it was in good condition. Her door was the same color as everyone else's but had been repainted more recently. Her house and yard wouldn't be featured on home and garden shows and her car wouldn't end up in *Hot Rod* magazine, but I liked that she had pride in what she owned and took care of it.

I knocked firmly on the door and held out my hero ID. A light came on in the hallway inside the house and Paula cautiously opened her door.

"Hi, Miss Priest, my name is Zack Stevens and my companion here is Olivia Dick, do you mind if we ask you a few questions?"

I offered the ID to her. While she studied it, I took the opportunity to check her out. Her appearance caught me off guard when she answered the door; I expected her to be shorter and heavier and have darker hair like her daughter. I also thought that having a seventeen-year-old she'd be older. Instead, I got a taller, rail thin blonde who was in her early thirties. She might even be younger than my thirty-three years.

A puzzled look appeared on her face. She handed back the ID and said, "You're a little outside your usual stomping grounds."

Her blue eyes stared intently at me, waiting for my answer. She might be younger than me but the lines around her eyes and the hardness in her gaze betrayed that her life hadn't been easy.

My hero ID had my name and my Hamilton Hurricane alias on it, and it was probably the Hamilton part that she was referring to. "Yes, ma'am, Kitchener isn't somewhere I usually patrol, but there was an incident in Hamilton that your daughter was involved in."

She perked up when I said 'daughter' and a range of emotions flashed across her face; there was concern, hope, sadness, and worry in her eyes.

"Carla? Do you know where my baby is?" she asked in almost a pleading tone.

"I'm sorry, I don't. We were hoping that maybe you could help us locate her."

Her face fell, and she shook her head, "I haven't seen her in—" she thought for a second "—it has to be nine months now. Look, why don't you come inside, and we can talk about it?"

I nodded, and she opened the door. Inside, the house was neat and tidy. The furniture was older but clean and in good shape. We took a seat on the couch in the front room and she sat down in an easy chair across from us.

Paula offered us coffee, but we declined. She then asked, "You've seen my daughter recently?"

"Yes, last night actually. I'm afraid she's involved with some bad people. Did you hear about the Hamilton police officer that was killed in the break-in a couple of nights ago?"

Paula nodded her head slowly and said, "I was sad to hear about that; his family must be devastated."

"That same group was involved in another break-in last night in Mississauga."

"I hadn't heard about that one; I just got off a double and haven't watched the news today. Was anyone hurt?" she asked.

"No, not seriously anyways," I said. "We were at the one in Mississauga and so was your daughter; she was one of thieves."

Paula gasped at this and said, "No, there must be some mistake. Carla is a shy, gentle girl; she wouldn't be involved in something like that."

I turned to Liv and held out my hand. She handed me the folder and I pulled out a picture of Carla and passed it to Paula. "Is this Carla?"

She examined the picture for a second and her hands started to shake. She nodded and tears started to flow silently down her cheeks.

After a few more seconds she wiped her eyes and said, "Sorry. I'm more relieved than upset; I didn't even know if she was alive or dead until seeing this."

I liked this woman. She seemed like a decent, caring individual and I couldn't imagine what it would be like to have your daughter disappear without a trace for almost a year.

"Look, Miss Priest—"

"Paula," she said cutting me off.

"Paula," I continued. "We want what you want—to bring your daughter home safely. The group she is a part of has killed one cop and put another in a coma. EIRT and local and provincial police are looking for this group, too, but they are more concerned at this point with stopping them than anything else. We'd like to get to them first. Nothing would make me happier than bringing them in peacefully without incident, but we need your help."

She nodded at this and said, "I'd like to help but I'm not sure what I can provide. As I said, I haven't seen or heard from her in months."

"Why don't we start there," I said. "When she disappeared. According to the police report, this wasn't the first time she left home…"

Paula sat up straighter at that, gripping the arms of her chair firmly. "I told them this time was different. The other two times she ran away, she took her phone and a knapsack full of clothes, but both were still here. She lived on that phone; there was no way she'd just leave it here if she ran away on her own."

"We think the person behind all of this recruited these kids. She was probably instructed not to bring her phone, as they can be traced. I'm guessing they were told to bring as little as possible. Did Carla mention any new opportunities or meeting someone new before she disappeared?"

"No, nothing out of the usual. I don't remember her mentioning anyone new or anything like that." Paula paused for a moment and a sad, regretful look crossed her face. "We had a big fight on the day she disappeared. She wanted a new phone; she'd cracked a small part of the screen on hers. I told her that if she wanted a new one then she'd have to get a job. Carla got upset at this and said she'd been looking for a job for months, but no one would hire her. I told her that it was her own fault; that with all her piercings she wasn't exactly 'employee of the month' material. I shouldn't have said that, and she lost it and stormed off to her room. I left for work shortly after that, and that was the last time I saw her."

She hadn't been in contact since then, unless the mom was lying, but it didn't feel like it. I could use Liv to whammy her to make sure, but my gut told me that she was being honest, and I didn't want to use Liv's mind control powers unless we had to. This was starting to look like a dead end.

Liv said, "Did Carla have any friends that she was close to?"

"Just Melvin," said Paula and then she laughed. "Carla was a shy but happy kid until she became a teen. Her power to control bugs emerged then, and she became obsessed with them. The kids at school picked on her and called her 'Creepy Carla.' She was upset at first but then seemed to embrace it. She dyed her hair black, started dressing in dark clothes, and went Goth. With each day she got moodier and more closed off. We argued more, as I wanted to help her, but she just kept shutting me out."

Paula paused for a moment. "I was concerned about her lack of friends, and all the time she'd spend in her room or out in the woods playing with insects. Just before she turned fifteen, she brought home Melvin. The kid was geeky and awkward but seemed bright and harmless enough. I was just glad that she had a friend. Unfortunately, things got worse once Melvin was involved. That kid was anything but harmless. He had a darkness about him, and you could just sense the resentment coming off him. She started skipping school and getting in trouble more. Each time, Melvin was involved. I'm pretty sure that both times she ran away, he went with her."

Paula sighed, and Liv asked, "Do you think Melvin went with her this time as well?"

"I don't know. I called Melvin's mom a few times. The first couple of calls she just hung up without saying anything. The last call I made she finally spoke but just said, 'that boy is no longer my son, don't call again.' I haven't seen or heard anything from Melvin since Carla disappeared."

What kind of parent just disowns a child? Melvin's mother sounded like a real winner.

A new thought hit me, and I asked, "Does Melvin have any sort of powers that you know of?"

Paula thought for a moment and said, "I don't know. He was freakishly good with electronics and computers. Carla dropped her phone in the toilet and fried it. We tried soaking it in rice to get the moisture out, but it was dead. Melvin came over, picked it up, and seconds later it came back to life in his hand."

My excitement grew, and I fumbled for the folder. I rifled through it and pulled out a picture of Terror-Byte and handed it to Paula. Her eyes widened, and she said, "Yeah, that's Melvin."

"Do you know his last name?"

"Coontz. Melvin Coontz," she said. I fished a pen out of my suit pocket and started writing the name inside the folder.

"Any chance we could get his mother's phone number or address?"

Paula nodded and got up from her chair and left the room. She returned with an older model smartphone and gave me the number, adding, "I don't have an address, but she lives near Hidden Valley in the southeast part of the city."

She looked down at my notes and said, "His last name is spelt K-U-N-T-Z."

I crossed out the last name and wrote in the correct spelling. As much as I hated Melvin for what he did to Rob, I was starting to feel a little sympathy for the kid. First, you probably can't find a nerdier name than Melvin. And second, I doubted that his school peers would have pronounced his last name as 'Coontz.'

It was coming up on nine already, and I wanted to talk to Mrs. Kuntz this evening, so I thanked Paula for her help. I also gave her my number and said to call me if she thought of anything else or if Carla contacted her. I added that she could also give my number to Carla if she called, and that if Carla wanted to get out, we could rescue her in minutes.

Just before we left, it hit me that Paula didn't have an aura. It was possible that other people in Paula's family tree had powers and it just skipped her, but it was more likely that Carla's powers came from her father, so I asked, "Does anyone in your family besides Carla have powers?"

Paula shook her head and said, "No, Carla got her power from her dad."

"Would she try and contact him?"

She got a sad, distant look on her face and said, "No, he died before she was born."

"Sorry," I said. I sensed there was a story there that I was curious about, but it was getting late and I wanted to talk to Melvin's mother tonight. I did, however, want to know one more thing, "What was his power?"

"Barry's powers were similar to Carla's, except it was small birds, not bugs that he could control."

Super class genetics were fascinating. The rest of the Enhanced Individuals were more predictable. Since my mother was an Air elemental, I only had two options when I hit puberty: I'd either be an Air elemental or a norm. Mages, witches, and other magic users were the same—either their kids would get magic abilities or not. When Supers had kids, you had no idea what the results would be; they could inherit their parents' powers or something similar, like Carla had, they could develop a completely new power, or they could just be normal.

Captain Awesome and Gravity-Girl were classic examples of this. They were two of the strongest Supers on the planet during the seventies. When they got married, everyone expected their kids to be incredibly powerful. They had four kids; three were normal and didn't have an ounce of power. The youngest daughter had power, but it was the ability to make herself faintly glow, which other than being useful as a night-light, wasn't good for much else.

I thanked Paula for her time, and she said, "Please, bring my little girl home safely."

I promised her we would try our best and she closed the door behind us.

Chapter 10

Thursday, May 1

Liv whistled and said, "Whoa, these are some nice houses."

They were expensive, and so far almost each one we had passed had a three-car garage and was big enough to comfortably house a family of twenty. I wasn't sure 'nice' was the right adjective; impressive, maybe, but their gargantuan size caused them to lose some of their charm. Most 'nice' homes had a welcoming feel; these felt more like looking out your rearview mirror and seeing a semi's grill filling up your back window. I did, however, appreciate the wide swatches of immaculate green lawns and the abundance of mature trees lining the quiet street.

At seeing these expensive homes, my anger at Melvin flared. I could sympathize with a kid who grew up in a shitty area with a single mom or as a foster kid bouncing from one bad place to another, turning to crime due to lack of options. This type of neighborhood, though, meant Melvin had the world as his oyster. He would never go hungry, his schooling would be paid for, and there may even have been a trust fund to boot. What excuse did he have to prey on other people?

Liv shot me a questioning look as sparks dripped off me. I waved her off and forced myself to take a deep breath. Maybe Melvin's life wasn't that rosy; his mother could be a violent alcoholic, or maybe his dad would come home from the office and take his frustrations out on him. Just because things looked wonderful from the outside didn't mean there weren't dark secrets underneath. I mean, Paula said that Melvin's mom disowned him. What type of person does that to their own kid?

We found Melvin's house and walked up the driveway. I glanced at my watch and saw it was just coming up on 9:30 p.m. A bit late to be making a random call on someone, but there were lights on inside the house, so they were still up.

We stepped up to the front landing, and I couldn't help but admire the intricate travertine stonework I was standing on. The double front doors were just as beautiful with their rich, dark stained wood and wrought iron design embedded in the glass. I pushed the brightly lit doorbell and a wispy chime echoed softly from inside the house.

The door opened, revealing a woman in her late forties or maybe early fifties—with the stretched Botox forehead, it was hard to tell.

I spotted an aura and readied my powers on instinct, but then relaxed. Her aura was barely there, meaning whatever her powers were, they were very weak. I was curious, however, about what her power was, as I had never seen this combination before. The core was orange, meaning Super-class. The second small ring was the same yellow as mine, which meant something Air or Electricity related. The outer ring was pale green, which usually meant telepath. I puzzled over what that combination could possibly be.

Her whole look puzzled me too. She was wearing a formal, conservative dress with a pearl necklace. Her make-up was done, and her nails were perfectly manicured a light pink color. She looked like she had just gotten home from a thousand-dollar-a-plate charity event. Oddly, though, her dark hair was in an up-do that looked like something from the sixties or seventies, and the big round eye glasses and outfit she wore fit that period too.

While I sized her up, she looked us both over and her face changed. She looked as though she had just stepped in some gum or something equally unpleasing.

"Can I help you?" she asked in a cold, brisk tone.

"Mrs. Kuntz—" I started to say but she cut me off.

"That was my married name. I now go by Mitchel."

"Sorry, Ms. Mitchel, we were hoping to talk to you about your son Melvin?"

"We have nothing to talk about; I no longer have a son by that name," and with that, she started to close the door in our faces.

Liv blurred forward, wedged her foot in the door and said, "You will invite us in and answer our questions." Her eyes glowed when she spoke, so I knew she was doing her vampire compulsion thing. Ms. Mitchel frowned in confusion but didn't get that blank look like most people did when under a vampire's thrall. Liv's eyes glowed brighter and she repeated herself.

This time it worked, and Ms. Mitchel said, her voice monotone, "Come in, and I will answer your questions." Her power must have let her resist Liv's initial push.

We stepped inside, and the house was tastefully decorated, but with its uniform marble floors, cream colored walls, and regimented appearance it seemed cold and clinical rather than welcoming.

We took off our shoes and followed her to a room just off the main hall. There were two black leather couches arranged in an L-shape with an antique wooden coffee table in front of them. The couches caught my attention, as they were oddly shiny. As I stepped closer, I noticed the leather was covered completely in a thick clear plastic.

A flashback from my childhood popped into my mind. When I was in grade school, my best friend was Paul Watson. We hung out all the time, and one day he invited me to spend the weekend up at his grandparents' house. They had covered all their furniture in plastic like this. They were also dour and felt children should been seen and not heard. That weekend sucked. I asked my mom why we didn't cover our furniture and stuff in plastic to protect them. She laughed and said, "That was a silly trend in the sixties. Why own nice leather or a soft material that feels wonderful if you are going to hide it under plastic? Besides it looks ugly too."

The plastic squeaked as we sat down. Liv looked down at the plastic coating and frowned.

I studied Ms. Mitchel for a moment and said, "I'm sorry, I didn't catch your first name…"

"I didn't offer it; it's Joannie, but only my priest and close friends call me that."

In this day and age, most people allowed you to use their first name. I found this odd, but continued, "Very well then, Ms. Mitchell, when was the last time you heard from your son, Melvin?"

She crossed her arms and said, "I don't have a son by that name anymore."

Joannie didn't offer anything else, and I gave Liv a nod. Her eyes glowed again, and she said, "When was the last time you heard from Melvin?"

Her stern expression was replaced by a neutral one and she said, "Nine months ago, when he ran away for the third and final time."

Interesting, it looked like Paula was right. Each time Carla ran away, Melvin did too. Were the two of them just friends or something more than that? "You said 'final time,' was that when you disowned him?"

She nodded but didn't add anything else. I went on a different track and asked, "What are your powers?"

Joannie frowned at that and said, "Powers? Don't be ridiculous; I'm not a freak. I'm the official secretary of the Kitchener-Waterloo Humans First chapter for heaven's sake!"

Liv made fists with her hands and clenched her jaw. I worried that she was going to leap out of her chair and attack the lady. Humans First was a group that believe Enhanced Individuals should either be killed or confined to guarded reservations. They were big in the fifties after 'Monsters' were exposed during World War II but faded in the sixties and seventies. In the last two decades, Enhanced communities lobbied and got more rights from various governments around the world, and Humans First and other hate groups like them had begun growing again.

"So, you don't have any talents that seem different from everyone else?" I asked.

She shook her head but then said, "Well, I always know exactly what the weather is going to do in the next twenty-four hours, but that is God's gift to me, so I can always dress appropriately and not ruin my hair."

A weather predictor. That would explain the yellow Air ring and the light green Telepathy ring. Sort of useful but with weather apps and how good they'd become at predicting short-term weather, it was kind of redundant.

"What did you think about Melvin's powers?"

She laughed coldly and said, "Melvin doesn't have any powers; he is just a very bright boy."

"So Melvin doesn't have any powers over electronics?"

"No, he is just handy with them. That isn't a power. I would know if he was one of *those*," she finished with a note of pure disdain in her tone.

I stopped myself from rolling my eyes. She was an Enhanced, albeit a very weak one, and her son certainly had power as well. The situation was kind of darkly amusing, like a KKK member finding out their grandmother was African American. My growing dislike of this lady overrode my sense of humor, and I just wanted to question her and get the hell out of there.

"Would Melvin contact his father?"

Joannie shook her head and said, "No, his father hasn't had time for him since moving in with his whore of a secretary and starting another family. Melvin and he were never that close. Herb was always working and never had much time for Melvin. Though now, I wonder how much 'work' he was doing."

I couldn't blame Herb for not wanting to come home if this woman was waiting for him. "Tell me about Melvin, what was he like as a kid?"

Joannie didn't answer, and I was about to get Liv to whammy her again when she said, "He was a mistake. I only had him because Herb wanted another kid. Our other two kids were in their early teens at the time, and Herb felt he missed out on them growing up due to working so much. Our marriage at the time wasn't a happy one. I hoped that having another child would fix that…"

She stared wistfully off into the distance for a moment and continued, "At first, when Melvin was born, Herb was home more, and things seemed better between us, but then with each passing month, he started working longer and longer hours again. My anger and resentment at him grew, but Melvin was a blessing. That boy was an exceptionally well behaved and bright child. My other two children were smart; Michael, my oldest, is a successful criminal lawyer in Toronto, and Melanie is a renowned surgeon in Toronto. Melvin, though, was on another level."

I interrupted and asked, "Would Melvin try and contact his brother or sister?"

Joannie thought about it and said, "No, due to the age differences between them, neither was that close to Melvin. They were both at university by the time he was five. Michael is like Herb in that he is always working. I constantly remind him that he needs to take some time and find a wife and start a family, but so far nothing. I swear, if I hadn't raised him to be such a good Christian, I might worry he was gay."

Liv tensed beside me at that and I put my hand on her leg to keep her in check. The bile this woman kept spewing was just too much. The worst part was how casually she'd say these things, like she was talking about the weather or something equally mundane.

Joannie continued, oblivious to Olivia's anger, "At least Melanie has given me two grandchildren, even though her husband is Asian, but at least he's also a doctor. I have to admit, though, that both of their kids are cute."

I felt Liv go even more rigid at the Asian comment and knew she was seething at this woman. I couldn't blame Liv; every time this woman opened her mouth, my disdain for her grew.

"Melvin as a child was a dream. He always did as he was told, got good grades, loved going to church, and was a prodigy with his violin. He was a concert-level violinist by eleven years old. That boy was going to be the Mozart of our time."

Joannie sighed and said, "And then puberty hit. Almost overnight he changed. He stopped picking up after himself, became willful and disobedient, his grades declined and all he wanted to do was play those silly video games and hang out with friends. The worst part was when he announced he was done with playing the violin. I tried to put him back on the right track; I threw out his video games, grounded him, and enrolled him in an after-school program the church had for troubled teens, but the harder I pushed, the worse he became. He then refused to go to church any more on Sundays. I found pot in his room. He constantly used foul language towards me.

"It became an ongoing war between us until Herb stepped in around Christmas when Melvin was fourteen. He sided with Melvin and said that he was just being a normal teenager. We fought about it, but in the end, I was forced to promise that I would clear any punishment of Melvin with Herb first. Herb bought him a new computer that Christmas. Melvin spent every waking moment on that computer."

She snorted and said, "That summer I had two RCMP officers show up at the house with a warrant to search the house. They were investigating a computer hack into a major bank. They confiscated the computer and several other electronic devices of Melvin's. He was charged, but thanks to connections Herb had in the legal community,

Melvin was only given three months' probation, and his record was cleared after the probation ended.

"Shortly after that, I caught Herb having an affair and filed for divorce. With Herb out of the way, I could properly discipline Melvin again. I got rid of that computer when we got it back. I grounded Melvin permanently until he brought his grades back up. That was the first time he ran away. No matter what I did, he refused to grow up and become a responsible young adult. After the third time, I was done with him, and as far as I'm concerned, he is dead to me."

With this cold, controlling cow of a mother and an absentee father, I actually felt sorry for Terror-Byte. I also knew that there was no way he would be in contact with her or any of his family. I had no doubt that he'd resent his father for leaving him to his mother's not-so-tender mercies, and the age gap between him and his siblings meant he wouldn't turn to them for help either.

I was about to thank her for her time when Liv asked, "In the days before Melvin disappeared, did he mention any new friends or opportunities?"

Joannie at first shook her head, but then smiled and said, "Yes, we had a visitor come by the house a couple of days before Melvin left. He was a distinguished English gentleman named James Niven. He was so charming..."

I perked up at this. Could this be the person behind the Acolytes, or was he just a recruiter?

Liv asked, "What did he want?"

"He wanted to talk to Melvin about what his plans for the future were. Melvin embarrassed me by just shrugging in response. I saved things by asking why he was here. He explained that he owned a technology company and was always looking for the best and brightest. He'd heard about Melvin's aptitude with electronics and felt that Melvin might be an asset to his firm. Melvin got more interested at that point, and James asked if he could talk with Melvin alone. I left them here to chat, and twenty minutes later, Melvin walked James to the door. He said goodbye to us and that he would be in touch. After he left, I asked Melvin about it, but Melvin just shrugged and said he had homework to do."

"Did he give you a business card or anything?" I asked.

Joannie shook her head and said, "Not to me, but he did give one to Melvin."

"Any chance that card is in his room?"

"A week after Melvin left and I disowned him, I had a charity come by and clean out all his stuff. If the card was there, it is gone now."

Liv piped up and asked, "Can you describe Mr. Niven?"

"Oh certainly," said Joannie, a dreamy look on her face. "Late fifties, piercing blue eyes, clean shaven, impeccably dressed, silver hair styled to perfection. He was in good shape, not an ounce of fat on him, and stood just over six feet tall. His English accent was crisp and precise; he sounded like a member of the royal family. He wore a stunning Patek Philippe watch and there was no wedding band on his finger."

I was impressed at the level of detail in her description, and it was obvious by her tone that she had been quite enamored by James Niven. I couldn't think of anything more to ask and looked over at Liv to see if she had any more to add. She shook her head. We said our goodbyes to Ms. Mitchel and left.

Liv called Blue for a ride, and after she hung up said, "I would have done the world a favor by draining that bitch and leaving her for dead."

"Yeah, she is a piece of work, but at least we got another lead. I also doubt Melvin will be contacting 'Mommy Dearest' or any of the rest his family."

Liv brightened and asked, "Do you think this James Niven is the one behind everything?"

"Not sure, he could just be the recruiter, but at least we have a name."

Chapter 11

Thursday, May 1

Ten minutes later, we were all sitting around the kitchen table back at the house. Liv updated the rest of the group regarding what we'd learned about Melvin and Carla. Stella said she would look into James Niven and added that since he was English, she would also touch base with Sarah at the English vampire court and get her to check into him as well.

An hour later, Stella and Blue excused themselves and headed for bed. We had just finished wishing them a good night when all our phones went off. There was a new text on my phone—Durham Regional Police were responding to an alarm at a chemical lab on the outskirts of Oshawa. The Acolytes had been spotted at the scene and EIRT was responding.

Oshawa was a good drive northeast of Toronto, which meant it would take EIRT a while to arrive. Durham Police would block off the roads around the lab, but as the Acolytes were Enhanced, they wouldn't engage them. "Okay, folks, it looks like we are getting another chance at the Acolytes. Gear up and meet in the living room. Blue, find a place to open a portal near the chemical lab."

Blue nodded and disappeared into the living room with Stella right behind her. Bree had already started stripping off her clothes when I'd been speaking so she could change. Liv blurred off to the basement, probably to grab her sword. I was glad I'd changed out of the suit and tie earlier, so all I needed to do to get ready was grab my balaclava from the front hallway.

Bree was already in her standing Werepanther form by the time I returned to the kitchen, and she gave me a growl of acknowledgement as we headed to the living room together. The rest of the team was there and waiting. Blue had a portal open and ready.

Blue said, "The portal comes out under a tree on the right side of the main parking lot in front of the building. I didn't see the Acolytes, but the police have all the roadways to the building blocked off."

"Good." I faced everyone and added, "We go through and hit them hard and fast. I will take care of the Bartender. Stella goes through first in her Hyde form, and then the rest of us follow. Stella, head straight for the building and take down anyone in your way. Bree, Liv follow behind her and back her up. Blue, hang back and use the shadows to figure out the best place to strike. Alteea, get high and film everything. Questions?"

Everyone shook their heads. Stella instantly changed into her massive Hyde form and lumbered forward. I was right behind her as she disappeared into the shadows, calling on my Air powers as I stepped through.

We emerged into a cool dark night. There were a few piles of grimy salt-stained snow at the edges of the parking lot, but the ground was mostly clear. The parking lot was a decent size and could hold thirty or so vehicles.

"That looks inviting...not!" exclaimed Liv as she appeared behind me.

I followed her gaze towards the main building. One look at the dark gray gothic-style building and I understood her concerns. There were almost no interior lights on. Two external spotlights shined up at the building, but they did little to diminish the place's creepy vibe. Even the large red glowing letters of 'AK Labs' at the top of the building cast a menacing blood red shroud over everything.

It looked like a fortress with its solid brickwork and small windows. I speculated that it had been built in the late-nineteenth century. I was willing to bet it hadn't started out as a chemical lab. I'd have put money on a prison or insane asylum.

I took to the air to get a better view and searched for any sign of the Acolytes. Behind us, the night sky was lit up with the flashing red and blue lights of the two cruisers blocking the driveways to the parking lot, and more sirens were closing in from a distance.

The main doors to the building were open. The door on the right had a gaping charred hole where the lock used to be. The lobby beyond the doors was dark and foreboding. A flash of bright white light came from within.

I cursed as I spotted four armored figures silhouetted briefly in the glow—we'd missed our shot; the Acolytes had teleported out.

Stella reached the edge of the parking lot, grunted loudly, and pointed to the left side of the building. I sped over to see what had caught her interest. My eyes widened at the sight of 'Hurricane' spray-painted in large neon green letters on the side of the building. There was smaller writing under that, but I couldn't make it out. I landed on the brown grass about thirty feet in front of the graffiti.

I thickened the air in front of me as a precaution and got closer to read the rest. I heard Stella's heavy footsteps farther behind me as I approached. The writing under 'Hurricane' was so small that I couldn't read it until I got within ten feet of it.

Hurricane, stop meddling!

I was puzzled at the message, as we'd only confronted them once. The only external investigations we'd done were our visits to Bug Girl's and Terror-Byte's mothers, and that had only been early this evening. Surely, they didn't know about that already, and why leave a message like this in the middle of nowhere?

There was a loud *beep* to my right, and I barely spotted two smartphones wedged into the ground, facing me, before I was engulfed in a series of huge explosions. The Air shield saved my life, but the force of the blasts was still enough to knock the wind out of me, toss me back like a ragdoll, and completely disorient me.

Seconds later, I hit the ground headfirst and everything went dark.

***

I awoke with a splitting headache and then immediately closed my eyes again due to the pain. The brief glimpse of orange couch I was lying on and the smell of incense with a slight undertone of pot confirmed that I was at Marion's apartment. By how bright the room had been, I also knew it was daytime, which made me wonder how long I'd been out for.

"Zack? Are you awake?" asked Stella in a soft tone.

"Yeah…" I groaned in reply.

"I'll get Marion."

Even Stella's light footsteps seemed like thunder in my poor aching head. This hadn't been a good week for me regarding mornings and throbbing head pain. I focused back on the here and now and started checking what else wasn't right. I was able to wiggle my toes and my fingers, which was a good sign. I did notice, though, that my pinky and the ring finger on my left hand tingled. That was a sign that Marion had healed them.

If a couple of broken fingers and a headache were the only damage from the bombs, then I figured I'd got off easy.

Marion returned with Stella. "How are you feeling?"

"Like a couple of giants played ping-pong with my head…"

"Not surprised. You got a nasty concussion last night."

At least last night meant I'd been out for less than a day. "What's the time?"

"Just coming up on one p.m. Can you open your eyes so I can take a look at them?"

I nodded, which was a mistake, and then opened my eyes, which was an even bigger mistake. The bright light of the room felt like daggers being driven into my eyes. The best I managed to do was squint.

Marion frowned as she studied me for a moment and then reluctantly nodded. "You can close your eyes again. You seem to be okay, but you'll need to take it easy for the next couple of days."

I heard her walk away. I sensed Stella was near and asked, "Is everyone else okay?"

"Yes. You and your Air-shield took the brunt of the blast, and you were the only one hurt."

I exhaled in relief and another question popped into my head. "What did the Acolytes take from the lab?"

"Nothing. It looks like the whole reason they where there was to lay that trap for us. The lab does water testing for the government, so other than a bit of fancy equipment, they really didn't have much to take. No dangerous or restricted chemicals, no secret formulas. EIRT thinks they set the trap on the outside of the building then cut the main locks to purposely set off the alarms before teleporting out once we arrived."

I didn't know what to say to that. I'd assumed that the trap was just a parting gift from Terror-Byte and the heist had been their primary goal for being at the lab. I thought back to the 'stop meddling' message. For them to act this quickly, they had to be monitoring either Terror-Byte's or Bug Girl's house. Either someone was watching them or, more likely, they'd planted some sort of electronic bug. The bug was probably set to listen for key words and then send an alert. I made a mental note to contact Bobby and have him send an EIRT tech team to do a sweep of both places. Maybe we'd get lucky and the bugs would lead us to where they were hiding.

Marion returned and said, "Hold still." I felt her put a pair of glasses on me and she added, "Not really your style but they'll help with the light sensitivity."

I cautiously opened my eyes and was pleased that the murderous pain was gone. Marion had another gift for me and handed me a couple of aspirins and a glass of water. "Thanks, Marion, you're a saint."

She rolled her eyes. "Just remember St. Marion when you get my bill for this little adventure…"

***

Even though I'd been passed out for most of the night and morning, I ended up going back to bed once Blue got us home and I had a quick lunch. Being that wiped and hungry had me wondering just how much healing Marion had done to me last night.

My alarm went off just before six. I was pleased that my earlier headache had been reduced to a dull throb.

Bobby had left a message on my cell to call him when he started his shift today at six.

"Hurricane, you are lucky to be alive. I read the report on the fake break-in. Those phone bombs blew ten-foot craters in the frozen ground…"

I winced at that. Terror-Byte certainly believed in overkill. That was another one I owed him. "Yeah, it takes more than a few exploding smartphones to kill me. Your message said you had news on the Acolytes?"

"I have the names of three of them."

"Which three?" I asked.

"Bug Girl, the Bartender, and the kid with the flaming knives."

"Bug Girl is Carla Priest, and the Bartender is Brandon Owens. Both are dead-ends. Tell me about knife guy."

There was a pause on the other end, like I'd caught him off guard, and he said, "His name is Ryan Conner, seventeen, grew up in Barrie. Had a couple of minor arson charges on his record from when he was younger—a dumpster fire and a garden shed. An EIRT agent stopped by earlier today and interviewed the parents. They filed a missing person's report on him eight and half months ago and haven't heard anything from him since."

I made a mental note to go to Barrie tomorrow and talk to the parents; maybe EIRT missed something. "I have another name for you. Melvin Kuntz, with a 'K,' is Terror-Byte's real name. He grew up in Kitchener. He and Carla are friends, or maybe something more. He has also been missing nine months, though his mother has disowned him and doesn't seem to care if he returns or not. Liv and I interviewed Carla's mom and Melvin's mom but neither has seen or heard from them since they disappeared."

I kicked around giving him James Niven's name as well but decided that I would keep that one to myself for the moment. My fear was that if it did lead somewhere, EIRT would use it to take the Acolytes down, and we wouldn't get an invite. That meant my team wouldn't get the bounty and, more importantly, I wouldn't get another shot at the Acolytes.

I couldn't resist giving him a hard time. "You know, for an elite law enforcement agency, coming with only three names like we did seems a little sad; either you guys are getting slow or my team is better than I think they are."

"Yeah, yeah. Thanks for the Terror-Byte lead; we'll send an agent out to investigate tomorrow."

"The only two we don't have names for are Meat-Shield and Hexadecimal. Hopefully someone will see the video and recognize one of them and get in touch with you. I bet someone will recognize Hexadecimal—a hot blonde who can clone herself is certainly something someone will remember. Any other leads or news on the Acolytes?"

"Other than those names," said Bobby, "nothing solid so far. I'll let you know if we get anything more."

I was just about to let him go and then remembered the possible bugs. I told him about my theory, and he agreed to send out a tech team. We exchanged goodbyes and I hung up.

Chapter 12

Friday, May 2

It was sweet to wake up without a headache for a change. After a late breakfast, Blue in her old man disguise and I went to Barrie. Stella and Blue had tracked down Ryan's parents and we went to visit his mom, Kelly, at her work.

Kelly worked for Barlow and Associates, which was a small family law firm. The building was a nondescript three-story office building close to downtown Barrie. Barlow and Associates took up half of the second floor.

Entering the office, I spotted a redhead behind the reception desk and knew this was Ryan's mom. Her hair color was the same as her son's, she had the same gray eyes, and her nose and cheekbones were also a close match with Ryan's.

I approached the desk and said, "Mrs. Conner?" She nodded, and I gave her my hero ID and added, "We'd like to talk to you about your son, can you spare a few minutes to talk?"

She nodded, and after getting someone to cover the desk for her, she led us deeper into the office to a small conference room.

The three of us sat down and Kelly said, "My husband, Dave, and I talked with EIRT yesterday, so I don't understand why you are here."

"We aren't with EIRT; we are private bounty hunters," I said and the confusion on her face deepened, so I added, "As a police officer has been killed by the Acolytes, law enforcement is more concerned about bringing them down than capturing them safely. We have fought against the Acolytes and all of them are about your son's age. I don't think these kids are hardened criminals, and we believe they are being used. We just want to stop them safely."

Kelly's eyes widened, and she said, "You are the ones in the video."

"Yeah, that wasn't our finest moment. We lost that fight because we were trying to use a minimum level of force against them. As I said earlier, they seemed like a bunch of scared kids." I paused and said,

"Look, I can't force you to talk to us, but I do feel we are the best hope for bringing all of them home safely. Would you mind answering a couple of questions?"

She studied me quietly for a few moments, and then nodded, "Ryan's a good kid. He's had his issues and his powers make him a bit of a fire-bug, but I know he doesn't want to hurt anyone."

I smiled at that and said, "With my power to control Air and Electricity, when I was Ryan's age my mother constantly had to chase me down when a thunderstorm was in the area. I'm sure if Fire was my element, I would also have been 'a bit of a fire-bug,' as you put it."

Kelly relaxed at that and I continued, "Ryan has been missing for eight and half months, have you had any contact with him in that time?"

She shook her head and said, "Nothing. Until seeing that video, we had no idea if he was even alive…"

"Does he have any siblings?"

"No, he is an only child."

"Any cousins or friends that he was close to that he might have tried to get in touch with?"

Kelly said, "His cousins are on the east and west coasts. He had met them a few times at family gatherings, but he isn't that close to any of them. As for friends, he and Peter were tight as can be until a year and half ago. They both fell for the same girl and she picked Peter. They had a falling out over that and stopped talking. After that, there wasn't anyone he was close to. I got the feeling the other kids at school shunned Ryan because of his powers. Even without that, Ryan has always been quiet and shy and didn't make friends easily."

I remembered Melvin and James Niven and asked, "Before he ran away, did he mention anything about meeting anyone new or any new opportunities?"

Kelly stared off into the distance for a moment and said, "No, not that I can recall. He was always quiet, but in the couple of days before he disappeared, he barely said anything at all. It was like his mind was elsewhere."

That was interesting. I wondered if he was approached by James Niven and then took a couple of days to consider the offer before accepting.

Blue asked, "Does he conjure the knives or just add flames to existing knives?"

"His power makes the knives and the flames," said Kelly. She smiled and added, "He loved that he could do that. Even before he got his power, he was into magic. He was constantly doing card tricks and sleight of hand stuff. Making flaming knives appear out of thin air was his greatest trick. He was determined to be the greatest magician ever. That was always the source of our biggest fights. Dave and I felt he needed something else to fall back on and pushed him to have a backup career in case the magician thing didn't work out..."

A vivid picture of a younger Ryan pulling a rabbit out of a hat with a big grin on his face popped into my head. It reminded me that these weren't just targets to be hunted down but real living, breathing humans with feelings and dreams. Ryan didn't sound like a bad kid. He was a loner who was dealt the double blow of losing his best friend and the girl he had a crush on at the same time. Add in kids at school picking on him because of his powers, and it was easy to see how he was recruited. My anger at James Niven, or whoever was behind all of this, grew. They were taking kids who felt lost and using them for their own gains.

Blue asked a couple more questions, but both led nowhere. We thanked Kelly for her time and headed home.

***

Later, Blue, Stella, and I sat around the kitchen table discussing the case. I was frustrated and puzzled. "We have to be missing something. Why would the Acolytes lay a trap for us if there was nothing to find? We know four of the six Acolytes' identities, and yet that hasn't gotten us anything..."

Blue turned her purple gaze in my direction and said, "The trap may have had nothing to do with covering their tracks. It might have just been misdirection."

I blinked at that. I wasn't sure what she was getting at. "Huh?"

"We are the only group that has a chance at arriving in time to deal with them before they teleport out. Whoever is behind the Acolytes may have ordered that we be eliminated so we can't interfere with their operations going forward."

I rubbed my temples. I was starting to miss our normal cases of rogue Weres, Enhanced Individuals with lengthy criminal records, and the occasional Fae creature that wandered into our world. Loners like that were much easier to deal with. International organized crime syndicates with plans within plans felt a bit above our paygrade, but we still had a job to do. "Speaking of masterminds, any luck finding James Niven?"

Stella shook her head and said, "There are a lot of James Nivens in Canada, and that is making the search difficult. We can eliminate most by age, race, or physical description. Blue is checking the ones we can't rule out by using the shadows to track them down and spy on them, but it is slow going. I also called Sarah in England and she is looking into it from her end."

I nodded and was pleased that they were turning over every stone looking for Niven. "Let's assume that the trap was set because we questioned Terror-Byte's and Bug Girl's mothers. That means they are worried about us finding out something about them or their operations. What are we missing?"

The table went quiet for a moment and then Blue asked, "These kids have all disappeared for eight or nine months before turning up now; where did they go? Did they leave the country to get their equipment and training or did they stay in Canada, out of sight?"

Stella tugged on one of her braids in thought and said, "Carla and Ryan are only seventeen. Even if they had passports, it would still be tricky to leave the country due to them being unaccompanied minors. You should ask Bobby if EIRT has any records of them leaving the country. If they did fly out, then there should be a record of where they went. Once we find that destination, we might be able to find their hideout."

I picked up my phone and texted Bobby Knight and hoped he'd get back to me with answers.

I pondered about where the Acolytes had been for the last eight months. If they had left the country, I doubted they flew commercially. The teleporters they'd used at the crime scenes came to mind. "What if they are teleporting in and out of the country?"

Blue frowned. "That would take an immense amount of power. With teleporting, unlike shadow-traveling, range and mass are a big part of the equation. Most Enhanceds that have the ability to teleport can only go short distances and take, at most, one or two people."

"Those are organic limitations," said Stella. The 'huh?' thought that came to mind must have been displayed on my face as she added, "The teleporters they are using are portable, and those are probably battery powered." She paused and I nodded at that. "What if they have a main unit somewhere that is connected to the power grid or its own generator?"

Blue's purple eyes widened, "If they have a main unit or gate and can teleport anywhere, why not teleport inside the places they are robbing rather than breaking in?"

"Maybe they can only teleport between devices?" offered Stella.

The table went quiet as the three of us pondered this. "If Stella's right and they can only teleport between devices, that raises another question—how are they getting to the crime scenes in the first place?"

"They have to have a van or truck," said Stella. "There have been no reports of stolen vehicles abandoned near the crime scenes. It's not like with that armor they wear they can take an Uber."

"If they have a vehicle, then they have to park it somewhere, which leads me to believe that even though the Acolytes are part of an international crime syndicate, they must have a base locally. If we can find that base, then we can take them down."

Stella nodded and added, "If they have a base, then there is probably a main teleportation unit at the base too."

This kicked off a discussion where we concluded that if there was a local base with a teleportation unit, then it stood to reason that the other Acolyte groups would have the same setup. It also meant that there was probably a main base somewhere that all three bases connected to via teleporters. This would allow them to move personnel and materials between the locations. That was probably how they were moving the stolen goods without being caught.

I was excited by the end of the discussion and said, "This means if we find our Acolytes' base, we can use their teleporter to travel to the main base and the other two local ones and take them all down."

Blue frowned and shook her head. "Do you really want to activate a gate or a portal device not knowing where it goes? The last time I did that, I ended up here with no chance of ever returning to my world."

I blanched a bit as I thought about what Blue said. Using something like that and having no idea how it worked would be a very bad idea. "Okay, getting back to the local base then, how do we find it?"

Stella was idly tugging on her braid again, which meant she was deep in thought. After a lengthy silence she said, "I could build a tracking device and make it look like a smartphone. If we could swap it with one of Terror-Byte's many phones, we could track him. If we set up three receivers in different spots, we could triangulate the exact position of their local base, and with Blue's shadow traveling abilities, we could hit them before they fled."

This plan assumed we got another shot at the Acolytes, but it made sense that they would strike again. If they weren't going to, why bother setting that trap for us in the first place? Ideally, if we got another shot at them, I wanted to take them down there and then, but if they did get away again, I liked the idea of being able to track them down. I approved Stella's idea.

Stella and Blue started talking about what they would need to build the device and the three receivers, and I left them to it.

***

A minute after the sun dropped over the horizon, Olivia and Alteea came up from the basement and joined us all at the kitchen table for dinner, or in their case, breakfast. Liv poured a bit of blood from her glass into a plastic shot glass for Alteea.

After draining half the glass, Liv asked, "Any new leads in the case or any change in Rob's condition?"

Stella was quicker off the mark than me and said, "We don't have any updates, but we are working on a plan to track the Acolytes back to their hideout." Stella explained about the tracking device and receivers.

To my surprise, Stella had already managed to get a working prototype completed and was looking to test it tomorrow.

"So, you want me to switch the tracker with one of Terror-Byte's phones?" asked Liv with a grin.

Stella nodded and said, "That is the plan; you could circle him in two passes, stealing a phone on the first pass and then slipping in the tracker on the second run. We'll practice it during team training."

"It should be pretty easy," I said. "Those suits that they wear seem pretty solid, so I doubt he will even feel you taking a phone."

Blue frowned and said, "A better plan might be for Alteea to do this instead of Liv. They don't know she exists and with her glamor can hide herself. If Liv blurs off, they will all be on high alert and looking for her."

Liv shook her head and said, "I don't want her getting close to them; she might get hurt. Besides, her glamor won't hide the tracker or the phone. A floating phone would catch their attention."

We debated it and by the end of dinner, the majority agreed that Liv would be the better choice for the job.

Chapter 13

Friday, May 2

Just before midnight, my phone buzzed. It was Bobby Knight calling.

"The Acolytes have hit another target. They are long gone, and we are on-site and investigating."

"Where? And what did they take?"

"Markham, at a place called PCL Inc. They make laser cutting machines for industrial manufacturing. It was a clean job; this time they disabled the alarm correctly. The cleaners showed up at 11 p.m. and noticed the melted front lock and called the police. Toronto Police arrived on scene and swept the building, but no one was found. The Acolytes broke into a secured room, and it was empty except for a black circle on the floor. The office manager has been contacted and we are waiting for her to show up so we can figure out what is missing."

"Okay, I'll be there shortly," I said.

"No, there are two EIRT teams on-site and my captain is here, too, so there's no way you'll be allowed in."

"That sucks. You'll let me know what they find?"

"If I can, I will," said Bobby. He then added, "Also, you were right about the mothers' houses being bugged. The tech team found a monitoring app on both of their phones." I started to get excited that this might be our break, but then Bobby added, "Unfortunately, as soon as the tech team tried to analyze the app, it erased itself. We sent another tech team to Barrie to look at Ryan Connor's parents' phones and those were clean."

I cursed at that. If it was only Carla and Melvin's mothers' phones, then the apps could have been installed even before they'd become Acolytes. Melvin had probably done it to spy on his parents and Carla's mom just to hear what they had to say about him. Though it did explain how the Acolytes found out so quickly that we'd been looking into their pasts. I told my theory to Bobby.

"Yeah, that was our thought too."

We ended the call shortly after that.

Liv and Bree looked at me, and Liv asked, "So, do we wake up Blue and go to Markham?"

I shook my head and said, "Let Blue sleep. I'll take Alteea and fly out to Markham."

"What about us?" asked Bree.

"You stay here and enjoy the movie."

They both looked disappointed, but it didn't make any sense for them to come too. Flying with them would also slow me down.

"Alteea, you up for a little recon?"

Her wings fluttered excitedly as she flew up from the couch and she nodded her tiny head.

After grabbing my jacket and balaclava and looking up the address on my phone, we were ready to go. The two of us stepped out the front door and had two different reactions to the unexpected light rain. Alteea opened her arms wide, tilted her head back and giggled as the steady spring shower washed over her. I just mumbled 'fuck' under my breath.

I loved thunderstorms, but this was just a plain old downpour. No vivid lightning to recharge and boost my powers, just plain old rain. Alteea did loops in the air, laughing the whole time. At least one of us was having fun. It took a bit of coaxing, but eventually I managed to convince her to stop playing in the rain and grab the collar of my coat and we were on our way.

It only took twenty minutes to fly to Markham, but I was soaked to the bone by the time we got there. I sighed as the rain stopped just as we reached Markham. I had no idea where PCL Inc. was but spotted the cluster of red and blue flashing lights off in the distance and figured that was a safe bet. I touched down a block away from the site and walked on foot the rest of the way.

The police had taped off the property, and I joined the edge of the small, sparse crowd that had gathered to see what all the fuss was about. It was a fair-sized property, but the large industrial building looked tired and old. As this company made laser cutting machines, I'd been expecting a more modern, high-tech location. On the other hand, their customers were industrial manufacturers and I doubted they got a lot of walk-in traffic. They probably had a sales team that went out to sell the company's equipment. That being the case, why spend money fixing up the place when no one came to you?

Alteea was perched on my shoulder with her glamor up, so no one other than me knew she was there.

She leaned in and whispered, "Should I go spy on them?"

I looked around and the nearest person to me was eight feet away. "Not yet," I said softly.

Bobby mentioned there were two EIRT teams on-site. EIRT teams only had one or two Enhanced Individuals, but I feared that one of them would be a Were or a vampire and either of those two would hear or smell Alteea in seconds. I spotted three auras and smiled; two were mages and the last was a Tank. Bobby's team only had a mage and five regular humans. The other team, therefore, had the Tank and the weaker mage as theirs. Luck was with us tonight.

"Okay, go," I said.

To my surprise, my pixie companion darted off in the exact opposite direction. I followed her small aura and the further she traveled away, the more confused I got. There was a brief small flare off in the distance and then her aura came darting back in my direction. She'd used her flame powers to dry herself off. Smart. She might have been noticed if she was dripping water everywhere.

She shot by me and ended up hovering above four people in suits. I recognized the large muscular frame of Bobby's captain as one of the four. The other two men, by their bearing and alert demeanors, were probably Toronto police detectives. The last one was a frazzled and upset brunette in modest heels. I assumed she was either the owner or manager of the place since her suit was the nicest of the bunch.

I yawned and decided to go find a Timmies and get a coffee. I knew this would take a while, so some caffeine to keep me awake wasn't a bad idea.

By the time I got back, the suits were gone, and I couldn't see Alteea's aura. I assumed they were all inside the building figuring out what had been damaged or stolen.

I was halfway through my large coffee when a heavy hand clamped down on my shoulder and I almost jumped out of my skin. I called on my powers by instinct but quickly dismissed them when I turned and saw Bobby's impressive form behind me.

"I thought I told you that you wouldn't be allowed on-site," said Bobby in an irritated tone.

"You did, and if you'll notice, I am well behind the police tape."

"Uh-huh. So, you flew all the way from Hamilton in the rain to just stand here and gawk like some bored civilian?"

I tried to look innocent and unassuming, but I don't think Bobby bought it for a moment and said, "I just wanted to get a better feel for the place and why they would hit it. To be honest, the place doesn't look like much. Any idea yet on what they took?"

Bobby's stern visage softened, and he grinned, "Yup, but it will cost you…"

"How much?"

"A dozen large black coffees from Tim's; it's cold and damp out here and some of us don't have your immunity to cold."

"Deal," I said and drained the rest of my coffee before heading off to get more.

Twenty minutes later, I returned with thirteen coffees and found Bobby waiting for me where I'd left him. I liberated mine from the stack and handed off my bribe.

"Let me hand these out and I'll be back," said Bobby.

He returned after a bit, carrying only his coffee and a smile. He slipped under the police tape and joined me again. "They stole a prototype laser cutting machine. The company debuted it in Las Vegas last month, and orders for it have been flowing in. Last week, they ironed out a few remaining bugs and are going into production next month."

"Any idea why it is so special?"

"Supposedly these laser cutting machines are power hungry monsters. This new version has reduced the power requirements to a third with no loss of cutting power. The monthly power savings make these new machines pay for themselves in a short period of time."

I was impressed. Reducing power requirements to a third would be a huge boon and give the company a massive edge over their competitors. "Any idea what the prototype is worth?"

"The manager said new machines will sell for six million each. Right now, that prototype is the only one in existence, so who knows how much it is worth."

I sipped my coffee and whistled at the number in my head; six million for an hour's work was a good haul for the Acolytes. I was puzzled at why they would steal it though. They either had a competitor lined up to buy it so they could reverse engineer it and stay relevant, or they were going to use it themselves.

"One other thing. Just before this call came in, I'd finished a search for three of the four Acolytes on whether they'd left the country in the last nine months, and it came back empty. I'll finish the search on the last one after this, but I expect I'll get the same results as the first three."

Before I could ask anything else, Bobby's radio went off, and he said he had to go. He told me he would text me if he learned anything new and disappeared under the police tape.

It would have been nice if Bobby had found a record of their flight, as that would have been a solid lead on where the main Acolyte base was. The futile search did mean it was more likely that they'd lived and trained locally for the last eight months, however.

I switched back to thinking about this crime. I wondered if they would use or sell the laser cutting machine. I'd have Blue spy on PCL's competitors tomorrow. If one of them was going to buy it from the Acolytes, then hopefully we could catch them at the buy. I suspected, though, that they were keeping the machine themselves. We speculated that whoever was behind the Acolytes was building something, and this might just be the thing they needed to help that process.

A good hour later, the brunette manager and the rest of them exited the plant with Altea's aura hovering just above them.

The manager and the EIRT captain got in their vehicles and left, and Altea returned to me. As we flew home, Altea shared what she had learned. She found out that there was a brief shot of Terror-Byte on one of the plant's security cameras before it went black. At least that confirmed it was the Acolytes, though the melted front lock and the blackened circle had already convinced me that it was them.

We told Liv and Bree what had happened when we got home. I left a detailed note for Blue and Stella to look into PCL's competition and went to bed.

Chapter 14

Saturday, May 3

The next morning when I joined Stella and Blue at the kitchen table, Stella had news for me; the other Acolyte teams had struck again. The European team hit an energy research company in Switzerland and stole two working fusion reactors. The Asian team had moved their operation to Japan. They stole the formula to a new metal alloy that was rumored to be stronger than steel but lighter than aluminum. They tortured and killed Dr. Tetsu Hamadate, the creator of the formula. They also destroyed all traces of the records of the formula and burned his lab to the ground. The Japanese government had condemned the attack and had added a million dollars US to the bounty on this group of Acolytes.

"That is a terrible waste and end to a brilliant man; he deserved better than this," said Stella sadly.

I finished my mouthful of coffee and said, "I'll be honest, I'd never heard of him, but you're right, no one deserves to go like that."

Stella nodded. "He isn't well known outside of Japan or the scientific community. I read about his work a couple of years ago and started following news on him. He'd scheduled a press conference for next week. Speculation was that he'd perfected the formula of the super alloy he'd been working on and was ready to announce it to the world."

"So, the Acolytes jumped the gun and got it first," I said, shaking my head.

They were getting bolder and more dangerous. The first killing here seemed almost accidental, but this one was intentional and disturbing. They needed to be stopped or more people were going to get hurt or killed. It was frustrating, as we knew the identities of two-thirds of our group of Acolytes, and yet none of those names led anywhere. Worse, our group was getting better at sneaking under the radar; last night they didn't trip any alarms, and their crime wasn't even noticed until after they were long gone.

Stella pulled me from my thoughts and said, "The bounty on the Asian team is now at three million dollars like the European team's bounty. Our group of Acolytes has been bumped to 1.5 million."

My eyes widened at that figure. That was a bump of a million dollars for Terror-Byte's group. It seemed excessive. Last night's job didn't seem to justify that increase. I guessed that since all three groups were connected, the hope was if the North American team was caught, they'd be interrogated and help bring down the other two groups.

"Stealing a formula is odd and a little disconcerting," said Blue. We both looked at her and she explained, "Smelting and combining metals isn't a small or inexpensive job. It hints at this group having bigger resources than I suspected."

"Well, they do have two hundred million in diamonds—that is a lot of startup capital..." I argued.

Blue countered with, "That is a fair sum of money, but serious metal production costs can be in the billions not millions. Not to mention that we have been guessing that they are building something. If that is the case, then the metal would only be one component of whatever they are making. If they are building an army of robots, tanks, drones or whatever, then that two hundred million is barely a drop in the bucket."

We all went quiet at that. There was no doubt that whoever was behind the Acolytes had serious resources, setting up three teams on three different continents with high-tech armor and teleport devices proved that. If we were right, they also had three local bases of operation and a main one hidden somewhere, and those wouldn't be cheap to operate either.

An idea hit me. "Was there any hint of what materials the formula needed? If one of the components was rare enough, we could watch the suppliers, as they might be the next target."

Stella shook her head and said, "Dr. Hamadate was incredibly secretive and reclusive. He eschewed having assistants for fear of them stealing his ideas. He'd be the type to order ten different rare elements to hide which one he was actually using."

I was disappointed at her answer but continued, "Okay, tell me about the Switzerland job."

"The Acolytes hit Infinity Power and Research Corporation after midnight. They disabled the alarms and made off with two fusion reactors. The theft wasn't noticed until staff arrived the next day."

I perked up at the Infinity Power name, as they made a big splash and caused a serious disruption in the stock markets for a short period almost a decade ago. They had created the world's first fusion power plant. Their CEO at the time talked about this being a breakthrough that would change the world. Clean, unlimited power that would end the world's dependence on fossil fuels.

The problem was they couldn't replicate their results. They built thousands of these small reactors but each one either melted or exploded when initiated. After five thousand failures, they finally created the second one, but then the ones that followed that failed too. I heard that in the last couple of years they'd raised the success rate from one in five thousand to one in two thousand. The issue was each reactor cost about $10,000, so having such a low success rate meant that a single working reactor cost twenty million dollars to build.

The reactors themselves were about the same size as a car battery and produced roughly the same amount of power. Granted, that power never diminished and was unlimited, but something with the same power as a car battery limited the applications for what you could do with just one of them. At one point, they built a small electric car to promote the new reactor and ran it non-stop on a track for weeks. The problem was the top speed was about five miles per hour. That original reactor, after a couple of years, ended up at the Deutsches Museum in Germany, continuously powering a light bulb on display for the last seven years.

Now the Acolytes had two of these reactors. I laughed to myself when I thought they could now make a small electric car that could do ten miles per hour, forever. On a more serious note, they had grabbed two $20 million reactors, which was a sweet haul for one job.

We discussed this job for a bit and then I asked Stella, "So far they have stolen a gyro, diamonds, GPUs, an advanced AI that has no ethical restraints, lithium-ion batteries, a laser cutting machine, two fusion reactors, and a formula for a super metal—any idea what they could be building?"

Stella tugged idly at one of her braids while she pondered this and said, "We can eliminate the diamonds; they were probably stolen for financial reasons rather than a building material. The AI can be eliminated too; it is probably being used to refine the design rather than being a part of what they are building. The same goes for the laser cutting machine. That leaves us with a gyro, GPUs, batteries, fusion reactors, and super metal as the components. It could be anything: a missile, a rocket, a robot, a tank, a drone, or about a thousand other things."

I banged my fist on the table in frustration and Stella added, "It was a good thought. The more items they steal, the more it will narrow down the list of possibilities."

I nodded and went in a different direction, "Let's focus on our little group of miscreants. Any updates on James Niven or on PCL's competitors as possible buyers for the stolen laser cutter?"

Blue shook her head and said, "We are still working on tracking down all possible 'James Nivens.' The list of possible matches is down to less than ten now. I will try and track them down via the shadows. I have just started on the PCL angle. There are four other major players. The two biggest have been putting together offers to buy PCL; the other two have been quiet. As today is Saturday, and all of them are closed, we'll probably have to wait until Monday to look into them further."

"The research is also our second priority," said Stella. "I wanted to test and refine our tracker first."

I couldn't argue with that. The James Niven search was a longshot; it could be an alias or even if it wasn't, there was a good chance he didn't live in Canada anyways. A PCL competitor being a buyer for the laser cutting machine was a hunch, and Blue was right that with it being the weekend, we'd probably not learn anything until Monday anyways.

We chatted for a few more minutes and then they left for the underground lab in London via the shadows.

***

A couple of hours later, I was at the hospital visiting Rob. I opened the door and was greeted by the steady beep of the machine monitoring his heart rate. The other bed beside him was empty and made. I wondered if Annette had gone home or was just getting something to eat.

He'd look so peaceful lying there if it weren't for all the tubes coming out of him. I was pleased to see that the pinkness of the healed skin had faded, and unless I looked closely, it was hard to tell that he'd even been injured.

I sat down gingerly on the edge of his bed and said, "Hey, buddy, miss you. We are due for a poker game soon…"

My eyes started to well up and I fought back the tears. He'd been in this coma for four days now and with each passing day my fears that he would never wake up grew. I forced those dire thoughts away; I didn't want that type of negative energy around him. I bowed my head and made a silent prayer to Eir, the Norse goddess of healing.

After my prayer, I started talking about all the stupid shit we'd been through over the years. I laughed at some of the verbal shots we'd exchanged and the old times barhopping together before he got married.

I lost track of time as I sat there rambling on; I think part of me kept expecting him to wake up and say something like, "make yourself useful and grab me a beer." Unfortunately, other than the steady beep and drone of the machines around him, the room stayed quiet.

In the end, I got up, squeezed his hand and said, "Love you, bro," and quietly left the room. I smacked my head for how stupid I was for trying to be quiet because I didn't want to wake him; I was tempted to go back into the room and stomp loudly and yell as I left but resisted the urge.

Outside the hospital, I found a secluded area, pulled on my balaclava and took to the sky. I hated seeing my friend lying there like that. There was nothing I could do to help Rob recover, but I could take down the people responsible.

***

Bobby called me early in the afternoon and had the two final Acolyte names for me: Brittany Tanner aka Hexadecimal and Jefferson Green aka Meat-Shield.

"Nice work; I knew all my tax dollars being wasted by EIRT were good for something."

"Ha-ha, very funny. You got anything new to share?"

I thought about it and James Niven's name popped into my head. I'd kept his name back originally as I wanted some time to investigate it and see if it went anywhere. Since Blue and Stella didn't seem to be getting anything, I figured it wouldn't hurt to spill and see if Bobby and EIRT could shake something loose. I told Bobby about him and gave him the same description we had.

The line went quiet for a moment and Bobby said, "You interviewed Terror-Byte's mom a couple of days ago and got this and you are just sharing it with me now?"

"Yeah, well," I said, trying to squirm my way out of this, "at the time, I wasn't sure if it was relevant to the case or not and wanted some time to check it out."

Bobby snorted and said, "Meaning you've looked into it and haven't found anything and decided to share, hoping that we might find something."

There were times when working with someone who knew me well could be annoying, and this was one of those times. "Yeah, Stella and Blue haven't found anything. We also have the English vampire court looking into him because of the English accent, but they haven't found anything either. James Niven is probably an alias and a dead-end but who knows. Did your investigators get a chance to talk to Hexadecimal's or Meat-Shield's friends and families?"

"Yeah, Jefferson Green is seventeen and grew up in Toronto. Raised by a single mom who died of a heart attack about a year ago. No known living relatives, he ended up in the system. Nine months ago, his foster parents reported him missing and no one has seen him since. No record and had decent grades. People who knew him said he was a shy, gentle giant of a kid."

Good kid, but all alone in the world; that isolation would make him a prime candidate for recruitment by the Acolytes. Being part of a team and being wanted would mean the world to a young man like that.

Bobby moved on to Hexadecimal. "Brittany Tanner is nineteen and grew up in Windsor, Ontario. Parents were divorced when she was eleven and her mom got custody. Dad moved out to California after the divorce and has had little to do with Brittany. Mom got remarried and had two more kids with the new dad. Both dads have serious money, so Brittany never lacked for anything."

"In her teens, the trouble began. A pot possession charge, followed by cocaine possession about a year later. Three public intoxication charges on her record as well. Friends described her as a party girl, and that was about all she lived for. Her grades got worse each year and her final year at high school she had a 70 percent absentee rate and failed every class. Her mom and stepfather decided some tough love was needed and kicked her out of the house when she was eighteen.

"She crashed at friends' houses until she wore out her welcome with them. For the first two months, she'd go home each week looking for money and then one day she stopped coming by for handouts. Last time anyone saw her was eight months ago."

I frowned and said, "The absentee rate seems odd; the girl has the ability to clone herself, why not send a clone to school instead if she didn't want to go?"

"Good point. Maybe the clones can't speak, or she needs to be a certain distance from them or they disappear or something?"

I thought back to our first encounter and realized that the clones didn't say anything other than their primal screams when they attacked. Bobby could be on to something here. Her aura wasn't that big and cloning sixteen copies of yourself would be enough to generate an aura the same size. Maybe the clones couldn't speak, weren't very bright, or couldn't think independently; if that was the case, then sending one to school would be pointless. The first time a teacher asked the clone a question, it would be obvious that it wasn't Brittany. The distance theory could also be true, which would also make it impossible for her to send one to school in her place. "Why did these two take so long to track down?"

The phone went quiet for a moment and I realized that Bobby probably thought I was giving him a hard time.

"Neither of them was listed as Enhanced on their missing person's report. Our first search was done by looking for any Enhanced Individual between sixteen and twenty-five that had been reported missing in the last nine months, and then we compared the results to the Acolytes' profiles for matches. Tracking Hexadecimal also got delayed by a false lead."

"False lead?"

"Another girl who closely matched her physical description and was listed as Enhanced went missing around eight months ago. The report didn't list what her powers were though, so we had to send out an investigation team to talk to the parents to find out what her power was. Once we found out it wasn't the ability clone herself, we moved on."

The other girl had my curiosity piqued. "Can you send me the file on the false lead?"

"Why?"

"She's Enhanced, so she might be an Acolyte we haven't met yet. If she is, getting a heads-up on her powers before we run into her would be useful."

"Sure."

"How did you find Hexadecimal and Meat-Shield if they weren't listed as Enhanced?"

Bobby laughed on the other end and said, "Old fashioned police work. Jefferson Green was fairly easy as there weren't too many six-foot-four teens that had disappeared around that time. Brittany was trickier. We made a list of girls matching her description that went missing around that time and then eliminated them until we found Brittany."

I told him that was good work and we ended the call shortly after that.

I considered the value of following up on Hexadecimal or Meat-Shield. Meat-Shield with no living family was probably a dead-end, as there wouldn't be anyone he'd contact. There might be a close friend that EIRT missed, but they were usually pretty thorough, so that was unlikely. Chances were good that when he joined the Acolytes, he'd left his old life behind, and I doubted there would be much to find there.

Since Hexadecimal had been kicked out, it seemed unlikely that she'd contacted someone from her old life in the nine months she'd been missing.

My phone chirped. I opened the e-mail that Bobby had sent me. The false lead was Madison Mazur. There was a photo of her in the file and I could see why EIRT thought she might be Hexadecimal.

They were both blue-eyed blondes with similar heights and builds. At eighteen, Madison was only a year younger than Brittany.

I scanned the file until I found her power and didn't like what I read. Madison could paralyze someone with fear by a simple touch. The fear-induced paralysis lasted thirty minutes to an hour. That was a very dangerous ability. The only upside was she had to make physical contact for it to work and couldn't project it. I wondered if it would affect me or not. As an Elemental, I had some resistance to mental attacks. Liv, with her vampire abilities, might be resistant too, ditto for Stella and Bree with their dual natures. Being resistant might just mean that we were paralyzed for less time, but any amount of time was too long in a fight.

I plugged in the kettle to make myself a coffee and kept reading. She was different from most of the Acolytes in that she was popular, outgoing, had good grades, and there were no discipline issues at school or with the police. Her parents were still married, and she had two younger siblings. With the seemingly happy home life, my first thought was that she was abducted rather than having run away, but I dismissed that immediately due to her power—anyone who grabbed this young lady was in for a rude surprise.

Coffee in hand, I headed up to the office upstairs and continued reading the report. On the next page I found something interesting. Madison, about four months ago, had called home. She talked to her mother and said she was fine but missed everyone and hoped to be home soon. Madison added that she was sorry for making everyone worry and was about to say something else, but the call abruptly ended.

The mother called the police thirty minutes later to report the call, hoping they could trace it. The police tried, but the number was a fake, and they couldn't find where it had originated from. Madison hadn't called back since then and was still listed as missing.

I wondered if she was connected to the Acolytes. To be on the safe side, I'd mention her description and powers to the team at dinner in case she did appear in a future battle.

I opened the file Stella and Blue had created for the Acolytes. I added Brittany and Jefferson's names to it and put Madison's name and details with a question mark at the bottom of the file.

We now knew all six of the Acolytes' real names, their histories before joining, their powers, and the name, or at least alias, of the suspected recruiter. We knew their methods of operation, from Terror-Byte disabling the alarms and cameras, to Flaming Knife Guy cutting the locks on doors and safes or secure areas, to them teleporting out at the end of a job and leaving a burnt circle on the floor. Their suits were high-tech and able to resist Elemental attacks, so that meant they were immune to heat, cold, and electricity, though I'd only tested the last one. There also had been no trace so far of anything they had stolen turning up on the open markets, which confirmed for me that they were building something.

We knew there was someone behind the Acolytes that was financing, recruiting, training, equipping and controlling them. Whoever this mystery person or persons were, they had deep pockets due to the armored suits and the fact that they had kept the Acolytes out of sight for eight to nine months before the operation began; clothing, feeding, equipping, training, and housing them during this period wouldn't have been cheap. The fact that they did this with three teams on three different continents also showed considerable resources.

We also knew that our group of Acolytes were locally born and raised. None of them were particularly powerful on their own, but combined, and with the protective suits, they were formidable. We speculated that after they were recruited, they stayed in Canada since EIRT had no record of them leaving the country. There was a chance that they left under false passports, but I'd put money on them not leaving. We were also guessing that they had a local base somewhere in Ontario due to all the crimes being committed here.

Despite all the things we'd learned, we weren't much closer to catching them than when we started. I focused on what we didn't know, and of those things, what would be the most important for taking them down.

Finding their hideout was paramount. If we knew where it was, we could hit them and end this. Stella's tracker, if it worked and we managed to slip it onto Terror-Byte, accomplished this goal.

We were assuming they must have a van or something that they owned that brought them to their targets.

The van likely dropped them off nearby and then left the area so as not to get caught up in a police roadblock after the crime. This meant there was a seventh member of the Acolytes; this person could be either a norm or Enhanced. I leaned towards them being Enhanced, since all the Acolytes we'd encountered were. The first job in Hamilton, only four members were used; there were six at the Lucifer AI heist, and I only saw four silhouettes at the chemical lab trap, and at PCL Inc., we only knew for sure that Terror-Byte and Flaming Knife Guy were there; Terror-Byte was on camera and the melted locks were a good indication that Flaming Knife Guy was involved. Did they configure the teams based on what skills were needed? If that were the case, then the next time we met them, there could be a surprise or two if the members had changed.

The last, and maybe the most important, unknown was the question of who was behind all of this. Even if we stopped our local team of Acolytes, there would still be two more teams out there hurting and killing people. My gut clenched as I realized that there very well could be other teams in training that might appear in the future. Why not? The cost of recruiting, training, and equipping a new team was probably paid for when the new team pulled off one big job. Hell, that diamond heist alone was probably enough to easily pay for ten to twenty teams just by itself.

The only way this would truly be over was if we nailed whoever was behind all of this, and that just made things seem even more daunting.

Chapter 15

Saturday, May 3

"**G**ood news, the tracker works and each of the receivers has a range of about 27 kilometers," said Stella as we stood around the kitchen building our plates of Chinese food.

I tossed a couple of chicken balls on my plate and said, "Good work. How many receivers do we have and where were you going to place them?"

Bree growled before Stella could answer and said, "Less talky-talky; food on plates first. Some of us are starving."

Stella shushed Bree but quickly put a couple more fried shrimp on her plate and then left. We had a rule that with any buffet-style dinner we had at home, Bree went last. That way the rest of us could actually get some food. Blue was just ahead of me and piled on a ton of an extremely spicy pork dish that was ordered mainly for her. My eyes watered just at the sight of all the angry-looking red flecks in that dish. I liked spicy food but not the same way Blue liked it. Blue's spice tolerance was so high that I was surprised her dish didn't melt its way out of the flimsy tinfoil container it was in, or that there weren't symbols for radioactivity painted on the container's side.

I tossed a large helping of beef chow mein on my plate and followed Blue to the table. Bree moaned in pleasure when she finally got access to the food and began heaping food on the three plates she was carrying. Alteea was at the table eating a pile of sugar granules the way a human would eat popcorn. Only Liv was absent, as the sun wouldn't set for another hour yet.

"I made five receivers," said Stella. "I was going to put one near each of the three break-ins—so Hamilton, Mississauga, and Markham. The last two I was going to use to cover the gaps to the north and south. I was going to put one in Burlington to take care of the gap between Hamilton and Mississauga and one in downtown Toronto to cover Mississauga to Markham."

I had a mouthful of rice, so I just nodded. Her logic made sense to me; to get a fix on the tracker, we needed two of the receivers to pick it up to pinpoint the location. The range from Hamilton to Mississauga as the crow flies was about 50 kilometers, so if the tracker was within 20 kilometers of Hamilton or Mississauga, it would only be picked up on one of the receivers. Adding Burlington in between them covered everything in that range. Same with downtown Toronto in the north with Markham.

"How long do the batteries last on the receivers?" I asked.

Stella finished chewing. "Forty-eight to seventy-two hours."

With Blue's shadow traveling ability, she'd be able to distribute all the receivers in less than ten minutes, so I said, "Okay, after dinner Blue and you can get them in place. After that we just need for the Acolytes to strike again and to plant the tracker on Terror-Byte, and we'll be all set."

Stella smiled and went back to eating. Bree joined us and smiled at the three massive plates she had built. I shook my head at how much food our little Were could pack away.

With all of us here except for Liv, I went over Bobby's call and covered what we now knew about Hexadecimal and Meat-Shield and my list of what we knew about the Acolytes.

Bree, at the end of my brief, frowned and said, "I feel sorry for Hexadecimal…"

I wasn't sure why Bree felt sorry for her. She came from a rich family. Okay, her parents got divorced, and she was kicked out of the house at eighteen, but neither of those things seemed that uncommon. "I think I feel sorrier for Meat-Shield than Hexadecimal; he's had a much harder life."

"No, not that. If the powers came from her dad's side or were random, she might not have been aware in her early life that she was Enhanced."

"Still not following," I said.

"Assume she didn't know that she would get powers. You said that extreme emotions could trigger her power, right?" I nodded, and she continued, "Well, I was thinking that in my teenage years, I'd get annoyed or pissed off at home, but the real emotional times came during school. So, what if at school she was stressed and scared about making a speech in class, or she was being bullied, or got dumped by a boy that she really liked, and her power manifested? Out pops a fully *naked* clone of yourself right in the middle of school. I used to have nightmares about walking the hallways naked and it was one of my greatest fears."

Without even thinking, I blurted out, "Funny that was your nightmare; it was probably the most popular fantasy of every hot-blooded boy at your school."

"Pig," said Bree with a suppressed smile.

"I can see what you mean though," I said. "Bad enough to be surprised by your power, but to have a naked copy of yourself in a public place and to have your power outed that way would be extremely traumatic for anyone. We also have no idea how her mom and stepdad would have reacted. They might have started treating her like some sort of freak on top of that humiliation. There are a lot of norms out there that wouldn't be comfortable finding out their daughter had powers."

The table went quiet as everyone continued eating. A few minutes later, I remembered Madison and filled the table in about her powers and her casefile.

Blue cocked her head at me. "You didn't bring this up with the other Acolyte news. Can I infer from this that you don't think she is connected to the Acolytes?"

I had a mouthful of food and just shrugged.

Stella answered for me, "I think she might be connected and that was why Zack warned us about her power. She is Enhanced, which isn't that common, and disappeared around the same time as the rest of the Acolytes."

Bree shook her head. "No, I don't think she is involved with the Acolytes. Her social life doesn't match the rest of them. Her life on paper looks perfect—popular, good grades, loving family, and no issues with the law. She doesn't fit the Acolyte profile…"

"I'm not sure if she is connected to the Acolytes or not. I brought her up because her power is dangerous, and if a new blonde girl does appear with them in the future, I wanted us to be prepared. If I had to bet on it, I'd guess she is not with them. As Bree pointed out, she doesn't fit their social profile. Also, if she is an Acolyte, why haven't we seen her yet?"

Blue's tail went still, and she said, "Because she's dead."

"Why would you think that?" I asked.

"Because of the phone call she made to her mother. If I was running the Acolytes, I would have killed her for that."

Bree gasped, and Stella seemed taken aback by Blue's cold statement. Most days with Blue I forgot that she came from a brutal world where life was cheap and that she had a darker side to her that she kept buried. That made it all the more shocking when she made a comment like that.

"That seems a tad extreme…" I argued.

Blue spent the next minute logically laying out her case. She pointed out that all the Acolytes were instructed to leave their phones when joining, yet at the first battle all of them had phones. This meant whoever recruited them provided them with phones. The lack of masks or helmets, which exposed the Acolytes' identities, was done to bind them to whoever was running this operation. That implied that loyalty was a core value with the organization. The provided phones were a test and were probably monitored. Once Madison called home, she failed that test and would have been deemed a security risk to the operation. By killing her for that transgression, the recruiter accomplished two goals: he eliminated a possible weakness and set an example of what would happen if anyone else stepped out of line.

The table went totally silent when Blue finished. The more I thought about it, the more what she said made sense. If they had killed her, it would certainly explain why we hadn't seen her at any of the encounters.

Bree said, "Your theory is the only thing that explains her brief phone call. If Madison called because she felt guilty about worrying her family, calling and then hanging up mid-way through and never calling again would have been just cruel."

I had to admit that they both had a point. The short, interrupted phone call had bothered me too. Another realization hit me. "This might be the thing that the Acolytes didn't want us to find and maybe even the reason they laid that trap."

Stella frowned. "I think you are reaching there, Zack. They have killed a police officer. Why would they care if we found out they'd killed one of their own?"

Stella had a point, but then Blue said, "The phones might be monitored, but maybe they just saw that a call was placed without knowing what was said…"

I smiled at that. "The Acolytes are worried that Madison might have mentioned where their base is or said something else that might give them away."

Blue added, "It is likely that the Acolytes, or whoever is behind them, tortured her before killing her to make sure that she hadn't said anything to her family that compromised them."

My smiled disappeared at that.

Blue got a small twinkle in her purple eyes and added, "It also shows that whoever is behind these Acolytes makes mistakes…"

"Why's that?"

"Because if I was running them, I'd have killed the family to make sure there hadn't been a leak."

Mental note—never piss off the ruthless blue alien! I thought to myself.

We finished the rest of the meal in silence. Bree, Alteea, and I cleaned up and Blue and Stella left to place the receivers.

Liv was up by the time Blue and Stella returned. After she'd downed a pint of blood and shared a saucer with Alteea, Blue announced that it was time for more training. We all groaned. Thankfully, this was tactical training and not physical training.

Blue shadow-traveled us out to our secret underground lab in London. I smiled as we entered the hangar, as there were six mannequins lined up in a row. Each of them had wigs and props to better reflect the Acolyte they were supposed to represent. Terror-Byte had a long black wig and three pouches hanging off his waist with a phone tucked into each one.

Hexadecimal's dummy was naked with a long blonde wig. Ryan's mannequin had short red hair, and he had two butter knives with paper flames on them. Bug Girl was in a short black wig, with metal thumbtacks in her nose, brow, and ears to represent her piercings, and there was a stuffed hornet on her shoulder. Meat-Shield was in a large shirt with a pillow stuffed down the front and back of it to mimic his larger size. The Bartender had a short blonde wig and an empty beer can in his hand.

"You two have been busy…" I said as I looked over the dummies.

I had no idea where Blue had procured the mannequins and decided it was probably better if I didn't ask where they came from.

"The main object of tonight's training is to get Olivia used to swapping the tracker for one of the phones," said Blue. "She needs to be able to do it at full speed, so she won't be detected. Before we do this as a group, I want Olivia to make a few practice runs while we watch."

Olivia asked, "Don't I need the tracker to do this?"

Stella shook her head and said, "No, for this exercise just steal a phone on the first pass and then put it back on the second. I only built one tracker and don't want to risk damaging it."

Olivia frowned at the damage part. I smiled to myself, as Stella's comments made it clear that she also didn't think this would go smoothly. It was time to have some fun. I turned to Bree and said, "Twenty bucks she doesn't pull this off in three passes."

Liv's vampire hearing picked up my comment and she flipped me the bird. Bree scratched her chin and then said, "You're on," which got a smile from Liv.

I turned my attention to Alteea, who was hovering just above Liv and said, "Alteea, make sure you get this on video, okay?"

Liv frowned at that and I added, "So we have it to review. That way we can all look at the recording and see where we can sharpen our skills."

Liv seemed to buy that, and I grinned to myself. My explanation was only partially true; I really wanted this recorded as I had a feeling it would be hilarious, and I wanted a copy for my own entertainment.

Blue, in the meantime, had moved the other five mannequins forward so they were out of the way. This would make it easier for Liv. I had twenty bucks on the line, so I said, "Terror-Byte isn't going to be by himself, so this is unrealistic."

Blue's lavender eyes turned towards me and her tail swished back and forth as she considered my point. She pulled Bug Girl's mannequin back and placed it beside Terror-Byte and then pulled back the Bartender one as well. The Bartender was now in line with Bug Girl and Terror-Byte but further down and off to the left of them on its own.

"The other three stay where they are as they will be coming out to engage us," said Blue. "But I acknowledge your point that Bug Girl and the Bartender with their ranged powers would stay back." I nodded at that and she focused her attention on Liv. "Come in from the left at full speed, retrieve a phone, and continue until you reach the far-right wall. Turn around, return at full speed, and put the 'tracker' back in the spot where you snatched the phone from."

Liv blurred off to the far left of the hangar. She glanced at Blue and Blue said, "Go!"

My jaw hung open in disbelief as less than a second later Liv was at the other side of the hangar with the phone in her hand and a grin on her face. She lifted the phone so perfectly that the Terror-Byte dummy hadn't even trembled in the slightest. I sighed and reached for my wallet.

She disappeared again for her return run. This time, though, there was a loud crash as the Terror-Byte mannequin tumbled to the floor and ended up on its back with one of its arms broken off. With a smile, I moved my hand away from my wallet. Liv had used too much force when she put the phone back.

Blue reattached the arm and stood the dummy back up. After adjusting the wig, she stepped away and returned to her observation spot.

"Go!"

Once again Liv pickpocketed the phone perfectly. She turned around and blurred back towards the dummy.

"Detected!" yelled Blue.

Liv had gotten the phone back in the pouch but had slowed right down to do it, so much so that we all saw her, hence Blue calling her out.

Liv moved back to her starting position for her third and final try for the bet.

Bree said, "C'mon, Liv, you can do this!"

Blue said, "Go," and Liv was off. A moment later she was on the other side of the hangar with the phone in hand. It hit me that if Liv decided bounty hunting wasn't her thing, she'd make a heck of a living pickpocketing. She was flawless in the lifting part of the exercise.

She turned and went for it. A moment later, a loud crack echoed in the hangar, and the Terror-Byte mannequin toppled forward, this time losing its head. I burst out laughing at the sight of a phone stuffed up the dummy's ass. She'd missed the back pouch completely and shoved the phone inside the dummy's shell.

"That is one way to make sure Terror-Byte takes the tracker back," I said between laughs.

Liv glared at me. Bree tried to smother her laugh, as did Stella. Blue just sighed and headed for the toolbox in the corner. I looked up to make sure that Alteea had recorded it and smiled when I saw she had her phone pointed directly at the sodomized dummy.

I turned to Bree and said, "That is twenty dollars you owe me. I'm also willing to take it in sexual favors."

Bree rolled her eyes, but then smiled and lifted her sweatshirt. She flashed her white sports bra at me. She held the shirt up for a few seconds and then lowered it and said, "That was your twenty dollars' worth!"

"What?" I asked. "Twenty bucks just gets me two seconds of bra?"

Bree smirked and countered with, "You think someone wouldn't pay me twenty bucks to flash my bra at them?"

She had me there; I had no doubt that many men would be willing to part with cash to see just her bra. I was about to complain when Blue came back and started duct taping up Terror-Byte's ass, which was amusing enough to leave me speechless.

Blue got the dummy fixed and righted and Liv made another pass. This time she got the phone back in the pouch but used too much force and broke off the pouch completely. On the upside, the dummy stayed upright. The fifth run, we all cheered as she pulled it off perfectly. To prove that wasn't a fluke, Blue had her do it again. The sixth and seventh runs she knocked over the mannequin again, but on runs eight, nine, and ten she nailed it.

Since Liv had pulled off three perfect runs in row, Blue decided it was time for the whole team to get involved.

"For the team drill, Stella and Bree can stay in their human forms," said Blue. "Our goal is to make as much noise and distraction as possible to keep the Acolytes focused on us and not on Olivia. Stella, Bree, and I will attack from the front. Bree, growl loudly; Stella, grunt and bang the ground and I will ignite my sword and wave it around as we approach. Zack, take to the air. Hit Bug Girl with a quick burst of lightning to neutralize her bug attack and then use your Air power to take out the Bartender. Liv, make your run as fast as possible, and then join the fight, but run back and make it look like you came from behind us. Any questions?"

We all shook our heads and took our places. Going over my role in my head, I realized that the timing on this would be tricky. The lightning attack had to be done before Liv was in the area or I would risk messing with her vampire speed and exposing her. The Air attack on the Bartender would also need careful timing or I could blow him back into her and screw up her run.

I readied my power and Blue called out, "Go!" I shot into the air and flicked a low-powered burst of lightning at Bug Girl's dummy. I laughed to myself as the mannequin rocked back and forth and knocked off the stuffed toy hornet on its shoulder without falling over. The hornet ended up lying 'dead' on the floor, which I thought was a nice realistic touch.

As I turned my focus to the Bartender, Liv started her run. Once she was by, I sent a burst of Air at the dummy. I pushed it back and used the Air to lower it gently to the ground. In a real attack, I'd hit it with a much more powerful blast, but for this exercise I didn't want to shatter the target.

Liv finished her run and a moment later appeared behind the rest of the team.

"Stop! Good run, people," said Blue. She set everything back up again and we did the drill over and over again until we could do it in our sleep.

Chapter 16

Sunday, May 4

Sunday was lazy and uneventful but that changed at about ten o'clock that night. Our phones all buzzed, and texts came in reporting that police were responding to suspicious individuals in black armored suits on Theodore Lane in Toronto. Toronto SWAT and EIRT were both en route.

The name Theodore Lane rang a bell with me, and it took a second for me to place it; when I did, I laughed, earning me odd looks from the rest of the team.

"The Acolytes are hitting Grundy's," I said and got blank stares in response. "None of you have heard of Grundy's?" They all shook their heads and I added, "Grundy's is a legend in the hero and law enforcement communities. They only serve registered heroes in good standing and law enforcement agencies. They make power-blocking cuffs and collars. They also make costumes, magic charms, potions, utility belts, gadgets, weapons, high-tech gear, and just about anything else you can imagine you'd need for taking on super villains and monsters. The founder, Theodore Grundy, came to Canada after marrying a Canadian girl he met in his home country of England during the war. He opened Grundy's in 1946 and supplied law enforcement with anti-monster gear. When he died in 2003, his daughter took over the business and Toronto renamed the street 'Theodore Lane' in his honor. Both he and his daughter were/are talented Mad Scientists. Their gear is top notch."

"Sounds expensive," said Stella. "I thought you were always broke when you were a hero, so how do you know about this place?"

"My mom took me when I was a kid. Also, those earpieces GRC13 loaned us while we were working with them to take down the demon were made by them. My retired hero status means I can't shop there. I have been trying to get EIRT to grant me clearance so I can go and get some gear for us. I'd been keeping that as a surprise."

Blue asked, "Why did you laugh earlier? It sounds like this place would be filled with priceless equipment."

I nodded, "It is but Grundy's has at least three wizards on staff and the building has seventy years of wards built into it. Even if you got around the wards, there are several automated Mad Scientist creations protecting the place too. This time the Acolytes have made a mistake; it would be easier to break into Fort Knox than Grundy's. For now, gear up and let's take them down."

Not even two minutes later, we were in the backyard, ready to go. Liv had the tracker on her, Bree was in her standing hybrid Were-panther form, and Stella was in her Hyde form.

I gave everyone a quick once over and said, "Okay, folks, do this just like we drilled. Alteea, stay high and film everything. Ready?"

They all nodded, and Blue opened a shadow portal. I popped out on the other side to the same cool clear night sky that we had in Hamilton. I took to the air and started searching for Bug Girl's aura. I frowned, as she wasn't among the group this time and focused on looking for the Bartender's colorful psychedelic aura. The Acolytes were in front of Grundy's, going to town on the building. Thankfully, the street was deserted other than four police cruisers blocking off either end of the street.

There was a golden energy bubble surrounding the building, which I assumed was the outer defensive wards. Flaming Knife Guy was slashing furiously away with his knives; Terror-Byte was tossing exploding phone after phone higher up the barrier; Hexadecimal's clones were clawing continuously at it; and a new Acolyte was jumping high into the air and crashing down with a loud *thud* against the barrier. Despite their efforts, it didn't look like it was making a lick of difference.

The new Acolyte's aura had an orange core with a hazy silver outline. The orange, of course, meant Super class, but hazy silver was new to me. I watched him leap off the ground like he was light as a feather. He'd get about fifteen feet high and then plunge down suddenly like he had a Brink's truck on his back. I guessed he could either change his weight or manipulate gravity in some fashion. Thankfully, his aura only radiated out a couple of inches, so he was a relative lightweight power-wise. For now, I just called him 'Mr. Bounce' in my head.

The Bartender was on the right flank and making hand gestures towards the cops at his end of the street. On the far left, Meat-Shield kept an eye on the cops on his end of the street. Behind him was a short, frail-looking kid with glasses. He was another Super class, judging by the orange core of his aura. The green and brown secondary ring was usually nature related and pale green meant telepathic or mental abilities. I speculated that he could control plants or manipulate earth with his mind. If his power was plant-related, I wasn't too concerned; we were in an urban environment and not a forest. The earth one had me more worried; if he had an Earth Elemental's ability to cause earthquakes, it might be an issue. His aura, though, was barely over an inch, so other than maybe rocking the ground a bit, I doubted he'd be that much of a threat. I dubbed him 'Nature Boy.'

"Boss, company!" yelled out Meat-Shield, and all the Acolytes turned their attention to Stella's angry lumbering form charging at them.

Meat-Shield and the naked blonde clones charged at Stella, and Terror-Byte tossed a phone in her direction as well. Mr. Bounce leapt up behind the clones and angled towards Stella. Flaming Knife Guy took up a defensive position on Terror-Byte's right.

The Bartender turned and started making hand gestures towards Stella, and that was my cue. I called on my Air power and focused a powerful but concentrated blast of air at him. I smiled grimly as it lifted him off his feet and he flew back. He hit the golden barrier like he'd been smashed by Thor's blessed hammer. His eyes rolled up in his head and he collapsed to the sidewalk like a puppet with his strings cut. He still had an aura around him, so I hadn't killed him, but he was out of this fight and he would certainly be feeling that tomorrow.

I spotted Liv's aura blur past Terror-Byte, and he seemed oblivious to her presence. If that was her first pass, she'd just grabbed one of his existing phones and would make another pass to slip the tracker in its place.

I was feeling pretty good at that moment. The Bartender was down, we would have a tracker on Terror-Byte in the next few seconds, and no civilians or cops had been hurt. But not a second later, everything turned to shit.

Bree made a loud, enraged growl that was unlike anything I'd ever heard from her before. She leapt up and began attacking the back of

Stella's Hyde form in an unrelenting fury. Liv called Bree's name in horror and she blurred over to assist Stella. The naked blonde wave crashed into our Hyde from the front. Stella ignored Bree and just stomped the clones into paste.

I wasn't worried about Stella; I knew that Bree could claw and bite at that Hyde form all night long and not make a scratch. I was puzzled at Bree's behavior though. The last time I'd seen her do something like this was when we took on the French master vampire. That time, she'd lost control of her beast and it looked like it was happening again. Her beast managed to gain control that time because the master vampire had put a contract out on Liv, and as far as the beast was concerned, Liv was pack and you didn't hurt the pack. This behavior now though made no sense. Stella was like a mom to Bree, and there was no way the beast wouldn't consider Stella pack.

I started calling on my Air power so I could lift Bree off and up into the air where she could do no harm when she suddenly leapt off Stella's Hyde form and went directly for Terror-Byte. I exhaled, relieved that she was now directing her anger at the right target. She dodged the clones and Acolytes like they weren't even there. Terror-Byte's face went pale and then Bree just stopped and knelt before him like an obedient dog.

What the fuck?

Worse, Terror-Byte pulled out the biggest freaking handgun I'd ever seen and pointed it at Bree's feline head.

"Everyone stand down unless you want to see kitty's brains blown out over the sidewalk; the silver bullets will make sure she stays there," said Terror-Byte, his voice loud and clear.

The battle instantly stopped, and all the Acolytes retreated, surrounding Terror-Byte and Bree while the rest of my team stood in shock.

I clenched my fists but lowered myself down from the air and landed beside Liv, Blue, and Stella. I spotted Nature Boy standing behind and off to the side of Terror-Byte. His eyes were closed, and he was sweating and shaking like he had a fever or was putting out a tremendous physical effort. I cursed under my breath as I looked at his aura again and realized what it meant: it wasn't plants or earth he could control—it was animals. The light green outer ring meant he had the ability to mentally control animals; Nature Boy was why Bree was acting so funny.

I could take Nature Boy out with another powerful gust of wind, but if I did that, Terror-Byte would kill Bree. I could do the same to Terror-Byte, but I couldn't do it to both at the same time. I also worried that it would only take him a split second to pull that trigger, and I couldn't guarantee that I could take him out that quickly.

I took a deep, resigned breath and said, "You win, Melvin. What do you want?"

His face went beet-red and he screamed, "That is not my name; I'm Terror-Byte and if you call me anything other than that, I will put a round into her leg."

I held up my hands in a gesture of surrender. "Sorry, Terror-Byte. Now, what do you want?"

His attention turned to the Toronto SWAT truck that screeched to a halt behind the cruisers that blocked the north end of the street.

"Hex, Meat-Shield, assemble the circle. We are leaving," ordered Melvin, and he turned his attention to me and said, "You have interrupted our job, and the Master won't be pleased. We are leaving and taking your cat with us. Interfere and she dies."

"Mel—" I started to say in anger but caught myself and said, "Terror-Byte, harm her and there will be no place on Earth you can hide; you will spend the rest of your short life looking over your shoulder."

He shrugged and said, "If she is harmed, it is because you didn't follow my instructions, so you'll have no one to blame but yourself."

The teleport circle was laid out now around Bree and Terror-Byte, and the rest of the Acolytes stepped inside it. Meat-Shield carried the Bartender's unconscious form over his shoulders.

Terror-Byte saw that Nature Boy was still outside the circle and said, "Beast Whisperer, get your ass in the circle."

The kid slowly nodded in response but didn't open his eyes. He was trembling with effort still but managed to shuffle closer to the rest of the Acolytes and crossed into the circle.

A white glow surrounded them, and Terror-Byte said, "I'll be in touch."

Then they were gone.

Chapter 17

Sunday, May 4

Bree

The beast paced back and forth in my head, and I could feel its rage coming off in waves. The odd thing was, under that anger there was fear, uncertainty, and doubt. In my entire time of being infected with lycanthropy, I'd never felt fear from my beast. My own fear started to rise in response, but I pushed it down.

Something had gone wrong. I always recalled everything from when I was in my beast forms, but this time all I remembered was arriving in Toronto, the beginning of the fight with the Acolytes, and then nothing. Judging by the coat of sweat across my body and the rapidly fading soreness in my bones and joints, I'd just changed back to human. I was also starving; changing between forms always burned a ton of calories. I needed food, but it would have to wait.

I had no idea where I was, but my nose started filling things in. By the musty scent, the cooler air across my skin, and slight pressure change, I knew I was in a basement somewhere. A plane loudly descended overhead. My skin itched as I sensed silver close by. Another scent caught my attention and Terror-Byte's image filled my mind. He was here and nearby. There was also another male scent.

The enhanced sense of smell was another mixed blessing of my Werepanther abilities. When I used to be human, scent was the weakest and least used of my five senses. Now, it was my most used and trusted. Eyes could be tricked but the nose never lied. I could walk into a room blindfolded and with earplugs and still easily tell a lot about who or what was in the room just from smell. The downside was the bad smells, like body odor, farts, cigarette smoke, and a host of other unpleasant scents that were harder to hide from.

I kept my eyes closed and stayed still. That was hard, as I knew I was naked and there were two men probably looking at me, but I didn't want to give away that I was conscious by covering myself.

The worst part was not knowing what happened to my friends. Were they okay? Did they get captured too? There was no way they would have let the Acolytes take me without putting up a fight. How did the Acolytes capture me?

"Is she awake?" asked a voice I didn't recognize.

The beast in my head snarled at the voice, and the hate coming from the beast was intense. It really didn't like this unknown man.

"How the fuck should I know? You're the Beast Whisperer. If anyone should know if she is awake or not, it should be you," said Terror-Byte.

Another airplane roared overhead. Wherever I was, it was close to an airport. The planes sounded low and two of them in less than a minute meant they had to be landing or taking off.

"She is fully human now, so I can't control or sense her animal half anymore," said the meek voice I didn't know.

A lightbulb went off in my head. Whoever this Beast Whisperer was, he had the ability to control animals. He must be the reason I didn't remember anything, as he was controlling the beast, not me. The beast nodded at me and then went back to pacing angrily. Oh God! If he was in control, did we hurt our pack mates? The beast stopped, shook its head, and relief filled me.

My stomach rumbled like thunder in my ears in the quiet space. For a moment, I worried that would give away that I was awake, but the two Acolytes didn't have my enhanced senses and wouldn't have heard it.

Another aircraft roared by overhead. Three planes in less than three minutes. There was no way this was Hamilton Airport. It didn't get this volume of traffic. The only airport that could be this busy was Pearson Airport in Toronto. *Assuming, of course, that I'm still in Ontario.*

"That is too bad..." said Terror-Byte.

"What's that?" asked the strange voice.

"That you can't control her anymore. Having that hot sexy body doing whatever you want would be a lot of fun for you," laughed Terror-Byte.

That's it! I flashed open my eyes and covered myself with my arms to stop the show they were getting. I was in a prison cell. Three solid walls and the opening was barred. The thick sturdy bars were either made from silver or coated with silver. The locked door was made of silver bars too. The cell was empty other than a metal toilet in the corner. I flipped around and sat up against one of the walls.

The room outside the cell was large. Terror-Byte and some nerdy looking Acolyte were standing about ten feet from the cell. At the far end, I could see paper targets. There was a garbage bin, a cot, and a small side table against the closer wall about fifteen feet away from my cell. Further down that wall there was a door with an Exit sign over it.

I stared at them and said, "If either of you want some fun, come in here with me, and I will give you something that you won't forget!"

Terror-Byte laughed and said, "Ah, our guest awakens."

"If I'm your guest, how about some clothes and some food?" I asked.

He shook his head. "And give you a way to touch the bars? I don't think so. I will get you some food though." He touched his ear and said, "Creepy, nuke up a dinner and bring it down here when it's done."

I perked up at the name 'Creepy,' as that was an alias we didn't know. Could this be the person who drove the truck that took them to the crime scenes? I'd worry about that later and asked, "Why am I here?"

"You're leverage. We have a couple of jobs coming up that the Master wants us to pull off, but we couldn't figure out how. Your team, particularly the shadow-traveler, however, is aptly suited for these jobs. So, they do these three jobs for us and they get you back."

"They won't break the law; The Hurricane is too good to do that!"

"We'll see. I have a feeling he might become more morally flexible to save you. If they don't do it, then you'll be going back to them—you just won't be breathing." Terror-Byte went quiet for a moment, as if to let his threat sink in and then with an arrogant smile added, "This chat has been fun, but I have things to do. I will leave you in the Beast Whisperer's care, and your food should be along shortly. Have fun, you two!" and with that he headed to the corner and exited the room.

Another plane flew low overhead. *I must be near Pearson, but how do I let Zack and the team know that?* I looked up as I heard a click and realized

123

that the Beast Whisperer had just taken a picture of me. My anger flared at that and I self-consciously pulled my arms tighter against me. I focused on that phone—if I could get that, I could text them.

I studied the so-called Beast Whisperer. My first impression was that he was a nerd. He was short, probably only a couple of inches taller than me. Even with the bulky black Acolyte armor he was wearing, it was obvious that he was scrawny. The thick glasses, slight acne, and bad haircut also reinforced my nerd assessment. I knew if I could get him close enough, that I could easily overpower him. By the way he was almost drooling over me, I got the feeling his social life was even more pathetic than Zack's.

The door in the corner opened and I saw the goth-looking girl who controlled bugs. She was carrying a steaming frozen dinner. I wasn't overly excited about microwaved dinner, but it was food and at this point, that was all I cared about.

The Beast Whisperer turned and intercepted her, "Thanks, Carla, I'll take that."

Goth-girl frowned and said, "I'm Creepy, William!"

"You certainly are," said the Beast Whisperer with a grin.

Creepy rolled her eyes and said, "That joke wasn't funny the first time, and it gets less funny each time." She handed off the food to him. She looked over at me and had an odd expression on her face, which was either sympathy or disdain.

I took a chance and said, "Your mom misses you, Carla."

For a brief second, a bit of remorse and longing flashed across her face, but then it was gone. She turned to me and said, "Carla is gone and so is that part of my life."

She made a beeline for the door and left. I hoped that maybe she might call her mom. I had no doubt that EIRT were monitoring her mom's calls. If she called, there was a chance that they could trace the cell phone and storm this place and take down Terror-Byte and his crew.

The Beast Whisperer walked towards me and had a grin on his face that made me nervous. He stopped a few feet in front of my cell and said, "Stand up and move to the far wall."

I carefully got to my feet, strategically using my arms to keep myself covered. I turned and walked to the back wall and William whistled.

I tensed up and my anger flared. The beast roared and rushed to the surface. I closed my eyes and forced myself to be calm. I was already starving; I couldn't afford to change again. I turned and rested my back up against the back wall.

William ogled me from head to toe, and I tried to ignore it. He was playing with fire—I barely had control of my beast. It hit me that that might be what he was trying to do—bring the beast out. He could control the beast but not me. Also, with those silver bars and the solid concrete walls, it wasn't like we could get out of here.

"You want this?" he asked, holding up the TV dinner. I nodded, and he said, "Drop your arms and flash me."

"Fuck you, go jerk off to *Star Wars* or something."

He flinched at that and went red. He stomped away and stopped at the garbage bin beside the cot against the wall.

He looked at me, smiled, and said, "Maybe tomorrow at breakfast you'll learn your place!" And with that, he dumped the entire tray in the garbage.

"NO!" I yelled. I needed that food. My rage flared uncontrollably, and this time I couldn't hold the beast back. I felt the change coming on.

We can't change; it will weaken us too much, I told the beast, trying to rein it in, but it was too far gone. It kept coming and I couldn't force it back into its mental cage. I could feel my body starting to change. I couldn't let that happen. I needed to stop this. Out of sheer desperation, I ran forward and grabbed the silver bars. The beast in my head screamed, and I echoed its cries with screams of my own. Tears ran down my face as I kept a hold of the bars. The beast backed down, and I pulled my hands away. My palms and fingers were red and blistered. I dashed over to the toilet and plunged my hands into the water in the bowl. Anything to stop the pain.

I sighed as the cool water coated my burned flesh.

"You're one crazy bitch," said William, but I ignored him and just kept rubbing my hands in the water.

After a good ten minutes, I pulled my hands from the water and they felt better. My Were healing was kicking in, but much slower than normal because of the silver. With no food and nothing better to do, I decided to go to sleep. I curled up on the cold concrete floor, positioning myself to reveal as little as possible to William, and closed my eyes.

I promised myself that as soon as I got out of there, William would die first. In my mind, the beast growled deeply in agreement. Mercifully, in my weakened state, sleep took me quickly.

Chapter 18

Sunday, May 4

I just stood there staring at the black, slightly smoldering circle, which only moments ago contained Bree and the Acolytes.

"Bree…" said Liv softly, distraught.

"We'll get her back," I said.

A bullhorn cut the air. "This is the Toronto Police, get down on the pavement and put your hands behind your head."

Really? What was it with SWAT types being assholes? They'd just witnessed us fighting with the Acolytes, so it should be obvious we were the good guys. I was starting to think the Murdocks of this world were the rule and not the exception. With how shitty this night had gone, couldn't I get a Bobby Knight type for a change?

"Stella, change back and look cute and cuddly for the nice police officers. Everyone, do as they ask," I said.

I had just hit the pavement when a familiar voice yelled, "Belay that. EIRT is taking over this crime scene. Hurricane, get your ass off that road and stand up, that goes for the rest of your team too."

Speak of the devil, I thought with a grin. I got to my feet and saw Bobby walking towards me with his team in tow. Losing Bree like that had shaken me, but the tracker flashed into my mind, giving me hope. With EIRT and Toronto SWAT here, all of us could hit the Acolytes' base so hard and fast that they wouldn't have a chance.

"Please tell me you got the tracker in place," I asked.

The silence made my stomach clench.

I looked over my shoulder at Liv; she had her head down and was shaking it back and forth. "I only had time for one pass…"

Which meant she stole one of Terror-Byte's phones but didn't make the switch. I cursed to myself silently but couldn't blame Liv; she went to help Stella when Bree went nuts. I would have done the same in her shoes.

"You're zero for two now; you're either getting old or losing your touch," said Bobby.

"More like the Acolytes are proving the saying, 'I'd rather be lucky than good.'"

He nodded and asked, "We just arrived, but the locals were saying something about one of your own attacking another team member?"

I sighed and said, "There are two new Acolytes to add to the list. One can change his weight or gravity around him, and the other has the ability to control animals."

Bobby's eyes widened. He glanced around and asked, "Where's your panther now?"

"They took her."

"I'm sorry, Hurricane. We'll get her back."

I turned at the sound of someone sobbing and saw Blue and Stella both comforting Liv. "Take Olivia home. Send Bobby a copy of the video and start looking into the two new Acolytes. See if there are any reports of people with similar powers."

"Wait, they are witnesses and we need statements from them," said Bobby with a frown.

"I'll give you my statement, and we are sending you a full recording of the encounter. Do you really need them?"

After a couple of long seconds, he waved them off and turned his attention back to me.

Blue said, "Call me when you are done."

"Don't worry about me; I'll fly home. I need some time to clear my head anyways."

Blue gave me a solemn nod of understanding and opened a shadow portal.

"This job didn't make sense," I said. "They have been getting better at this. Heck, their last job was so clean that nobody even saw them do it. Now they hit Grundy's? They had no chance of even cracking the magic wards, never mind the automated defenses. They staked out their previous jobs and were in and out in less than ten minutes. They knew where to go and what to grab, and yet here they just fumble around like idiots outside one of the most well-protected places in Canada?"

Bobby rubbed his chin and said, "Unless they weren't trying to break in."

I groaned and then swore; this was a setup. They wanted Bree for some reason—that's why they brought the Acolyte that could control animals. Why Bree though? Werepanthers were rare in Canada, but they were common in South America. Was this Terror-Byte's plan for keeping us from interfering with his operation? As they were usually in and out in less than ten minutes, there was no way the local SWAT team or EIRT could respond in that short amount of time; we were the only team that could get to them that quickly. With Bree as his hostage, he could keep us off the board going forward. At least that meant Bree would be safe; if he killed her, he lost his leverage.

I gave Bobby descriptions of the Beast Whisperer and Mr. Bounce and an overview of the encounter, which was kind of redundant once the video showed up fifteen minutes later. We watched the video on his phone, and he asked me a couple of questions as we did.

Towards the end of his questioning, the Toronto Five showed up. The Five were the city's resident superheroes. They were founded in the sixties by five local superheroes. They were based out of the Hall of Heroes in downtown Toronto. As a kid, I got a tour of the Hall when they were trying to recruit my mother to their team. She turned them down. Most of that team had retired or died. The only active member left from those days was Kid Canada who was now Captain Canada and the current leader of the Five.

Captain Canada landed dramatically, lowering two of his team members who couldn't fly. "Who dares to attack Grundy's?"

Bobby rolled his eyes and walked over to deal with them. I had to admit that Captain Canada was the poster boy for what a hero should be. He was tall, blonde, handsome, probably had more muscles in his one arm than I did in my entire body. Heck, his prominent chiseled chin was almost big enough to house a family of four. Add in a commanding baritone voice and a sterling reputation for good, and he was just about perfect. His powers were intimidating too; he was a flying tank that could dish out powerful blows that could level a building. His presence here instantly annoyed the shit out of me.

The Five were extremely powerful, but they were posers. I had no doubt they'd wipe the floor with me and my team, but they were more like professional athletes than heroes. They spent more time doing interviews than they did stopping crime or saving people. Sure, they would show up and save the day if something big was happening, but only once the TV cameras were rolling. I knew they trained constantly to stay in peak form, but they didn't go out on active patrols very often.

It was a shame what they'd become. It hadn't always been like that. In the sixties and seventies, they were always out on patrol at night, keeping the city safe. The Five saved countless lives during the freezing winter of '76. They played a huge role during the Mississauga train derailment and saved a lot of people. Their finest moment was in the early eighties when they stopped a massive Fae invasion. After that though, the corporate sponsorships started. As the money and fame grew, they became less like heroes and more like celebrities. They were more concerned about their image and their brand than they were about doing actual hero work.

I was kind of shocked that they showed up here, as there were no news crews on scene yet. I kicked this thought around and realized that Grundy's must be a sponsor. That made sense. Grundy's was the premier superhero equipment supplier in Canada, so I had no doubt that the Five shopped here frequently. They probably got things at cost or below and in return they'd list Grundy's as a sponsor.

I glanced at the Toronto Temptress and felt like an awkward teenager again. I had her poster on my bedroom wall back then and had a bit of a crush on her. She was a telepath and a martial arts expert. It was said that no man, and a good number of women for that matter, could resist her call. Comic books usually caught shit for overemphasizing a heroine's, um, *assets* and sexuality, and the Temptress seemed like a living embodiment of that stereotype. She was tall, lean, and had a chest any stripper would kill for. She was currently wearing thigh-high heeled boots and a black leather corset that showed more than it covered. She changed her costume a few times a year, and each time the new scandalous costume made the front pages of all the papers.

Everything about her was beautiful and sexy. Her lush, dark hair flowed down her neck and back and contrasted amazingly against her flawless pale skin. The emerald green eyes, the small refined nose, and the full pouty lips gave her a look that models would die for. She was over forty and yet I had no doubt that her poster was still the most common one on teen boys' walls.

Beside her was an Ice elemental called the Snowman. His pure blue aura extended out a good nine or ten inches and he was easily one of the more powerful elementals I'd ever seen. He tipped his head at me and turned his attention back to Captain Canada and Bobby.

Above me was another elemental, the Eternal Flame, and her element was fire. She was the newest member of the Five and not much was known about her. I could just barely make out her feminine shape through the flames that engulfed her, but I couldn't tell her hair color, ethnicity, or anything else about her.

Thankfully she was high enough that I couldn't sense her power. As the opposite of my minor Ice power, it would have been distracting. That was one of the most impressive things about the Five—they had a Fire and Ice elemental on the same team. Usually opposite powers didn't get anywhere near each other, as the feeling of the other's power was extremely uncomfortable. The discipline it took for those two to work together was amazing.

The last member of the Five was invisible and was perched atop a nearby ten-story building. I only knew he was there due to his aura. The Phantom was incorporeal, and out of all the Five, he was the one I would least like to take on. How do you fight something that is invisible and has no physical mass?

"It looks like you have everything under control here, we will leave it in your capable hands, officer," announced Captain Canada.

The Temptress snuggled up to his right side and grabbed the Snowman by his left arm before taking to the sky.

Bobby came back to me and we finished up shortly after that. He said he would let me know if he found out anything about the new Acolytes or anything else related to them and wished me luck on getting Bree back.

It was my turn to take to the skies. I told Blue earlier that I would fly home as I needed to think. That was true, but I was also a mess of emotions. Bree was gone, and I'd lost to freaking Melvin for the second time—maybe three times if I counted the exploding trap. I lost my control; the local morning news would be reporting about a freak lightning storm that happened overnight.

Once I got that out of my system, I felt better and actually did use the last part of the trip to clear my mind and focus.

Twice now we'd faced the Acolytes in combat and lost, and it was because I'd underestimated them. Sure, their auras were pathetic in size and individually any one of us could wipe the floor with any of them. A single raindrop wasn't much either, but enough of them together could wear down mountains and wipe out entire cities. I vowed that I wasn't going to make that mistake again.

I forced myself to stop thinking about them as scared and nervous teenagers and classed them as organized international criminals with unknown resources behind them. They killed a Hamilton police officer, put Rob in a coma, and kidnapped Bree. The kid gloves were coming off, and we were going to take them down no matter the cost.

Chapter 19

Monday, May 5

It was past midnight by the time I got home. Blue and Stella were still up and that caught me a bit off guard. The whole team was around the kitchen table with a couple of laptops.

Liv blurred over to me, threw her arms around me, and said, "I'm sorry. I should have planted that tracker. How are we going to get Bree back?"

I held her and stroked her long dark hair, "Shush, that wasn't your fault. For now, chin up and let's focus on what we can do to find Bree."

Liv nodded, and we joined Stella, Blue, and Alteea at the table.

"After you guys left, Bobby and I came up with a theory; they weren't trying to break into Grundy's. That was a ploy to draw us out so they could capture Bree."

Liv gasped softly at that, but Stella and Blue both nodded in agreement. Blue said, "That would be logical. They had no chance of breaking those wards with the resources they had there. It also explains why they brought along someone who can control animals in an urban environment."

Liv asked, "Why do they want Bree?"

"I think it is to keep us from interfering with them going forward," I said. "Thanks to Blue's shadow powers, we are the only Enhanced group around that is able to get to one of their break-ins in time. By taking Bree, they can use her to keep us on the sidelines. I expect Terror-Byte will contact us soon. He'll probably demand that we stay away, and if we are good, they will return Bree to us unharmed."

"That is good news," said Stella. "If that is why they took her, then it is in their best interest to keep her alive."

Olivia looked relieved at that. I nodded in support, but deep down, I worried that was only half true. They would keep Bree alive as a hostage to keep us out of the way, but what happened when they finished their operations here? Bree would have seen their base, overheard conversations and would know too much about them. Sure, they could keep her isolated somewhere, but it was hard to hide from Were hearing and scent abilities. They were already looking at murder charges for killing the Hamilton cop earlier, breaking and entering, grand theft, weapons charges and Odin-only-knew what else. What was one more murder charge on top of that? If I was in their shoes, I'd kill Bree at the end of their crime spree. Melvin may not be that ruthless, but whoever was behind all of this certainly was.

Blue gave me a sidelong glance. Her tail was straight down, and I knew she was thinking what I'd been thinking. I subtly shook my head at her, and she gave me a small nod in response; we'd talk about this later.

"Alright, we probably won't be able to interfere when they are doing a break-in, but that doesn't mean we can't still work to figure out where they are hiding. We have two new Acolytes: Beast Whisperer, and I named the other guy Mr. Bounce; we should start trying to figure out their real identities. Also, we should take another look at the video to see if we missed anything there."

Stella said, "Your 'Mr. Bounce' is Austin Woodson aka Air Austin aka Gravatron the Great. He is eighteen, grew up in St. Catharines, and has been missing for nine months. There is also a warrant out for his arrest that was issued about nine months ago. A bounty was put out for him eight months ago on the UN website for $12,000 US."

I blinked in surprise at Stella and said, "That was quick."

"Blue and I had already looked into him months back when I found his bounty online. Tonight, I didn't place him immediately, but he seemed familiar to me. As soon as we got home, I went through the UN website and when I spotted his bounty, it all came back to me. His reward was small, but it was local, so we investigated him. There hadn't been any sign of him online, or with his family or friends and we came up with no leads, so we moved on."

"Okay, what is his story?"

"He made a big splash in the competitive skateboarding scene a few years ago. He was able to do moves that no one thought were even possible. He got endorsement deals and built up a following quickly. He branded himself, 'Air Austin,' and was very active on social media. About a year and a half ago, he was outed as being Enhanced. He was prohibited from competing and his sponsorships were revoked. He shut down his Twitter and Instagram accounts due to the negative comments and stayed out of the public eye for a bit. Ten months ago, he reappeared as Gravatron the Great, stuntman extraordinaire."

"Wait," I said to Stella, "I remember this guy now. He was the idiot who jumped off the Peace Bridge in Niagara but rather than drowning, he miraculously bounced off the water and floated right back up to the spot on the bridge he started from. It was a cool stunt, but it was unauthorized and caused an 18-wheeler driver to be distracted; the truck crashed into the back of a minivan and severely injured the two kids in the back seats."

She nodded and added, "Blue and I did a thorough search for him back then and there was nothing. That means he is just like the rest; once he was recruited, he completely left his old life behind."

Another dead end then. This case was starting to piss me off. Normally there were leads when you were tracking someone down; you'd do the research, follow the leads, and you'd find your target. With this one, every lead went nowhere, and we still weren't any closer to catching them than when we started. We now knew who seven of the eight Acolytes were, and not one of those seven contacted a friend or loved one after they disappeared. There was an old expression, 'three can keep a secret, if two of them are dead,' and that usually turned out to be the case in the bounty business, yet seven people had managed to keep a secret this time.

"Anything on the Beast Whisperer?" I asked.

"We haven't had time to look into him much," answered Stella with a yawn.

It was coming up on one in the morning, and Blue and Stella were both morning people, so I said, "Why don't you two go to bed and get a fresh start in the morning. Liv, Alteea, and I will give the video another look. I will leave you a note if we find anything."

Stella shut down her laptop and she and Blue disappeared upstairs shortly after that. I moved the other laptop to the living room and hooked it up to the big screen. We played the video twice, the second time in slow motion, but didn't see anything new.

I opened a browser and we did some searches for the Beast Whisperer, but nothing seemed to match our guy. After an hour we gave up. Stella and Blue were better at this sort of thing and if there was anything out there, they would find it tomorrow.

I worried about Liv; she was subdued and focused while we watched the video and did the searches, and that wasn't like her. Bree meant the world to her, and not knowing where Bree was or what the Acolytes might be doing to her must have been tearing her up inside.

We sat on the couch and watched a movie; I hoped this might take her mind off Bree. I was tired and suppressed yawn after yawn, but I didn't want to leave Liv alone. This was the time she and Bree usually hung out together and I wanted to be there for her.

"Go to bed, Zack. I'll be fine here with Alteea," said Liv as she muted the sound with the remote.

"I'm fine." She lifted an eyebrow at me. "Yeah, okay, you're right. I'm tired but I don't want you to be alone."

She smiled and said, "That's sweet, but you need your sleep. If we want to get Bree back, we need to be sharp, and you being exhausted helps no one. Get some sleep, I'll see you tomorrow."

"You sure?"

She nodded firmly. I gave her a warm hug and wished her and Alteea a good night and headed to bed.

I was wiped, but sleep was a long time in coming. Lying there in bed, alone with my thoughts, it was hard not to worry about Bree. I took this case because I wanted to stop the people who hurt Rob from hurting anyone else, and if I was completely honest, to dish out some payback too. Now Rob was still in a coma and Bree was missing. Worse, if I was right, missing would turn to dead once they were finished here.

Chapter 20

Monday, May 5

Bree

The next morning, I awoke to an almost overwhelming feeling of hunger. The lack of food was making it harder to control the beast, which was right at the surface of my mind and itching to break free. My body ached from sleeping on the concrete floor.

Even without opening my eyes, I knew William was up, as I could smell his scent and hear the noises of whatever game he was playing on his phone.

I got up and used the toilet, which was mortifying and annoying. William's gaze was on me the whole time. Even worse was the fact that there was no toilet paper.

After I finished, William came over carrying a paper plate that had two muffins and a small container of orange juice. I couldn't tear my eyes away from the food, and I don't think I'd ever wanted a muffin more in my life.

"Move to the back of the cell," said William.

I stepped back, not taking my eyes off the food he was carrying.

I felt his eyes lingering on me and my anger surged, causing the beast to rise to the surface of my mind. I closed my eyes and forced myself to be calm. I pictured grabbing the silver bars again and the beast's pressure in my head relented at my threat.

My eyes started to well up at the humiliation, but I forced myself not to cry. I sensed him get closer to the bars, and I was tempted to spring forward and see if I could catch him. I so wanted to get him by the neck and slam his face into the bars until it was mush. The beast stopped its pacing and growled in approval at my dark thoughts. The thought of food was the only thing keeping me in check. I couldn't risk not getting those muffins. I felt as weak as a kitten at this moment and needed food.

"Enjoy your breakfast," said William as he walked away.

I blinked my eyes open and almost cried at the sight in front of me. I leapt forward and scooped up the plate. I inhaled the two muffins and downed the OJ in less than a minute. God, they tasted good, but they were gone, and I needed more.

I hated myself at that moment but asked, "Please, Beast Whisperer, can I have some more?" and carefully pushed the empty plate and juice carton back under the silver bars to him.

He put down his phone and looked over at me. "That was the last of the muffins for today."

"It doesn't have to be another muffin; any food will do. I'm starving and need calories…"

He stared at me for bit and then touched the neck of his suit, "Gravatron, the Were needs more food, can you heat up a dinner and bring it down?" There was a pause and he added, "Your food will be here shortly."

I forced a smile. "Thank you."

He smiled at that and went back to his phone. I wondered how much he'd smile when I tore his beating heart from his chest and showed it to him. Despite my dark wishes, I kept my face neutral. I needed that food and needed more information. He lusted after me, and I was going to use that to my advantage. Once I had gotten more food, my next goal was to escape, but I also had an opportunity here to get more information on their operation.

A few minutes later, Gravatron came down and handed the steaming TV dinner off to William. To my surprise, Gravatron didn't even look my way, and once he handed off the food, he immediately headed for the exit. I wondered if Gravatron disagreed with taking me prisoner and didn't want to be reminded that I was here. My stomach knotted as another thought hit me; maybe he knew what they had planned for me. Terror-Byte said that he was going to leverage me to get Zack and everyone to do some jobs for him. What if after the jobs, they decided to break the deal and just kill me? If that was the case, then I needed to escape before that happened.

William approached my cage and said, "Move to the back wall."

He pushed the food under the bars and quickly moved back. I ignored him and just grabbed the food. There were plastic utensils on top of the dinner. I sat against the wall and dug in.

I was shocked at how much I enjoyed the crappy previously frozen food.

My thoughts drifted to my friends. I missed them. Liv was probably going crazy with worry about me. I wished I could let her know I was okay. I knew that they would move heaven and earth to find me. I cringed at that last thought as that meant they probably would do whatever Terror-Byte asked to get me back. At least Zack would make sure that they didn't hurt anyone while stealing whatever thing Terror-Byte wanted.

I looked down at the now empty plastic container, and my stomach rumbled. I still needed more food. I sighed and channeled my inner Olivia. I tried to pretend what I was about to do was no different than when I worked at Gil's as a shooter-girl. Men there would blatantly check me out in the low-cut crop top I wore then. I slid the container back under the bars and stood up. I didn't bother covering myself and said, "Beast Whisperer, thank you for the food but I'm still hungry, can I have another one?"

He looked up from his phone with an annoyed look on his face for a second until he noticed how I was standing.

"You just ate. How can you still be hungry?"

"Downside to being a Were—we need a lot of calories. Kind of like a pregnant woman; I'm eating for two here."

He smiled at that and then touched his ear to activate the communicator. "Gravatron, can you heat up another dinner?" He paused and added, "I know but she is still hungry...Thanks, man."

Ten minutes later, I was done the next frozen dinner. I felt better but still wanted more food. I decided not to ask for a third one and hoped that lunch wouldn't be too long. I pushed the empty tray under the bars and stood up against the far wall. William noticed I was done and came over to clear away the tray.

After he dumped the tray in the garbage, I asked, "Why did you join the Acolytes?"

He turned back towards me and his eyes stayed focused on my exposed chest. After a long pause he said, "Because the Master recruited me."

"What is the Master like?"

An expression of awe and reverence instantly came to his face and he said, "The Master is our savior. He is preparing us for the upcoming war with the humans. He sees the threat to the Enhanced community and when humans move against us, we'll be ready. We are superior to normal humans, and they are jealous of our abilities. Groups like Humans First want to kill or imprison us, and those groups are growing and getting stronger every day; we need to be ready."

I rolled my eyes a bit at the last part and said, "Humans First are just an oddball fringe group; most people are decent."

William snorted and said, "Right, people are decent… How long have you been a Were?"

"Just over a year now; what does that have to do with anything?"

"So, you didn't have to grow up as one; that explains why you think humans are decent. My power manifested when I was in grade seven. I didn't have any control over it. Squirrels, raccoons, rabbits—they would all show up at the windows to my class and try to get in. The other kids figured out I was the one the animals were attracted to. They called me a freak and worse, and a day didn't go by that I didn't get beat up. I was twelve and it got so bad I wanted to kill myself. My parents pulled me from public school, and I got homeschooled until the Master found me. I think the only reason my parents homeschooled me was because they were ashamed that I was a freak and wanted to hide me away."

He gazed off into the distance and said, "There is nothing decent about humans. I wish people were more like animals. They talk about wild animals being unpredictable but they're not; humans are. Humans First are bigger and more dangerous than you think, but the human-controlled media is careful not to let that secret out. The day is coming when you and your team will have to decide: be puppets for the human regime or take your rightful place as one of the rulers of humanity."

I still hated William but a part of me did feel sorry for him. How bad were those kids that William at age twelve wanted to kill himself?

I did want to know more about the Master, and he seemed happy when he talked about him, so I asked, "Is the Master Enhanced? What makes him so special?"

William's whole demeanor changed. "He is the greatest scientist the world has ever seen. This suit, which is bullet, fire, electrical, and ice resistant, he created. It is amazing, it weighs almost nothing, and it self-regulates the internal temperature. I have been out in minus thirty-degree weather, and it feels like a perfect spring day inside of it. The suit can also handle human waste with no problem. Our teleporting circles and gates were designed by him. He has many other amazing inventions, but you're not an Acolyte, so I can't tell you about them."

I probably would have been more impressed if I hadn't seen Sir Reginald's underground lab. His inventions were just as impressive, but he was more than a hundred years ahead of this so-called Master.

"His real genius though was planning for when the humans turn on us. Without his guidance and his preparation, we would be overwhelmed by the mass of humanity. Enhanceds are the next step in human evolution; we are the superior race."

"Hitler thought the German people were the superior race, too, look how that turned out..."

William's face went red and he angrily said, "You dare to compare the Master to that monster?"

I had touched a nerve. "You have to admit that the whole 'superior race' thing does have a lot in common with Nazi Germany..." William seemed to get even angrier at that, and I didn't want that, so I quickly added, "To be fair, you've had the chance to listen directly to the Master, whereas I'm only getting this secondhand. Maybe the Master explains this better than you do."

"Of course he explains things better; he's the Master," said William, who seemed to instantly calm down at my praise of the Master.

The level of devotion William had for the Master was scary. I wondered if the rest of the Acolytes were as fanatical. I asked, "The Master does seem to be impressive, but what happens if you fail in one of his tasks?"

William's face went ghost white at that and he said, "The Master doesn't tolerate failure. He loves all of us, but the entire fate of the Enhanced community is riding on us, so we can't fail."

"Is that what happened to Madison?"

A look of shock and surprise appeared on William's face. "She was a traitor and was dealt with accordingly."

It was nice confirming that she was once an Acolyte, but I felt bad that Blue was right, and they'd killed her. "She was a girl who missed her family..."

"She broke her oath with that call! If she'd been more dedicated to the Master and our cause, she'd still be with us today."

William had gotten worked up, and I needed to calm him down. "What were you playing on your phone? It sounded cool."

William beamed at this and said, "Fudge Force. I'm up to level 967. You have to match three of the same colors together to clear a row..."

William excitedly went over the details of the game and I pretended to care. The alternative was staring at the walls of my cell, though after fifteen minutes of him ranting about his stupid game, the walls were starting to look good.

Chapter 21

Monday, May 5

I checked my phone when I woke up. There was nothing from Terror-Byte, but Annette had sent me a text. My excitement diminished when I read that there had been no change in Rob's condition.

The weather was overcast and dull and matched how I felt. Stella and Blue hadn't found out who the Beast Whisperer was yet but were still looking into it.

The day dragged, and with each passing minute, I was growing more anxious. I was convinced Melvin had taken Bree as leverage and would contact us to tell us to keep out of his way. If he didn't call, that meant they took Bree for another reason. Did they take her and just kill her after they left us? Were they going to sell her to someone? Was she going to be a part of some freakish science experiment? Were they torturing her for information? I also worried about how she was and if she was getting enough food. As the day went on, I came up with more and more frightening possibilities and was becoming a total basket case.

I tried distracting myself by doing some model building but gave up after five minutes; my heart wasn't in it and it wasn't helping.

For the rest of the day, I hid in my office doing fruitless Internet searches on the Acolytes.

Just after six that evening, my phone rang, and I almost dropped it in my haste to answer. I was disappointed when I saw it was Bobby calling.

We exchanged greetings and he got right down to business. "I have the names of the two new Acolytes."

"You can skip Austin Woodson, unless he has been in contact with someone in the last nine months."

"Okay, so you already figured out one of them; 50 percent as a success rate isn't too bad, but 100 percent is better," said Bobby, and I could picture the smug grin on his face.

"Yeah, yeah, score one for EIRT and your huge resources for a change. Now, who is the Beast Whisperer?"

"William Sidney, seventeen, grew up in Brantford. Clean record, we found him through a missing person's report his parents filed nine months ago. Unfortunately, no one has heard a peep from or about him during that time; just like the rest."

"Anything interesting in his background?" I asked.

"Not really. He was homeschooled from grade eight onwards. Seems his power manifested near the end of grade seven. Animals kept showing up outside any classroom he was in and tried to get in. The kids in his school figured out that he was causing it and the bullying escalated. His parents pulled him from school after it got to be too much."

William's story wasn't that uncommon among young Enhanced Individuals. There'd been a lot of talk over the years about starting special schools for them in Canada like some other countries had done. I had mixed feelings about it. My main issue was it exposed anyone with powers to the government. There was also the issue of putting that much uncontrolled power in a small area, and I didn't like that it created another barrier between normal humans and Enhanceds. It might cut down on bullying and make Enhanced Individuals feel less like outsiders. It would also give Enhanced kids better access to resources and specialists to help them cope and learn to control their powers better.

"Anything else?"

"Not about the Acolytes," said Bobby. "Um, not sure how to bring this up, but I also put out an alert to all law enforcement agencies, hospitals, and morgues about Bree. So far no one matching her description has turned up."

"Thanks, Bobby, I appreciate the effort."

We ended the call shortly after that. I gave the information to Blue and Stella and they updated their files and said they would look more into William just in case EIRT missed something.

Dinner that night was a subdued and somber affair. Liv was abnormally quiet and the rest of us followed her lead. I knew Bree being gone was eating at her, but I couldn't think of anything to say or do to make things better, so I just ate in silence.

Just as we finished dinner, I got an e-mail from a random numbered G-mail account with the subject line 'Werepanther.' It contained no other information or text other than a Skype link. After grabbing and putting on my balaclava, I clicked it and after a few seconds, Melvin's annoying face popped up on my screen.

"Ah, the Hopeless Hurricane, I thought you'd be quick in getting back to me."

"What do you want…Terror-Byte?" I'd almost called him 'Melvin' but caught myself.

"As you know, I have your Werepanther, and as you can see, she is alive and well." He turned the phone and standing in a barred cell was Bree in her human form, naked and awkwardly trying to cover herself with her arms.

My anger flared at that as I knew Bree was sensitive about her body being exposed.

"Give her some clothes," I said through clenched teeth.

"And give her a way to touch those silver bars? I don't think so."

"Tell Melvin to go fuck himself… Don't do want he wants," yelled Bree defiantly.

That's my girl.

"Shut up, bitch! Call me Melvin one more time and I'll use you for silver bullet target practice!"

She just glared at him but stayed quiet.

Melvin turned the phone back to him and said, "Feisty little kitten."

"Touch her and I will kill you."

Melvin laughed and said, "You can try, but I won't lay a finger on her. She is too useful to me at this moment." He paused and added, "The Canadian Mint has 80-million-dollars' worth of gold bullion for a new gold maple leaf coin they are going to make next month. You and the rest of your remaining team are going to steal it for me. Do this and I will give you back your friend alive and unharmed."

Motherfucker. I had underestimated the little bastard again. I'd been right that he was going to use Bree as leverage, but not to keep us out of his way. It was to make us do his work for him.

"I need to discuss this with my team," I said, trying to stall and figure a way out of this.

"I don't care what you have to do. In forty-eight hours, I will e-mail you another link. You will show me the gold and I will give you directions for the exchange. Fail to do this and I will send your panther back to you in pieces." And then he cut the connection.

I yanked off my balaclava and tossed it and my phone on the table and everyone looked at me.

Liv broke the silence. "We have no choice. We need to get that gold."

Stella and Blue nodded at that, but I didn't say anything for the moment. This wasn't an easy decision, and if we did this, we would become wanted criminals. At that point, our options would be to run or turn ourselves in and spend a long time in jail. If we didn't do this, there was a good chance that Melvin would follow through on his threat and kill Bree.

I briefly kicked around contacting EIRT or GRC13 for help. They might be able to help us get the gold and set a trap for the Acolytes. I dismissed it when I realized that an operation like this would need approval from Director Smyth. Due to our history, I knew he wouldn't approve it and would be likely to double the security at the Mint to make sure we couldn't access the gold.

I wondered if we could raise the money to buy eighty million in gold; if Terror-Byte got the gold, it shouldn't matter how we got it and we'd get Bree back. With the bounties we'd done in the last few months together, my savings, and any money I could get for the house, we'd probably have about six to eight million. That still left us seventy-two or so million short.

The only people I knew of with that sort of money would be the English vampire court. I had no idea if Elizabeth, the Master of the English vampire court, would be willing to loan us that amount, and even if she did, she would own us for the rest of our lives. If she was generous, she might allow us to pay it off by continuing to do bounties.

However, to continue making the amount of money we'd need to stay ahead of the interest, we'd have to take on the most dangerous bounties out there. It would only be a matter of time before one of us ended up dead.

That also assumed Terror-Byte honored the deal and returned Bree; he could very well double-cross us and then we still wouldn't have Bree and we'd owe the English vampire court a ton of money.

A small part of me was also bothered that if we did steal the gold, I'd be flushing my mother's and my hero legacies down the drain. Mom was a hero until the day she died, and I'd spent a good chunk of my life upholding the law and protecting the public. The idea of me becoming a criminal didn't sit comfortably with me.

Liv frowned at me and asked, "We are going to get the gold and get Bree back, aren't we?"

"We're talking about breaking the law. The Mint is well protected, and we might hurt or kill one of the guards in our attempt."

"This is Bree's life we are talking about!" yelled Liv.

"I know. I want her back too, but if we go down this route, there is no turning back. We'd be no better than Terror-Byte and the Acolytes..." Liv was about to interrupt, and I held up my hand and said, "We have forty-eight hours, so we don't need to go steal the gold right now."

Liv crossed her arms but reluctantly nodded. I turned to Stella and Blue and asked, "You've both been quiet, what are your thoughts on this?"

"We don't have any choice," said Stella. "We are a family and Bree is a part of that. Nothing is more important than family..."

Blue nodded in agreement, and with that my fate was sealed. If we put this to a vote, it would be three to one. And deep down, I knew I couldn't let Bree die and if we voted, I probably would vote with them too.

I felt my shoulders slump, and I sighed. "Alright then, it looks like we have some gold to steal." Liv smiled and Blue and Stella nodded. "This isn't going to be easy. There have been two successful break-ins to the Canadian Mint, one in the seventies and one in the eighties. Both were done by powerful super-villain teams. After the second one, the Canadian government got serious about protecting the Mint and its security was radically enhanced. There have been many attempts since then, but none have been successful. It is one of the most secure places in the country and probably would make the list of the top one hundred most secure places in the world."

I paused to let that sink in. "If we had months, we might be able to pull this off undetected, but as we have less than two days, we are going to have to do this quick and dirty. The second we pull this off, we become wanted criminals. We'll need to abandon the house and move to the secret lab. The first thing we need to do is move anything important we want from here to the lab to prepare for this."

I turned to Blue and said, "I need you to start spying on the Mint from the shadows. Figure out guard schedules, where the gold is and how we can access it, what defenses we need to worry about and anything else that will help us plan out this job. The rest of us will pack. Tomorrow morning, we'll take what you learned and put together a plan to hit the Mint tomorrow night."

Stella said, "We'll need money to get by when we are on the run. You'll need to hit the bank and pull out as much as you can in cash."

I frowned at this and said, "We'll be lucky to get $50,000 on such short notice. That isn't going to get us very far."

I had $25,000 in cash in my safe up in the office, plus the $20,000 from Walter and the $50,000 from the bank. That would give us $95,000. I knew Blue and Stella had some English pounds tucked away in the lab that would put us at just over $110,000. It wasn't a bad sum of money. The Food-O-Tron would keep us fed and Liv and Alteea in blood, so we could stretch that money out for a good while. The problem was if we did this we'd be wanted and hunted for the rest of our lives and the money wouldn't last that long. Also, if the Food-O-Tron broke, we'd drain that money fast.

Stella tugged at her braid, deep in thought, and then said, "What if we transferred all of our individual cash to the main company account. Once the money is there, we move it all to the English vampire court."

I doubted the English vampire court would get involved in something like this, but then I remembered that the vampire courts had ties to organized crime. Vampire courts were the first to do organized crime in a big way, and the rumor was that most of the jobs pulled by big crime syndicates were run by them from the shadows. Moving a little money for us would barely register with them. They'd also take a fee for their services.

I thought about that and found myself slowly nodding in agreement. Our personal accounts and company accounts were all with the same bank branch so there wouldn't be any delays there. There would be a delay of twenty-four to forty-eight hours in moving the money electronically between the main company account and the English vampire court's account due to the large amount. It would be a race from the time we pulled off the heist to when the authorities froze our accounts.

We'd also take a bath on the currency exchange, as the English vampire court would give us the money in US dollars or English pounds and not Canadian. But even after their fee and the exchange, at least we'd still have 90 percent of our money, which was a hell of a lot better than $110,000.

"Make the call and see if they will do this for us," I said.

A few minutes later, Stella came back into the room with a smile. We all moved our money, and as I expected, it showed up immediately in the main business account. Stella then moved the bulk of it to the English vampire court. The race had begun.

Chapter 22

Tuesday, May 6

Just before noon the next day, Stella, Blue and I sat around the kitchen table and started planning out the heist. All of us were tired. Stella and I had been up most of the night with Olivia, packing up our stuff and moving it to the lab. Blue was working on even less sleep; she'd been up the entire night either opening shadow portals between here and the secret underground lab in London or remotely viewing inside the Mint from the shadows.

Blue began going over what she had learned and most of it wasn't good. "There are just over two dozen officers on-site. They are well armed and are using SWI composite rounds."

SWI rounds were made from silver, wood, and iron. That combination meant they were lethal against Weres, vamps, and fae. Those rounds were only available to government agencies and militaries around the world and were strictly controlled. If Liv took one of those to the heart, it would kill her just the same as driving a wooden stake through it would. For Blue and me, they'd be just as deadly, but then a normal bullet would also kill us. The only one this didn't affect was Stella in her Hyde form, but if they had higher caliber rounds, then she too could be taken down. There were large gun emplacements on the roof of the Mint, and those would be dangerous to her. Thankfully those same guns couldn't be used inside the Mint.

The officers in the Mint were also a concern; they were all RCMP officers and most were from EIRT teams or even GRC13. They were well trained and not to be taken lightly.

"They also had a Fire elemental on staff," continued Blue.

That was annoying. Depending on where the elemental was, it would sense my presence as soon as I entered the building. The elemental would also be GRC13 or EIRT, which meant highly trained and capable.

"The gold is kept in the main vault. The vault is well lit and there are only two small shadows in the entire vault. They are under the two security cameras mounted in each corner on the entrance side of the vault. The inside of the vault is about one hundred and fifty feet square and about eight feet high. There are three barred cages on the far side of the vault. The left cage is filled with silver bars, the center has the gold bars, and the right one is empty. The vault is shut at the end of the day and is on a time lock that won't open until the next morning. There are overrides; you need two people with the right codes, keys, and thumbprints to open it during the time lock."

Blue paused and Stella immediately asked, "How big are the shadows?"

Blue shook her head and said, "No bigger than six inches in diameter."

I smiled and held up my hands about two feet apart and said, "So about this big."

Blue gave me a confused look and Stella just rolled her eyes at my attempted humor. Bree and Liv would have laughed. It was from a joke I'd told them, 'why can't women parallel park? Because men always tell them this is six inches…' Any time a six-inch reference came up, Liv or Bree would always hold their hands wide apart and grin.

"Ignore him. So, too small for me to fit through," said Stella, and Blue nodded. Stella perked up and added, "But not too small for Alteea!"

"She would be able to get through, but that doesn't help us," Blue said. "The gold bars are twenty-five pounds. That is too heavy for her to lift. I also thought about Alteea when I found those two shadows. Even if we could boost her strength somehow, her flying back and forth in the vault as she moved the gold bars would quickly be noticed. There is no way she could move them all out in time. There is a red button under glass in the main monitoring area marked 'gas,' and I can only assume that means they would flood the vault with gas as soon as they caught wind of what was going on. I haven't been able to find the canisters, so I have no idea if the gas is lethal, knockout, or tear gas."

Stella's expression fell at hearing Blue's answer, but she was tugging on her braid, so I assumed she was pondering our options.

I'd never been around gold before, so I asked, "How many gold bars are we talking about here?"

151

"There are one hundred and twenty of them."

Holy shit. I thought we'd be stealing ten to twenty gold bars. A hundred and twenty bars at twenty-five pounds each was about a ton and half of gold. Even if we got into the vault, it would take us time to load them on a cart and get them out of the vault and through a shadow portal. This was time that we didn't have. Even if we took out all the guards, the GRC13 base was less than ten minutes away by helicopter. There was no way we could take out all the guards without one of them sending out an alert. The Mint being attacked would have GRC13 responding with at least one team, if not both.

Blue continued on with her briefing, "We need to open the vault. The two officers with keys and codes are in the main monitoring area. The monitoring center always has at least eight officers there and the Elemental is always nearby. The rest of the guards are manning the gun emplacements on the roof or patrolling the grounds inside and outside the Mint. The main monitoring area is also well lit and has limited shadows, but there is a supply closet nearby that we could portal into. But the main monitoring area is secured. To get in, someone inside needs to buzz you in. Stella's Hyde strength should be enough to smash through one of the entrances though."

I started going over all of this in my mind and my gut knotted up.

"Okay, hold on," I said. "I'm sorry but this isn't happening. There is no way we can hit that main monitoring room and take out eight trained officers in a non-lethal way. I love Bree but I'm not willing to kill cops who are just doing their jobs. Also, the keys and thumbprints are easy enough to get if we take them down, but to get the codes, we'd need to take both of those officers alive and conscious. They also won't give up the codes willingly, so we'd either have to torture it out of them or start killing others until they gave them up. Bree would never forgive us for doing something like that."

Blue looked down at the table and nodded. Stella suddenly got up from the table and left the kitchen, heading towards the front hall.

She returned less than a minute later and was holding something behind her back. She smiled and said, "We are going to get that gold—" she paused and held up an umbrella and said "—with this!"

It's a real shame when the bright ones go nuts. Stella's solution to robbing one of the most secure places in the country was a black ten-dollar Home Depot umbrella.

Blue's alien face morphed into a huge grin and she said, "You're a genius!"

In response, Stella smiled and gave a playful bow. In the meantime, yours truly sat there trying to figure out how the umbrella helped or why both my teammates had lost their freaking minds. "Can someone clue me in?"

Stella took her seat and said, "We send Alteea into the vault from one of the two small shadows with the umbrella. She flies it across the vault and into the gold cage and opens it. This will create a shadow big enough so we can open a portal that the rest of us can use…"

"Oh, that is clever," I said. "What about if we send her in first with a can of spray-paint to black out the cameras?"

Blue shook her head and said, "Won't work; the gas, remember?"

She had a point. The guards may not notice an umbrella darting across the vault, but the second one of the cameras went dark they'd go on full alert. Alteea wouldn't have enough time to paint both cameras, return for the umbrella, fly across the vault, open it in the cage and then hold it up long enough for us to get through the portal and take it from her before the gas got her.

I cursed silently at not being able to disable the cameras. If we could have done that, then we would have had a good chance of getting away clean. Now they'd have us on film stealing the gold and too many people at EIRT and GRC13 knew us.

"The gas also means it will only be Liv and me going into the vault," I said.

Blue frowned but nodded her head. We could have gotten gasmasks for Blue and Stella if we had enough time. But with Blue's alien physique and Stella's oddly shaped Hyde form, we would have to get custom ones for them, and we didn't have that sort of time.

We had a rough plan and got down to hashing out the details. We estimated that it would take at least three minutes for the guards to gear up, leave the monitoring center, get all the way down to the vault, open it, and engage us. We needed to get in and out before that happened.

Luck was with us as Blue had noticed in her spying last night that one of the two officers with the keys and codes to get into the vault drank a lot of water and left the monitoring center almost hourly to pee. We would hold off sending Alteea through until he left to go to the bathroom, and that would buy us another thirty seconds to a minute, as the bathroom was in the opposite direction of the vault.

I pointed out that the officer with the weak bladder might not be on duty and Blue just shrugged. I was also concerned that it might be another Enhanced Individual on duty tonight rather than the Fire elemental. A mage or a tank could really throw a wrench in our plans. But we didn't have a choice—we had to hit the Mint tonight.

Our final plan would have us hitting the Mint after 1:00 a.m. If Officer Pees-a-lot was on duty, we would start the heist once he left his station. Alteea would portal into the vault, fly to the gold cage, and open the umbrella. I'd go through the shadow portal, clear the air and keep the gas back, and take the umbrella from Alteea. Liv would be right on my heels. Alteea would fly out through the portal. Liv would then start tossing the gold bars through the portal using her vampire speed. Once she had cleared out the gold, she would go back through the portal. I'd use my Air powers to keep the umbrella in place, step back through the portal, and we'd be done.

If everything went smoothly, then we should be in and out in just under two and half minutes, well before they would be able to get the vault open.

"We have a plan," I said. "We'll mockup the vault in the hangar of the secret lab and do some practice runs later when Olivia is up. For now, let's all get some more sleep—tonight is going to be a long night."

Chapter 23

Tuesday, May 6

By six o'clock, Blue, Stella, and I were seated at the kitchen table having dinner. I was enjoying my dinner right up until Blue said, "I do not believe that Terror-Byte will return Bree to us when we give him the gold. They will make us do more jobs for them."

The more I thought about what Blue said, the more it made sense. Making us rob the rest of their targets would be ideal for them. With Blue's shadow traveling abilities, we could teleport right inside a place, which they couldn't do with their teleport device. Also, there was no risk to them; they could keep stringing us along with Bree until their work was complete. However, once we got the gold, we had leverage of our own. "Then we won't give them the gold until he does."

Blue shook her head. "What if he starts torturing Bree? How long will you be able to refuse to hand over the gold?"

Stella gasped and I cursed under my breath at that. Blue was right. If they started harming Bree, we'd hand over the gold. "You've obviously given this some thought, what do you suggest we do?"

Blue gave us a pointy-toothed grin. "We cheat. We plant a tracker in with the gold. Once we know where their base is, we rescue Bree and then take them down."

Stella added, "Not in with the gold, under it. We can put the tracker on the underside of the cart we got to move the gold."

I agreed to Blue's plan to use the tracker. That way, even if he stuck to the deal, this would still give us a chance to nail him, recover the gold, and clear our names.

My dinner mood improved when Blue also said that she had been using the shadows to spy on the Mint since it closed and the same people were on duty again tonight, including the officer with the weak bladder. That meant we still had an extra thirty seconds and we didn't have to adjust our plan for a different Enhanced Individual.

Once Olivia and Alteea were up, Blue used the shadows to transport us to our secret underground lab in London. I smiled as I spotted the well-used but sturdy looking handcart off to the side of the hangar which was going to be our Trojan horse for the tracker. I wondered for a moment where Blue had gotten it but, as usual, figured I was better off not knowing.

Blue and Stella had been busy in the couple of hours they had before dinner. In addition to the handcart, they'd already built a mock vault. Spray paint markings stood in for the outside of the vault and the three cages. In the middle cage there were red clay bricks neatly stacked to represent the gold bars.

In the right-hand corner near the vault door stood a five-foot pole with a six-inch wire circle on top of it. In front of the stack of bricks there was another pole, but this one was three-feet high, and the wire was rectangular. I puzzled over that and asked, "What is the pole in front of the cage for and why is it rectangular and the first one is circular?"

Blue said, "It is to represent one of the gaps in the bars of the cage that Alteea will need to fly though. The bars are in a grid pattern and the gaps are rectangular in shape. The one by the entrance is circular because that is the shape of the shadows the cameras cast."

That made sense. It would actually be easier with the real thing, as there would be multiple openings through the bars on the real cage, so Alteea wouldn't have to aim for a specific one and just go through whichever one she wanted to.

At the back of the middle cage there was a four-foot wooden archway that represented the portal created from the umbrella shadow.

Blue walked us step by step through the plan. She then had us go through our roles at a slow pace. Alteea picked up the umbrella and flew through the wire opening that denoted the shadow portal under the camera. She made good time and cleared the wire opening to the cage flawlessly. Things slowed down as she tried to open the umbrella. It took her a good fifteen seconds to move the runner down the tube and lock the umbrella open. She flipped the umbrella upright and flew up into the air.

Blue nodded at me. I ducked under the archway and took the shaking umbrella from the struggling Alteea. I called on my Air power and created a cushion around us that would push the gas away. Liv darted through behind me and Alteea fluttered out of the archway a second before Liv tossed the first brick through. She casually tossed a couple more bricks through the fake portal.

As this wasn't a timed drill, there was no need for Liv to toss all the bricks though, so after throwing a few, she blurred out through the archway again. I shifted my Air power to hold up the umbrella and then ducked and walked backwards through the archway. The umbrella then fell to the floor when I cut my power.

We lined up for another run-through, but this time Stella got out her phone, started the stopwatch app and said, "Go!"

Alteea darted through the mini fake shadow portal and flew across the vault. The next part didn't go as smoothly.

"Hairy troll's balls!" cursed Alteea as she caught the crook of the umbrella handle on the wire of the cage opening, causing it, her, and the umbrella to hit the ground.

Stella stopped the clock and Liv blurred over to check on her small friend.

"Are you okay, little one?" asked Liv with concern.

Alteea got up, brushed herself off, shook her wings out, and nodded. "I'm fine, sorry Mistress!"

Liv smiled warmly and said, "It's fine—that is why we practice these things. Are you up for another run-through?"

Alteea nodded.

Blue picked up the umbrella, drew her sword and ignited it, and then, in the blink of an eye, lopped off the U-shaped handle at the bottom. The handle, while useful for humans, was detrimental for Alteea. Now it wouldn't get caught on anything and Blue had also made it lighter and more manageable. It would be trickier for me to hold but that was a minor issue.

On the next run-through, Alteea was flawless. I bumped my head on the short wooden archway but got through and grabbed the umbrella without much delay and activated my Air powers. Liv came through behind me and got in position by the bricks.

As soon as Alteea cleared the archway, Liv tossed the first brick through. The brick shot past me, missing me by inches. She had put so much gusto into the throw that it flew through the opening like a missile and exploded into dust against the back wall.

With her vampire speed, two more bricks were in the air before that first one disintegrated. Blue yelled "Stop!" and Liv let one more brick go before coming to a halt.

"Speed is important but if you throw that hard, one miss, and you will kill or injure Zack. Everyone take a break while I get more bricks," said Blue.

She opened a portal in one of the darkened corners of the hangar and disappeared. Stella left and returned with two large blankets. She hung one up on the wall where the bricks had smashed and put the other on the floor in front of it.

Blue stepped out of the shadows with four new red clay bricks in her hand and added them neatly to the stack in the cage.

The next timed run-through went smoothly, and we pulled off a time of one minute and forty seconds. Better yet, Liv managed to lessen the power of her throws and almost all the bricks survived.

We spent the next hour doing timed practice drills of the heist. During our penultimate drill, we pulled off a time of one minute and twenty-three seconds, which was our best time yet. On the last run-through we made some mistakes and it took us almost two minutes to finish.

Blue called an end to the practice due to our regression. We cleaned up and retired to the main area of the lab to grab some drinks and snacks from the Food-O-Tron. I also used this time to fly up between the two Tesla coils arcing away in the corner of the lab to recharge my powers.

"Thanks for setting up the practice vault," I said to Blue and Stella. "I'm feeling better about our chances now. Our worst time was two minutes, which gives a good cushion in case we run into any surprises."

"It is the surprises I'm worried about," said Blue. "I only had last night to monitor the Mint, so chances are I have missed something. And we still don't know what type of gas they are using in there."

"I'll keep the gas away from Liv and me, so it really doesn't matter what it is," I said, trying to reassure everyone, including myself.

"After this, I'll visit the shadows again to spy; hopefully I will find out more, so we don't get surprised," said Blue.

I nodded and added, "Look, none of us wanted to become criminals. We have a good plan that hopefully will pull this job off without anyone getting hurt, but if the plan does go sideways, under no circumstance do I want anyone to attack the guards. Bree wouldn't want us to hurt or kill innocents to rescue her, so if we get in that type of engagement, just surrender, understood?"

Blue and Stella nodded but Liv lifted her head like she was about to argue. She stared hard at me and I matched her gaze. She lowered her head and softly said, "Understood." Alteea looked up from the saucer of blood she'd been drinking from and nodded her small head as well.

Chapter 24

Wednesday, May 7

At just before one in the morning, we all gathered in the hangar near one of the shadowed corners. I was wearing my balaclava to hide my face and Liv had one covering hers as well. I'd wiped the stem of the umbrella down to remove any fingerprints on it. I was also wearing thin black leather gloves, so I didn't leave any more. We'd argued about Liv wearing gloves too, but she was worried it would slow her down moving the gold. She argued that the only thing she would be touching was the gold and we were taking that.

I doubted these precautions would even slow down the authorities for a second. The use of the shadow portals would make us prime suspects. Add in that their Fire elemental would know I was an Air elemental, and there was a vampire moving the gold, and anyone familiar with our team would know it was us. Despite that, I figured I'd at least try and leave behind the least amount of physical evidence. Without seeing our faces, they might give us the benefit of the doubt for a few hours until they contacted us. That time might be enough for the money transfer to clear before they froze the accounts.

Blue was standing there almost in a trance, staring at the shadows, using them to spy on the Mint.

The team was ready to go. We just needed Officer Pees-a-lot and his bladder to do their part.

The minutes ticked by slowly and I looked down at my watch: 1:45 a.m. Since the top of the hour, I'd been mentally urging Officer Pees-a-lot to go to the bathroom. The problem was the only thing I'd managed to stimulate was my own bladder and I sheepishly said, "I need to pee."

Stella rolled her eyes. "Really?"

"Sorry, look, has he even gotten up yet? Even if he gets up to go, it will take him thirty seconds to reach the bathroom and the first twenty seconds after that is up to Alteea anyways, so I'll be back in plenty of time, okay?"

She sighed and said, "Go."

I sprinted out of the hangar and hit the bathroom. My usual luck was with me and not a second after I started to pee, Liv yelled that he was getting up. *Fuck.* I finished as quick as I could, ran back, and put my gloves back on as I went. I entered the hangar just as Alteea disappeared into the shadows with the umbrella.

I took my spot in front of the shadows and waited. Blue tapped me on the shoulder and said, "Go."

I held my breath and called on my Air powers just before stepping through the shadows. I popped out in the gold cage and paused for a second at the sight of all those gleaming bars stacked neatly in front of me before getting my head back in the game.

I used my powers to check the Air and so far, it was just a usual mix of nitrogen, oxygen, and other trace gases that were normally there. I stepped out of the way and grabbed the umbrella from Alteea, using my powers to prevent any incoming gas from getting near us. Liv came in and was hunched over the gold, looking back at the portal. Alteea flew out and I said, "Clear."

Liv struggled to get a good grip on the first smooth shiny bar but then lifted it and tossed it towards the portal. It only went half through. I used my foot to push it the rest of the way.

"Sorry, these are heavier than the practice bricks," said Liv.

Her next toss had more juice and the bar sailed by me and through the portal with ease. The next bar was right on its heels.

We were running behind at this point, and a hissing sound started inside the vault. Thick green smoke began pluming out of small holes at each of the corners of the vault; they'd started with the gas. I focused more on my power to make sure none of it got to us.

Liv was getting faster with her throws, but we'd been in here just over thirty seconds now and only moved a quarter of the gold. Add in Alteea's twenty seconds and our total time for this job would be over two minutes and thirty seconds. That still gave us a cushion of less than a minute.

The gas was now swirling around and thickening outside the circle of my Air power, but I managed to keep it out. Not a second later, I dropped that barrier as Liv missed with one of her throws and a gold bar grazed painfully off my shin. I quickly put the Air barrier back up and concentrated on cleaning the air around us.

"Sorry," said Liv.

She blurred over, picked up the stray bar, and tossed it through, wasting more time. Liv returned to the gold and resumed tossing bars through the portal.

Once she was about halfway through the pile, I checked my watch and we were coming up on a minute forty-five. It had taken her a minute and twenty-five seconds to move half the gold. At this rate, we'd be done in three minutes and ten seconds. We'd figured the fastest they'd be able to get down and open the vault would be three minutes but that didn't add in the time it took Officer Pees-a-lot to get back from the bathroom to his station. That would buy us another thirty seconds to a minute, so we should be okay. I hoped.

That hope quickly deflated when a hatch opened in the ceiling of the vault and a lethal-looking twin mounted machine gun descended from the opening.

Liv paused mid-toss, glanced up, and yelled, "Zack!" before going prone behind the stack of gold.

"I got it, keep tossing," I said as I hardened the Air between us and the guns.

Not even a second later, a deafening roar filled the vault as the guns started firing. Inches in front of the gold, a wall of metal appeared as the bullets sat suspended in the air. Liv gulped and started tossing faster. The bullets were a dull gray and brown with silver specks, which meant they were SWI rounds; if I let any get through, we were dead.

In short order, I was starting to sweat. Thickening the Air to stop the bullets was hard enough, but I also had to keep a barrier around us to keep the gas out.

A gold bar whizzed by my waist so close that I felt it pass before disappearing through the portal. My fear grew; if Liv had hit me with that, there was a good chance I'd have faltered with the bullet shield, and we would have died. I made a silent prayer to Odin to keep her aim true.

I was now shaking with effort, and I was also draining my reserves quicker than I was comfortable with. If they had another surprise in here, we were done.

The guns continued pouring rounds down on us and the Air-shield in front of us was now so thick with bullets that I couldn't even see the guns firing anymore.

There were less than ten bars left, and I was almost out of power. I willed her to toss faster and I was weakening with each bar that sailed by.

Just as Liv tossed the last bar, the guns went silent. A loud *clunk* filled the air and the main vault door slowly started to swing open; we'd run out of time.

Liv blurred forward, and I dropped the umbrella as she crashed into me like a freight train and pulled us both through the closing portal. The wind was knocked out of me as I hit the floor in the hangar, and I groaned in pain.

I'd have some nasty bruises tomorrow, but we were alive. On the upside, I currently had a lovely young vampire draped nicely on top of me and we weren't going to jail.

I grinned and said, "I know you are excited that we pulled it off, but maybe we can wait until there are less people around to celebrate."

Liv's green eyes twinkled back at me with mischief for a moment, but then she nodded and got off me.

She stood up and just said, "Wow!"

I flipped over and got to my feet. I stopped and stared at the gleaming gold bars scattered on the blankets in front of us.

"Maybe we missed our calling by doing bounty hunting instead of crime…" said Liv as she stood there taking in the sight of our haul.

"Don't go there," I warned. "This was a one-time thing just to get Bree back, understand?"

Blue and Stella joined us, and Blue said, "Olivia has a logical point. Even if we only got fifty cents on the dollar for this, it would still be more money than we ever made bounty hunting."

Alteea buzzed happily from one gold bar to another. She landed on one, rubbed it, and said, "Shiny!" in an excited, high-pitched voice.

Great, three of the four of them had gold fever. I turned to Stella and said, "Help me out here, will you?"

Stella nodded sagely and said, "It is impressive, but I was raised by a career criminal. I know where that path leads. A hundred times this amount of gold wouldn't make me go down that road."

"Thank you," I said. "Now let's get this loaded on the cart and then we can call it a night."

Liv yawned and said, "I'd love to help but the sun is coming up..."

That threw me for a second, but then I realized London was five hours ahead, so the sun would indeed be rising shortly. We wished her a good night and she blurred out of the hangar with Alteea on her heels.

Blue wheeled over the cart and we all got to work stacking it with the gold. I was sweating like a pig by the time we were done. Those bars were heavier than they looked. The gold made a nice sight, stacked there neatly on the cart, and there was a small part of me that wondered if Liv had a point earlier. I shook my head as I realized that the pile of gold also meant we were now wanted criminals. We'd be spending the rest of our lives on the run, or behind bars, if we didn't take Terror-Byte down, rescue Bree, and get the gold back. We'd been hunted before, and I had no desire for that constant state of fear and paranoia to become the norm.

We had the gold, now we just needed Terror-Byte to contact us and arrange the trade for Bree.

Chapter 25

Wednesday, May 7

Bree

They marched me back into the cell and locked the door behind me. I barely noticed the few of them that took one last glance at my nakedness before heading for the stairs. I was clean, and it was nice to have had a hot shower, but I felt violated. All the male Acolytes, except for Gravatron, were on the 'security detail' as Terror-Byte had called it, to make sure I couldn't escape. They kept the door to the shower area open, and all of them watched me while I showered; once again for 'security purposes,' but by the crude comments they were making while I was showering that hadn't been the only reason.

I sat down in my empty cell and covered my body self-consciously.

Meat-Shield was the only Acolyte left now, other than William. They were talking in hushed voices between themselves, but with my Were hearing, they might as well have been yelling across the room to one another.

"C'mon, Will, you've been down here for two days. I'll get Creepy to cover here for you and we can go up to the roof and watch the planes coming into Pearson," said Meat-Shield.

I kept my head down and tried not to show that I heard anything, but I'd certainly perked up at the word Pearson. I'd been right that we were near Pearson Airport. It did make my earlier detective work seem small and inadequate. I'd determined that we were still in Canada when they brought me food from Harvey's—a Canadian food chain—for lunch yesterday.

William sighed and said, "I'd love to, Meat, but if she changes, I'm the only one who can control her."

Meat-Shield laughed and said, "She is in a cage with silver bars, so what if she changes?"

"I know, but according to Terror-Byte, it was the Master himself who said I should be down here watching her at all times…"

Whatever mirth was on Meat-Shield's face instantly disappeared at that. As much as William seemed to adore the Master, it was clear that all the Acolytes seemed to fear him.

"Oh, I will leave you to it then," said Meat-Shield as he made a beeline for the exit.

My stomach rumbled, and I tried to ignore it; I was always hungry but at least playing nice with William or shaking 'the girls' for him usually got me an extra serving of food at each meal. The extra portions helped, but I needed more food. I was losing weight and felt weaker than usual. The other problem was each time I played William for more food, he got bolder in his requests. The bolder he got, the more uncomfortable and degraded I felt.

I was still trying to find ways to escape, or somehow let everyone know where I was. Confirming that I was close to Pearson was more useful than just knowing I was in Canada somewhere, but I wasn't sure how I would use that information yet. William was relaxing his vigilance with me. Last night and this morning he pushed the food under the bars without having me back up against the wall. I'd been tempted to grab him last night, but I didn't since I didn't know if he had a key to my cell or not. I got the answer to that question this morning. Earlier I had been going a little stir crazy from being in this cell and paced back and forth for a long time before asking William if he could let me out to run around the basement. He said that only Terror-Byte had the key.

From the trip upstairs to shower, I now knew we were in a warehouse. I'd suspected as much, but it was nice to have it confirmed. The warehouse had three exits, a fire door not far from where we came up from the basement, and a main entrance at the front that was large enough for the big white truck they had up there to drive in and out of. There was a door right beside the truck entrance as well. Terror-Byte had placed Meat-Shield directly in front of the fire door, which prevented me from making a break for it. There were a few windows around the warehouse, but they were blacked out and too high for me to get to quickly. They'd built small, wood-framed living quarters down the one side of the warehouse. There was also a futuristic looking archway against the opposite wall, which I assumed was the main teleport gate.

From chatting with William, I learned that he and the Acolytes had been based here and trained here for the last eight or nine months. William's powers only allowed him to control a few small animals or one large one at a time. He'd learned how to control his powers when he was fourteen so that he didn't keep attracting nearby animals to him unintentionally.

William was quite the little gossip, and he spilled tons of details about the Acolytes. The two girls, Creepy and Hexadecimal, didn't get along at all. That could have been useful if I were ever in the same room with them, as I could start playing them against each other. The problem was Creepy had only come down that one time to deliver food, and I hadn't seen Hexadecimal since I had gotten here.

Creepy and Terror-Byte were a couple. The rest of the guys, except for Gravatron, all vied for Hexadecimal's affections, but she had declined all of them. Gravatron was gay or at least William suspected he was. Hexadecimal and Gravatron were close friends. William was close with Meat-Shield, and he liked everyone but the Bartender. Nobody seemed to like the Bartender, who kept to himself most of the time, other than hitting on Hexadecimal. That too would have been useful, as maybe I could have turned the Bartender against everyone, but I'd only seen him once just now as part of Terror-Byte's shower security detail. Also, it was hard enough to fake being nice to William. I'd probably throw up if I had to be nice to the Bartender. Even if I didn't know about the date rapes he was wanted for, there was something super creepy about that asshole.

I cringed when William told me that Terror-Byte would order Hexadecimal, on occasion, to create some clones to 'keep up the morale' of the male Acolytes. At seeing my reaction to this, William explained that the clones weren't very bright and just took basic instructions. Hexadecimal also had to be within five hundred feet of them or they'd dissolve. They also liquefied after two hours of being created. William laughed and said that Bartender once lost track of time with his clone and in the middle of him screwing it, the clone liquefied. He had to shower to get the goop off him and spent the next couple of hours washing his bedding. I'll admit, I giggled at that image.

I learned that Gravatron could manipulate gravity around him but only out a couple of feet. He could make himself as light as a feather or up to three times heavier than usual. Terror-Byte's power was that he could manipulate any electronic device. All of the Acolytes' smartphones were older models, but Terror-Byte had boosted them, so they were faster than even the latest models on the market. He could also make them explode. Creepy could control up to a thousand insects at a time, but they all had to be the same species. The Bartender could change the alcohol level in someone's blood at will but only out to one hundred and fifty feet, and it took him some time to do this. Cutter, the Flaming Knife Guy, could conjure the flaming knives at will but once he did, he had to wait another ten minutes before he could do it again. He was also immune to fire.

I knew some of those things he'd told me already but there was a lot of new and useful information. But for it to be any good I needed to get out of there. I'd faked some tears after he told me all of this and he asked what was wrong. I replied that he was only telling me all of this because Terror-Byte was going to kill me in the end anyways. He shook his head and said, "No, he is going to make your team do our last three jobs, and then we'll give you back. We are being relocated after that to another country, so it doesn't matter what you know about us anyways."

I stopped crying at that and put on a fake smile and he looked relieved. By his tone, I think he honestly believed that, but I suspected that Terror-Byte and the Master had other plans. Being here, I'd learned too much about their operation, and there was no way they were letting me live.

I tried a couple times to borrow William's phone. I'd said I wanted to play a game because I was bored but he wouldn't go for it. The last time I'd asked for it, he said that Terror-Byte would kill him if he gave me his phone.

I kicked around what William had told me about using my friends for three jobs. When he first contacted Zack, Terror-Byte turned his phone towards me to show I was still alive. I had to assume Zack would insist on seeing me alive before the next job. Knowing that there were three jobs gave me a deadline. If I wasn't rescued after the second job, then I had to get out of here no matter what the cost or, at the very least, I had to take a few of the bastards down before they killed me.

I wanted to tip Zack off about my location without Terror-Byte realizing. If I yelled out that we were near Pearson, Terror-Byte would just move us somewhere else. The best idea I came up with was to angle the hand on the arm covering my breasts up like a plane taking off. If I knew Zack, he'd be staring at my boobs anyways, and hopefully he'd see my hand at an odd angle and puzzle it out. He would likely hear a plane overhead and maybe he'd put it all together. Blue would be able to search all the buildings near the airport and hopefully this place was close enough that she'd find it. It was a longshot, but it was the best I had for now.

Chapter 26

Wednesday, May 7

"You aren't going to be able to Skype down here, so how are you going to show Terror-Byte the gold?" asked Stella. She and Blue were having lunch, and I'd barely sat down before she questioned me.

She had a point; the reception was terrible down here. We barely could get voice calls and texts, never mind trying to do video conferencing. I'd also had everyone turn off their phones as I didn't want the authorities tracing them.

"After lunch," I said, "you and Blue can use the shadows to travel to some place random in Canada. I'm sure our little heist last night will be front page news. Pick up a paper. We'll take a picture of the paper on top of the gold and that should be good enough. Tonight, at just before nine, Blue and I will use the shadows to go somewhere that has Wi-Fi. I will take my laptop and we'll use that to Skype with Terror-Byte."

"Smart," said Stella. "The laptop won't be as traceable as the phones." I nodded, and Stella continued, "When we get the paper, we'll also hit the receiver sites. We'll check that they are still there and change the batteries, so we are ready for when the tracker goes off."

"Have you attached the receiver to the cart yet?" I asked.

Stella shook her head and said, "We'll do that after lunch. I checked the cart last night and it has a one-inch lip under it, which will hide the receiver nicely."

"Have you heard anything from Sarah about whether our money cleared?"

Stella shook her head. "She, like Liv, is down until the sun comes up…"

I should have known that, but I was still so worried about the money being frozen, us being hunted, and the upcoming exchange with Terror-Byte that I wasn't thinking clearly.

***

Blue caught me off guard as she came out of the shadows as her old man hologram. Stella was right behind her and held up a copy of the *Toronto Post*. On the cover was a full color picture of the empty gold cage from the Royal Canadian Mint. The headline read 'Hero goes Bad!' and there was also a small picture of me in my Hamilton Hurricane costume in the bottom corner and another of my face beside that.

She handed me the paper and I shook my head; we were officially wanted now. "All the receivers were still in place and now have fresh batteries."

"Good," I said, not looking up from the paper. "Did you guys read this?"

"No, we just picked up the paper and went directly from there to check the receivers, why?"

"We weren't the only ones busy last night," I said. "It says here that the Acolyte team in Asia struck again last night. They hit a Chinese military research complex in northern China and stole a dozen newly designed portable missiles. The missiles were developed as an infantry weapon. They use a large quadcopter drone that can be remotely controlled by troops on the ground. The drone carries a single anti-personnel missile. They can use the whisper-silent drone to fly behind enemy positions and use it to laser lock onto a target. The missile then launches and homes in on the laser and destroys the target."

Stella tugged at her braid and said, "We'll add it and the gold to the list of stolen items. The missiles really don't help narrow down what they are building. What does it say about us?"

"Nothing we didn't already know. We stole eight million dollars' worth of gold in a well-orchestrated heist. No one was injured. They did publish our full names and descriptions and said we are wanted in connection with the crime. They added that as of going to print, no bounty has been posted, but one is expected shortly. It also says that both GRC13 teams hit our house early this morning, but it had been abandoned."

Being outed by the paper was annoying, but I'd known that would be one of the consequences of breaking the law on such a grand scale.

Hero secret identities were protected but criminals or villains were not. GRC13 hitting the house also meant that if we ever got this mess cleared up, I'd have to contact Walter the wizard to redo the wards, but that was a distant worry at this moment.

I moved on and found that the *Post* had also done an editorial about us. They'd used last night's crime to further their anti-Enhanced agenda. The *Toronto Post* wasn't openly Humans First, but they weren't far off. They were always pushing for more controls and oversight on Enhanced Individuals. The only reason the *Post* didn't officially endorse Humans First was because they had been condemned as a hate group and the paper didn't want to be associated with that.

I stopped reading when the subject matter turned to local news and politics. We moved to the hangar and I used the laptop to take a picture of the gold with the paper on top of it. Once I was out of the way, Stella attached the receiver under the cart with double-sided tape.

An hour later, Liv rose from the dead with Alteea in tow and joined us. They had just sat down at the table with a pint of blood from the Food-O-Tron when a phone started ringing.

My head shot up and I said, "I told everyone to turn off their phones."

"We did. That is the one the English vampire court provided us," said Stella as she hustled over to the other workbench to answer it.

I was mollified by that. Blue did transport work for the English vampire court and they gave her that phone, so they could contact her. It was registered to them, so there shouldn't be any way Canadian authorities even knew it existed and therefore wouldn't be traced.

Stella answered the phone, listened for a few seconds and then said, "Okay, we'll be there shortly," and hung up.

She turned back to us, smiled and said, "That was Sarah, our money cleared, and she has our cash ready and waiting."

***

An hour later, we were waiting on Liv to finish getting ready, so we could visit the English vampire court. I was in a formal black fitted tux, Stella had ditched her usual white *Little House on the Prairie* dress for a more elegant bright blue gown, and Blue was in her usual ensemble: scale mail and combat boots—the outfit for all occasions.

This wasn't a formal visit, as we'd just be visiting with Sarah, but I'd made the mistake once of attending court underdressed and vowed never to do that again. I was convinced it would be just like Elizabeth, the master of the English vampire court, to grant us a surprise audience if I ever showed up in casual clothes just to make me squirm.

I almost moaned as Liv entered the room. She was in a formfitting, emerald green semi-sheer lace gown that hugged her lovely body like a second skin and a pair of matching green high heels that made her long, lean body look even more so. Her dark hair was up, exposing her sensuous neck. Her makeup was subtle and made her sparkling green eyes pop.

I was pretty sure my mouth was hanging open at the sight of her, and she took one look at my expression and smiled, pleased that her outfit had the intended effect.

She took her time for a change, and slowly sauntered over to us, letting me get my money's worth as I continued admiring her.

I tugged at my tie, trying to make it easier to breathe, and said, "I hate wearing this shit, but I'd strongly consider wearing it every day just to see you in that outfit."

"This old thing? You, sir, are too kind," teased Liv with mock formality.

"If you two are done," chided Stella, "we have money to pick up."

Blue opened a shadow portal and we all stepped through. I'd been getting déjà vu during the last twenty-four hours from being hunted and hiding out in the secret lab, and it struck again when we stepped out of the shadows into the same library that we entered the first time we visited the court. Hargraves was waiting for us just like that first time too.

He and Stella exchanged pleasantries, and he then said, "I was instructed by Lady Sarah to bring you to her immediately once you arrived. One does not keep the court's champion waiting; if you'll follow me?"

Stella nodded, and he led us through the ornately decorated corridors to Sarah's office. He knocked, and Sarah's sultry voice said, "Come in, Hargraves."

He opened the door for us, and we all filed in behind Stella. The office hadn't changed, but there might have been one or two more turtle-themed knickknacks stuffed in between the monitors on her desk. I spied the two live turtles in the fish tank behind her desk. The cute turtle fixation was an interesting contrast to the plethora of antique, yet deadly weapons crammed on to every wall around the office.

"That will be all, Hargraves, thank you," said Sarah.

My attention was drawn to Sarah in her usual black leather body suit that showed off every one of her sensuous curves. I spotted the daggers she kept tucked into the outsides of her thigh-high black boots and a sword handle peeking out from over her left shoulder. She was as beautiful as she was deadly. The fact that I noticed the office décor before Sarah showed just how many interesting things there were to see in here.

Hargraves gave a small, polite nod and closed the door. Sarah blurred over and lifted Stella from her feet and embraced her in a warm hug. Sarah's scarred face lit up with a smile of pure joy as she held Stella.

"It has been too long, my little one; you look lovely," said Sarah, still not breaking the embrace.

"It has been less than two weeks, and thank you."

Sarah laughed and added, "Like I said, too long!"

Stella giggled at that, and Sarah reluctantly put her down. Sarah moved down the line and she and Blue clasped forearms and nodded at each other.

"I have missed our sparring sessions; you also need to visit more often."

Blue gave Sarah a full grin of sharp teeth and said, "As have I. You are always a worthy challenge."

Sarah turned her attention to me and looked at me like a predator would its prey. She licked her lip and slid tightly up against me. I almost shivered when she ran her tongue lightly along my neck and upon reaching my ear said in a sultry whisper, "So, have you considered my offer?"

Sarah once had a relationship with an Air elemental and loved how he'd tasted. As soon as she sensed my powers, she had wanted me.

Her offer was if I'd let her feed from me, she would give me a night of unforgettable sex.

I cursed as the feel of her body against me, the pure lust in her tone, and the images of her offer had my body starting to react.

Before I could answer, Liv said, "Back off, grandma, he's mine!"

Sarah sighed but backed away and said, wearily, "Oh you brought the *child* along too, how lovely…"

The two of them faced off and Liv added, "Nice to see you up and around without your walker. You probably have a bingo game or a shuffleboard tournament to get to, so give us the money and we'll let you get back to it."

"Oh, how droll, and in complete sentences too. Stella, you have been training her well. Can she go to the bathroom on her own like a big girl now as well?"

"You're the only one in adult diapers here, honey!" snarled back Liv.

Sarah was about to say something else when Stella pushed herself between them and said, "Liv, Sarah, knock it off!"

Both looked down at Stella glaring fiercely at them. They lowered their heads and said, "Sorry," in unison.

Sarah strolled around the large, elaborate desk, lifting four metal briefcases and placing them on the desk with a thud. "A million pounds in this one, and the other three have just shy of one million US in each. We took a small fee for our service, but the briefcases are yours to keep."

Blue lifted them two at a time off the desk and placed them on our side of it.

"Thank you for doing this," said Stella.

"Anything for you, little one," said Sarah with a smile. "I know you are anxious to get out of here and get back into hiding, but stay for a moment; you are quite safe here, I assure you. I also have information that might be relevant to your situation."

Stella took one of the two chairs in front of the desk and Blue took the other. I stood behind them and Liv snuggled up to me and possessively put her arm around my waist. Sarah tipped her head at Liv and said, "You may or may not be aware that a bounty has been issued for a million US dollars for your capture. Elizabeth has decreed that you and your team are friends of the court and no court member may pursue that bounty."

Stella said, "Please give her majesty our thanks."

Sarah nodded and continued, "You will always be welcome here. If your hideout is ever compromised, you are welcome to seek sanctuary here."

My eyes shot up at that; it was an exceptionally generous offer. Harboring us would put the court in possible conflict with the law. On the other hand, vampire courts had a long history of criminal activity, so I shouldn't have been that surprised. If we did shelter here, it would also bind us to the English vampire court, and they would have full use of our talents while we were their guests. We'd bolster their already formidable daytime defenses, and they'd have more access to Blue's shadow talents. So the offer wasn't as generous as it first appeared. Vampire gifts were always something you had to look closely at—there were always strings attached.

Stella said, "Thank you again. We will keep that in mind."

Sarah's face softened again, and she added, "Even if you are just going stir crazy being cooped up in your hideout, come for a visit, okay?" Stella nodded, and she continued, "Have you seen YouTube today?"

Stella shook her head and said, "No, as you know the lab has limited connection to the outside world, why?"

Sarah turned the middle monitor around and said, "Then you'll want to see this," and she hit play.

An elderly man in a lab coat and a monocle appeared in the video, and I instantly recognized Doctor Bubbles. The trademark wild hair and monocle made him distinct, but I was still shocked to see him. No one had seen in him in more than a decade and most people, including myself, assumed he was dead.

He was the most well-known evil Mad Scientist on the planet. He'd been active since the mid-sixties and had gone on an unparalleled forty-year crime spree. The current bounty on him was twenty-five million US, but no one in their right mind would ever think about going after it. The only thing superior to his genius was his ruthlessness. He'd killed hundreds of people over the years in some truly horrible ways.

It was ironic that a guy named Doctor Bubbles who looked like a crazy retired high school science teacher was that feared. He wasn't originally called Doctor Bubbles. I'd forgotten the grand name and title he'd given himself originally, but after the press branded him Doctor Bubbles, he just went with it.

His signature weapon was his bubble gun. As a little kid watching the news with my mom after one of his heists, I laughed as I thought the reporter said, 'bubblegum.' Mom, never one to find any crime amusing, scolded me for my laughter at first. When I explained that I thought the reporter said "He took out the guards with his famous bubblegum," she cracked a small smile, and when I started giggling uncontrollably, she joined in.

The gun shot out bubbles, but those bubbles were lethal and multipurpose. He could fire a small stream of them through a lock or the crack under a door. The bubbles would keep expanding until they cracked open a building like an egg. He could also use them to trap people. The bubbles were just about impenetrable, and the only thing that could eventually cut through them was fire, like from a welding torch, and even that took time. Most of the time, people couldn't get free and suffocated to death inside of them. He could even use them defensively as a barrier to protect himself from bullets.

He traveled on a cool-looking stealth sled that people speculated worked by anti-gravity, and he had a belt that let him teleport short distances. Those were just his three most famous inventions, but there had been tons of gizmos over the years.

In German-accented English he said, "Today a group of people were foolish enough to invade my lair; they have paid the price for that foolishness."

The camera panned out, and there were eight large bubbles lined up in a row with tan, red, and black blobs inside of them. I struggled to figure out what I was seeing. The camera zoomed in closer, and I heard Stella and Olivia gasp. It was a person inside the bubble, but it looked like someone had poured acid on them. The flesh and bone were melted, and the black Acolyte uniform was almost unrecognizable. You could just make out the stylistic 'A,' but it was deformed. The camera panned along the row of bubbles and each one contained a mangled Acolyte corpse.

My heart sped up as I worried this was Melvin and his group. If they were dead, our chances of getting Bree back were all but gone. I remembered that Doctor Bubbles only worked in Europe, and with relief, figured this must be Melvin's European counterparts.

Doctor Bubbles finished with, "Let this be a warning to any who would dare to disturb me," and then the camera went black.

"Well that's one three-million-dollar bounty we won't be collecting," I quipped darkly.

Sarah and Olivia laughed, but Stella said, "That's terrible, Zack; those people were bad, but no one deserves to die like that."

"Sorry," I mumbled, shrinking under the weight of her stern visage. Stella nodded and turned to Sarah and said, "Is Doctor Bubble's lair somewhere in Europe then?"

Sarah nodded and said, "It is rumored to be somewhere in the Swiss Alps, but we are unaware of its exact location."

Stella looked relieved. She must have had the same fear that it was Melvin's group that I did.

Sarah didn't have anything else to add but we spent twenty minutes with her discussing our plan to get Bree back to get her insight. She'd been a warrior for over four hundred years and her input was always incisive. She gave us a few suggestions and we were on our way. Blue took two of the cases, and I took the other two. Carrying two million US dollars was heavier than I expected.

Blue opened a shadow portal in the corner of Sarah's office, and after we said our goodbyes and thanks, we stepped through.

Chapter 27

Wednesday, May 7

At 8:30 p.m. Eastern, Blue, in her holographic old man disguise, and I were in a coffee shop in Cleveland. After buying a coffee and tea, we left and headed to the alley behind the shop. The Wi-Fi password was on the receipt, and it was strong enough to extend outside. The sun was just going down as I fired up the laptop, connected to the Wi-Fi, and waited for Melvin's e-mail.

Since I'd been outed in the media, I skipped bringing along my balaclava—might as well be comfortable. It did feel odd to be out on a job in public though without it. I also had an itch between my shoulder blades from being out in public and knowing there was a million dollar bounty on our heads.

I passed the time by trying to spot flaws in Blue's elderly man illusion and had to admit that it was an impressive piece of technology. It would also be handy if we ended up on the run long term. With it, she would be the only one of us who could easily go out in public with little to no risk.

At almost nine on the dot, my laptop chimed as the e-mail from Melvin arrived. I clicked on the link and in short order Melvin's grinning face appeared.

His expression turned to one of surprise at seeing me without my mask and he said, "With that ugly face you should keep wearing the mask, Hurricane." I rolled my eyes and he continued, "It sounds like you got my gold." I nodded. "Good, show me."

I held up the printout of the gold to the camera and Melvin yelled, "What's this? A picture? I want to see the real gold."

"Yeah, and I would like a busty redhead with loose morals, but neither one of us is getting what we want today."

Melvin frowned at that. "You will show me that gold or your panther will pay."

"Since pulling your job last night, we have been on the run and where we are keeping the gold has no Internet, so I have no way to show it to you. Look at the picture again. It has today's paper on it. You've seen the news reports; you know we cleaned out the Mint, so obviously we have the gold."

I held up the picture and after a bit Melvin said, "Okay, this had better not be a trick…" The 'or else' was implied by Melvin's tone.

I pulled the picture away, faced the screen again, and asked, "Where do we meet to do the swap?"

"We don't. I will give you an address, and you will bring the gold there and leave it. You will exit the premises and I will recover the gold. Once I have the gold, I will return your panther."

I smiled to myself, as Blue had been right—the little bastard was going to screw us. "Yeah, that is not happening. Once you have the gold, you have no reason to give us Bree."

Something loud like a motorcycle, truck, or maybe an airplane overwhelmed the audio for a few seconds and then Melvin said, "Let me try this another way…" He turned the phone so Bree in her cell was visible, and in his other hand was that hand-cannon he had last time. He pointed it at Bree but was aiming low and said, "In five seconds, I'm going to fire, and I will keep shooting until I hit her. Hopefully it doesn't kill her. After that I will count to five again and take another shot. I will continue until either she is dead, or you agree to my terms."

"Let him shoot me! Don't give him what he wants!" said Bree. She made an odd movement with her head and I noticed her hand across her breasts was at a weird angle. I worried that it was broken but she lowered it when Melvin focused more on her and yelled, "Shut up."

Melvin started counting.

I waited until he hit three, as I didn't want to seem too eager to give in and said, "Okay, okay, don't shoot. We'll do it your way."

Melvin lowered the gun and turned the camera back to himself. "There is an abandoned warehouse at 42 Applewood Drive in Brampton. It is locked, but that shouldn't be an issue for your shadow-traveler. In the next ten minutes, take the gold and leave it there. Once you are gone, we will pick it up, and then at ten I will e-mail you another Skype link explaining how to get your panther back."

He cut the call as soon as he finished.

I turned to Blue and said, "Look at this. I think Bree was trying to tell us something." I replayed the odd head movement and the angled hand.

"What do you think it means?" asked Blue.

"I don't know. Maybe the head movement means she bumped her head and the angled hand means she went down a ramp. So, the entrance to their base is tight and they are underground?"

Blue frowned and said, "A staircase with a low ceiling? That could mean wherever she is isn't built to code. So maybe the Acolytes have built off of, or under, an existing structure, like our secret lab?"

I kicked it around and said, "We'll show it to the rest of the gang when we get home. Maybe they will have better ideas. We have less than ten minutes to get the gold delivered."

Blue nodded and opened a portal. We stepped back into the lab. Liv, Stella, and Alteea were waiting for us.

"Like we thought, it looks like he is going to screw us over," I said and then went over Melvin's instructions.

Stella got on the floor of the hangar, reached under the cart, and said, "What should I set the timer to?"

"Make it an hour and a half. That will give enough time for him to get the gold and for Melvin and I to have our chat at ten. Hopefully after that he'll think he has us beat and will let his guard down. Once they are celebrating their victory, we'll hit them."

She reached up and a couple of soft beeps later had planted the tracker. Blue opened a shadow portal, and I started pushing the cart towards it.

"Everyone stay here. I'll drop off the gold and come back."

I pushed the cart into the shadows and emerged into a dimly lit open warehouse. There were a few discarded broken wooden pallets in one corner and a few large moldy boxes, but other than that it was empty. Or so I thought. I spotted a large white plastic circle set up in the far corner—it was one of the Acolytes' teleport circles.

I reluctantly let go of the cart and prayed the tracker worked as we planned. I thought about giving the boxes and the pallets a quick once over, in case they were hiding a hatch to an underground lair like Blue and I thought Bree was hinting about in the video. I decided against it. Blue would see where they'd come from when they arrived anyway.

I turned and exited the warehouse by the same shadow portal I came in from.

"It's done. Now we just have to wait and see what they do," I said as I returned to the hangar in the lab. "Use the shadows to keep an eye on the warehouse. It would be my luck some homeless person was watching and steals the gold before Melvin gets there."

Blue nodded and stared off into the shadows in a trance. The wait stretched out, but ten long minutes later, Blue perked up. "Terror-Byte, Hexadecimal, and Meat-Shield just teleported into the circle. He is talking over a mike to someone."

I cursed to myself about them teleporting in, as that meant their base wasn't hidden under this warehouse like I'd hoped. Terror-Byte communicating with someone was probably just his insurance. He knew we could pop out of the shadows instantly from anywhere around that dimly lit warehouse. He probably left instructions that if the line went dead, they were to kill Bree.

Blue continued giving us a play-by-play, "Hexadecimal just made at least a dozen clones of herself, and they are spreading out in a protective circle around the rest of them. They are now walking over to the gold. Terror-Byte is still talking nonstop. Meat-Shield and Hexadecimal are now putting together a new teleportation circle around the gold. Terror-Byte is staring at the gold. He just frowned and…oh no…"

Blue cursed in her native language and said, "He just pulled the tracker from under the cart and destroyed it. The new circle is active, and they are gone."

Liv looked at me in horror and I had no idea what to say. With the tracker gone, so was our hope of getting Bree back.

Chapter 28

Wednesday, May 7

A short time later, Blue and I were back in the alley outside the coffee shop in Cleveland. We startled a homeless guy who was dumpster diving nearby. He grunted at us, but quickly turned his battered shopping cart around and skittered away. It was fully dark now, but there were enough lights in the alley that I could see well enough. Blue's night vision meant she could see clear as day, so I doubted anyone could sneak up on us.

I opened the laptop and we waited. My worries increased as ten o'clock came and went and no e-mail appeared from Melvin. I knew he wasn't giving us Bree back now, especially since he found our tracker. I still hoped that he would make us do another job for him because if he didn't then he had no use for Bree anymore.

The minutes dragged by. "He will e-mail us," Blue reassured me. I nodded and prayed she was right. It would be just like Melvin to make us squirm for a bit before sending the e-mail; at least that was what I kept telling myself. I started to worry that he wouldn't, and he'd just kill Bree and do the jobs himself. Maybe after what happened to the European team, whoever was behind all of this would pull the other two teams back to regroup.

After a good twenty minutes, which seemed like hours, the laptop chimed as a new e-mail arrived. I anxiously went to click it and cursed as it was a spam e-mail offering to add inches to my penis size. Damn those e-mails were annoying, and for some reason I received at least a couple of them per day. I was starting to get a complex. I wondered if they knew something. I was sorely tempted to have Stella track down where the spam came from, pay them a visit, and fry all their equipment for the general good of humanity.

The laptop chimed again and this time it was Melvin. I clicked the link and I was relieved to see Melvin's pimply smug face staring back at me.

"Really, Hopeless Hurricane, an electronic tracker? You think a master of electronics like me wouldn't sense it?" said Melvin.

I shrugged and said, "Thought it was worth a shot."

"Well you missed your shot, and that little stunt means you aren't getting your panther back until you do one more job for me."

"We had a deal, Melvin," I argued.

"It's Terror-Byte!" he yelled.

By Odin's beard, it was too easy to get a rise out of the little shit.

He took a breath and smiled. "I'm in a generous mood today, so I will let that slide. After all you did just give me eighty million in gold."

"Exactly, you got the gold, now give us Bree!"

He shook his head and said, "I am altering the deal. Pray I don't alter it any further."

I blinked as I realized he'd just quoted Darth Vader at me. The inner geek in me approved, but I was also annoyed that Melvin would use one of my favorite films against me.

"Fine, what's the job?" I asked.

"You are to steal the Arctic Avenger's freeze ray for me."

I hadn't been expecting that. Seymour Potts, aka the Arctic Avenger, was a one-trick Mad Scientist who invented a potent freeze ray. The freeze ray would instantly make anything so cold that even the smallest tap would shatter it into a million pieces. Seymour was a Canadian eco-terrorist who believed that corporations and their disregard for the environment were killing the planet. He went on a crime spree in Toronto a few years ago with the gun, robbing banks and destroying corporate headquarters that were based in Toronto.

The Toronto Five eventually stopped him, but he did a lot of damage and killed more than ten people in the process. He was currently a guest of the federal government's Enhanced super-max prison up north in the Canadian Arctic. I'd found it amusing that at least he was now living in his namesake, though I doubted he'd see much of the scenery from his cell.

"He's in jail, and I have no idea where his freeze ray is or if it's still even intact," I said.

Melvin smiled, and I knew I wouldn't like whatever he was about to say. I was right. "Lucky for you, I happen to know where it is. It is in the vault at the Toronto Hall of Heroes. Get it for me and I'll give you back your panther." I opened my mouth to argue and he added, "You have forty-eight hours, I will e-mail you then. Get it, or your panther dies slowly."

The video went black as he cut the feed. I slammed the laptop shut and cursed. Blue lifted a purple eyebrow at me, but I just shook my head and said, "Let's go home."

We emerged from the shadows into the lab's hangar and Liv looked at us in excitement, which turned to confusion. "Where's Bree?" I lowered my head, and she said, "But we got the gold!"

"I know, but he changed the deal. Let's go to the main lab and get a drink and we'll discuss his latest demand."

Less than ten minutes later, the five of us were all gathered around one of the workbenches that doubled as our dining table. Normally it would have taken longer, but without Bree here to monopolize the Food-O-Tron it went faster than usual. Her absence was felt by everyone, and made worse by the fact that we had been so close to getting her back.

I took a long pull from my beer and said, "He wants us to steal a freeze gun from the vault in the Hall of Heroes in Toronto. We get him the gun and he'll give us Bree."

Liv said, "He was supposed to give us Bree this time, what is to stop him from changing the deal again?"

"Nothing, but what choice do we have? If we don't get the gun, he'll kill Bree."

The room went silent at that.

Liv sighed. "I guess we have a gun to steal. How much time do we have?"

"Less than two days, but this isn't going to be easy…"

"We just broke into one of the most secure places in Canada and stole eighty million in gold, how hard can grabbing one freeze ray be?" asked Liv.

I rubbed my temples and sighed. "Yeah, but this is the second most secure place in Canada, and unlike the Mint, there are eight Enhanceds living there. Any one of the Five would wipe the floor with us. Against the Five and their three auxiliary members who call the Hall their home, we don't have a chance."

Stella frowned and said, "What if we staged some sort of diversion to get the Five to respond?"

I rubbed my chin and said, "That would get rid of the Five but not the three auxiliary members. The place also has human guards, cameras everywhere, and a host of other defenses. The guards only carry stun-sticks and not guns but in some ways that is worse. We know your Hyde form can shrug off small arms fire, but we don't know if those stun-sticks would work against you. I only know this from a tour I took as a kid twenty-five years ago, so they have probably upgraded things since then."

Blue nodded and said, "Let me go use the shadows to take a look, so we'll get a better idea of what we are dealing with, okay?"

I nodded, and she got up and left the room while the rest of us discussed the plan.

"The Hall is built like a fortress and most of it is underground. The vault is six floors down. When I did the tour with my mom, they just opened the elevator but wouldn't let us get off. The sixth floor is open and well lit, and the vault is in the center of the floor. There are motion and thermal sensors. Robotic guards circle around the vault on constant patrol. The robots are armed with stun-beams, but I'd bet they also have more lethal weapons too. The vault door was imposing and not something that will be easy to crack."

Stella said, "We may get lucky and the vault itself may have lots of shadows and we can just jump in and out."

I shook my head and said, "I doubt we'll be that lucky. It makes no sense that they would go to the effort of securing the floor around it so well and leave that type of hole in their security in the vault itself. There has been an active bounty on the thief in Europe that has the same type of powers as Blue for almost a decade now, so I can't see them overlooking that."

Stella nodded and asked, "Alright, assuming we can create a diversion to pull the Five away from the Hall, what are the powers of the remaining three?"

"We are going to need something major to get the Five to respond. They won't go flying out to deal with a small fire or something like that."

Stella interrupted and said, "Would a Hyde rampage be enough?"

I thought about that and nodded. "That could do it, but you won't be able to take on the Five by yourself. I doubt you'd be able to beat Captain Canada, never mind the other four as well."

"I don't need to take them on; we just need them to respond. Just as they arrive, I will jump into the shadows and disappear. If we pick somewhere on the edges of Toronto, that will take them five or so minutes to get there and the same to get back. Can we beat the remaining three during that time?"

"They have the Speedster, Dr. James Davidson and his armored suit, and the Sonic Screamer as their three reserve members. The Speedster is fast, quick enough that she'll make Liv's vampire speed look like the movements of an old lady with a walker in comparison. The Sonic Screamer uses her voice as a weapon. Even with earplugs, the wall of sound she can produce will still knock someone on their ass. Dr. Davidson is a Mad Scientist but the good kind not the evil kind. He is older now, but most of the defenses in the Hall were designed by him. The armored suit he wears flies, but being indoors will neutralize that, and the suit has claws and stun-beams as its main offensive weapons."

Stella tugged her braid and said, "I should be able to handle the armor suit in my Hyde form. You should be able to neutralize the Sonic Screamer by deadening the air with your Air powers, and that leaves Blue, Liv, and Alteea to take on the Speedster. Maybe we can lay down some oil or something to trip her up."

I shook my head and argued, "We don't know if the stun-beams work against your Hyde form or not. If they do, one blast and you're out. If you're down, it will be a short fight. The other three might be able to take down the Speedster but that assumes we can take them on separately. They will try to stick together and work as a team."

"What if we attempt this late enough that those three members are sleeping?" said Stella. "I doubt Dr. Davidson sleeps in his armor, so what if we hit him in his quarters and take him out before he can change into it. Maybe we can weld the Speedster's door shut or something; if we trap her in her room, she can't bother us. That would only leave us with the Sonic Screamer and your powers can neutralize hers and the rest of us can take her down with no problems then..."

Stella had an interesting point; with Blue's shadow powers we could hit several different places quickly. Dr. Davidson was in his sixties, so if we caught him without his armor on, Blue or Liv could easily handle him. The Speedster was fast, but she wasn't any stronger than a normal human woman, so if we could bar her door, she probably wouldn't be able to get to us in time.

"Okay, let's say you are right and we can get the Five out of the building and take down the three reserve members, that still leaves us with the robotic guards on the sixth floor, the human guards throughout the building, and an impenetrable vault to break into before the Five return…"

Liv piped up and said, "Hard or not, it is the only chance we have of getting Bree back, so we have no choice!"

A moment later Blue entered the room. "Here's what I found." She lifted her arm from behind her back and held up a three-foot-long shiny silver-colored freeze gun.

Stella, Liv, and Alteea cheered, and I just sat there blinking stupidly at the sight of the Arctic Avenger's freeze gun in Blue hand.

"But…why…how?" I stammered.

Blue smiled and showed off her shark-like teeth. "The vault should have been fully lit but someone forgot to change a burnt-out light bulb…"

Well, shit! It was about time some luck went our way for a change. I smiled and finished my beer.

Chapter 29

Wednesday, May 7

Bree

Terror-Byte came down wearing a cocky grin and carrying a shiny gold bar. I groaned to myself at the sight of the gold; my friends were now fugitives. Even if I got out of this, we'd be living our lives on the run or they would be in jail and I'd be on my own. I wished they hadn't done this, but I realized they had no choice; if any other member of the team was in my predicament, I would have done the same.

"Beast Whisperer, take a break for ten minutes. Go upstairs and check out the gold. I'll watch the prisoner."

William nodded and scurried away.

Terror-Byte approached my cell and eyed me for a moment. His smile got bigger as he held up the gold bar and said, "I wouldn't have valued you at eighty million dollars, but your friends seem to think you're worth it. Unfortunately, they tried to place a tracker on the gold, so you'll be staying with us a while longer while they do another job to make up for that."

The beast roared in my head, and it wanted to kill him. My own temper flared but I forced myself to calm; I couldn't afford to change.

"Cat got your tongue?" taunted Terror-Byte.

"You weren't going to let me go for one job. I know that you have three jobs planned for my friends, so stop pretending the tracker made the difference."

Terror-Byte frowned. "I see the Beast Whisperer has been gossiping again. No matter. I have given them their second job and we'll see if they can pull it off in the next two days."

A chill ran down my spine. Terror-Byte only needed the team for three jobs, which meant the next one after this would be the last. He

189

probably wouldn't kill me until after the third job in case Zack played hardball and insisted that I be there for the trade, but that wasn't a sure thing. I needed to try and get out of here.

Even though the tracker attempt had failed, I was glad they tried it. It showed that they weren't just rolling over and doing whatever Terror-Byte asked. Blue, being her usual ruthless self, had probably figured out that Terror-Byte would kill me and not hand me back. I hoped she didn't share that with Liv—it would just freak her out.

"I have to stay I'm disappointed in the Hopeless Hurricane. As a kid I was a fan, but it is obvious that his reputation was overhyped. We've beaten your team twice now, three times if you include me thwarting their foolish attempt to use a tracker to catch a master of electronics."

I laughed at that and Terror-Byte got a confused look on his face, so I explained, "You haven't seen the full Hamilton Hurricane; he's been taking it easy on you. He thinks you and your team are a bunch of kids that are being used. In those two fights, he was pulling his punches and trying for non-lethal takedowns. Trust me—he won't make that mistake again in the next fight."

I smiled to myself as Melvin's smug smile slipped a little.

"There won't be another fight. After they do these next two jobs, we are being moved to another country."

"What about me?" I asked.

"What about you? After they pull off the jobs, you'll be returned to your friends," said Terror-Byte, but he broke eye contact when he said it.

I knew he was lying and called him on it, "Bullshit. You and I both know at the end of this you or one of your lackeys is going to kill me. I've seen too much and know too much about your operation. You've killed twice—"

"I've only killed once!"

"So, you weren't the one to kill Madison?"

A look of surprise appeared on Terror-Byte's face. "Beast Whisperer really needs to shut his mouth, but to answer your question, I didn't kill Madison. The Master did for breaking her oath."

I smiled to myself at the Beast Whisperer getting blamed even though it was something we'd already known. "Okay, once then, but I'm betting that after she was killed that bothered you. I also think you killed that cop by accident. You probably tossed the phone at the cops as a distraction but put a bit too much on it in your nervousness and threw it too far. How have you been sleeping since that happened?"

Melvin looked away and I continued, "Thought so. It is easy to kill but not so easy to live with the consequences, is it? How well do you think you will sleep after you come down here, put a bullet in me, and kill me in cold blood?"

"I'm not going to shoot you," said Terror-Byte in a soft voice.

I believed him and for a moment was relieved until it hit me what he would do. The little coward was just going to leave me here to starve to death. With my Were metabolism and its constant need for food, I'd last maybe a day or two before my body consumed itself and I would die. The bullet would be kinder. I wanted so badly to tear his throat out, but I went a different way, "Don't do this. It will haunt you for the rest of your life. It isn't too late. Turn yourself in. If you cooperate and give them information to take down the Master and the other two Acolyte teams, they'll go easy on you. You could live a normal life again…"

For a brief second, it looked like he considered it, but then he shook his head and said, "A normal life? We are freaks and no one will allow us a normal life…" He paused for a bit and added in a soft voice, "Besides, the Master doesn't tolerate failure. I'll end up like Madison the second I try to betray him."

The door to the stairway opened. William had returned.

Terror-Byte's sad expression changed, and he loudly said, "The Master knows the war with the humans is coming and that is why this is so important. We are laying the foundation for the New World Order where Enhanceds will take their rightful spots as rulers over the weakling humans!"

William's smile grew at Terror-Byte's words and I sighed. Whatever moment we'd had, it was gone. Terror-Byte was back to his usual self. He turned his attention to William and said, "The Master will be pleased with the gold. Just like he is pleased with the good work you are doing guarding this prisoner, Beast Whisperer. I'll leave you to it."

Terror-Byte gave the team forty-eight hours on the first job and would probably give them the same amount of time for the second. If that was true, then I had four days until the last job was done and the Acolytes bugged out and left me here to die…

Chapter 30

Thursday, May 8

"Stella, what are you doing?"

Stella had the freeze ray clamped to one of the workbenches and was examining it in detail. Blue was standing behind her with an amused look on her face, her tail playfully swishing behind her.

She looked up and lifted her brass magnifying goggles. "Seeing how this gadget works."

"Are you nuts? You more than anyone should know how delicate Mad Scientist creations can be. One wrong turn of a dial or tweak of a wire and that thing will be a useless hunk of metal and plastic. If that happens, Bree is dead."

"Calm yourself, I'm taking all precautions," replied Stella while continuing to poke around it. "Come here, and let me show you what I've found."

Curiosity got the better of me, and I wandered over. The freeze ray looked similar to a modern assault rifle, well, other than being shiny silver with a two-inch wide mouth at the end of the barrel. Stella did something, and a hatch on the stock of the gun popped open. Inside was a decent sized storage compartment that was currently empty.

"There is a hidden button on the underside that opens this."

Part of me shuddered that she was randomly pressing buttons on this thing, but another part of me wondered why she seemed so excited about this. "Yeah, so what?"

Stella sighed and said, "So, that means we have a place to hide another tracking device."

"Yeah, that's great, but Terror-Byte found the last one in seconds. He will sense this one too. If he knows there is a tracking device on it, he won't take it back to their hideout and Bree is dead."

Stella smiled and said, "But this time he won't know there is a tracking device on it!"

"How? He can sense electronics and what they do, so how are you going to stop him from sensing it?"

Stella smiled and held up what looked like a small two-inch brass clamp with gears and springs. "With this! He can sense electronics when they are powered up and working. But if we put a tracker in here that is completely powered off, there is nothing to sense. We set the tracker to go off as soon as it is turned on. This device will turn it on, watch."

She fiddled with a gear and then held the clamping mechanism up. Nothing happened for a good few seconds and then suddenly the mouth of the clamp sprung shut. "I can set the time it takes for it to go off by twisting the gears further around; up to two hours. We place a powered off tracker, attach the clamp over the on/off button on the tracker, and twist the gear to set our timer. Once the timer is up, the clamp springs shut, it turns on the tracker, the tracker goes off, and we can nail them!" finished Stella with a smile.

Holy shit. Stella went old school to get around Terror-Byte's power. She was right, he wouldn't be able to detect some springs and gears, and if the device was off then he wouldn't sense it either.

"You're a genius; I'd hug you but well, you know. So how about a 'great job' and a thumb's up instead," I said with a grin.

Stella, with her history, didn't like physical contact. She nodded and smiled at my gesture.

"Do we have another tracker?" I asked.

Stella shook her head and said, "I was going to build another right after I was done examining the freeze ray."

"How about you stop playing with it and get to work on that tracker. As a matter of fact, build two so we have a spare," I said.

Stella stopped tinkering with the freeze ray and sighed. "Alright, I guess that makes sense. I still want to figure this thing out though, so once the trackers are done..."

"Sure, if you must, just be careful, okay?"

She nodded and started talking to Blue about getting parts for the two trackers. Satisfied that Stella wasn't going to incase us in an icy tomb, I went to find breakfast.

The last time we hid down here, the greatest challenge was boredom. While the lab had amenities like the Food-O-Tron, fridge, freezer, washer, dryer, showers, and bathrooms, it lacked modern conveniences like music, TVs, and computers. I fixed that oversight by having an electrician install power converters and outlets, so now we had a TV and places to plug in computers and other modern electrical devices. I couldn't stream Internet content on the TV, but it did have a Blu-ray player attached to it, and we had a huge library of titles on hand. The lack of Internet also meant the computer options were limited, but I had a local collection of MP3s on my laptop's hard drive so I could listen to music.

In our preparation for moving here, I had also moved most of my model building stuff down here. We had a day and half to kill before Terror-Byte would be e-mailing us for the exchange, so I decided I might as well enjoy myself and started building a new 1/72nd scale Zero fighter. I opened up my forties playlist on the laptop and got down to business.

As I cut pieces out of their plastic frames, I started considering Bree, Terror-Byte, and the whole mess that we found ourselves in. It bothered me that Terror-Byte had waited until after ten last night to contact us. In that twenty or so minutes he delayed, I'd truly feared we'd blown our shot at getting Bree back and we'd never see her again. I knew he wouldn't honor the deal tomorrow night either, but if he didn't have another job for us, what then? We had the tracker as our insurance and if everything went right, Melvin and company would be in for a rude surprise when we popped out of the shadows and stormed their base.

With the pieces cut out, I picked up each one and gently sanded down the rough bits. This part of model building was mindless grunt work, but it gave me time to think. I was worried about the tracker. What if their base wasn't in range of the receivers? And what if there were more Acolytes at the base than we could handle?

I addressed my first concern by asking Stella to build ten more receivers. With those ten new ones, we could cover a good chunk of the province and increase our odds of finding them.

The second problem was trickier, Melvin had beaten us twice already, and we couldn't afford to fail a third time. If we hit them in their base and failed, we were dead—they wouldn't let us live after we discovered where they were hiding.

I decided that tomorrow night, all of this was going to end one way or another, and I had an insurance policy that would make sure of it.

***

The upside to being in London and yet staying on Eastern Time meant Liv rose four hours earlier than she usually did. Having dinner at six was nice for a change, rather than having to wait until after eight as we did when we were back home.

"The two trackers are done, and I've started building the ten new trackers you wanted," said Stella. "I'll have them done sometime tomorrow."

I was pleased at that and smiled to myself as the more time Stella was tied up with the receivers, the less time she would have to tinker with the freeze ray and either break it or kill us all by mistake.

I took a deep breath and said, "I have made a decision that tomorrow night this is all ending one way or another. After dinner, Blue will transport me to somewhere remote in Alberta and I'm going to make a call to Dmitri," I said.

Dmitri was Dmitri Petrov, leader of one of the two GRC13 teams. GRC13 was Canada's elite anti-monster squad, and like EIRT, they were part of the Royal Canadian Mounted Police or RCMP as they were more commonly known. We'd worked with GRC13 last month to take down a demon and had gotten pretty close. Dmitri and Blue had started dating. They had been taking things slow, but it seemed to be going well. At least it had until Blue, like the rest of us, ended up on the run from the law which had probably put a small kink in their budding relationship.

"I'm going to ask him to have his team on stand-by at EIRT headquarters in Toronto. Once we find where the Acolytes are hiding, I will call him and give him the location. We'll hit them first, but this way if we fail, then the cavalry will save us. Even if we win, I'm going to stay at the warehouse and wait for GRC13 to take me into custody along with the Acolytes."

Liv gasped. "No, you can't do that. You'll go to jail."

"Maybe," I said. "Okay, probably, but I knew that when we hit the Mint. Liv, my whole life I was raised to be a hero. This being a wanted criminal thing doesn't sit well with me. We had to do it to rescue Bree, and I'm good with that. Tomorrow night though, it ends; I will face the consequences of my actions. We might get lucky, and if the gold is still at Terror-Byte's base and we recover it as well as Bree, I may not face much jail time. If we do take down the Acolytes before GRC13 arrives, you are all welcome to take Bree and go. I'm not asking you guys to stay as well. But this is something I have to do."

"Your actions are made with honor. I, too, will stay and face the consequences," said Blue.

I was floored at that; Blue always tended to defer to Stella and let Stella make the decisions for her. Yet, here she didn't hesitate and immediately followed my lead.

Stella nodded and said, "I was raised by a career criminal and have seen where that path leads, I will also stay."

Liv looked at us like we had all lost our minds and said, "You know we have like five million in cash sitting over there and we could hide for the rest of lives quite comfortably, right?" I nodded, and Liv sighed and said, "Alright, if everyone is going to be all noble and shit, I guess I'm in too."

Alteea said, "I'm too small to go to prison, so I'm out. I'll find where they are keeping you and smuggle in drugs or cigarettes to you so you can trade them for favors. Hopefully that will make your lives easier in the Big House and stop you from becoming someone's bitch."

Liv laughed at our 'street-wise' pixie and shook her head. "We really have to cut down on the TV you've been watching recently."

I smiled and was so proud of this team. I hadn't expected them to join me and figured they would take off once we'd rescued Bree. Now, I had a call to make.

Ten minutes later, Blue in her old man disguise and I were standing at the edge of a small town in northern Alberta. The streetlights sparkled off the freshly fallen snow on the ground. I powered up my iPhone for the first time since we'd bugged out from Hamilton.

I had some new texts and e-mails but other than a quick look at Annette's texts to check on Rob's status, which as of this morning was the same, I went straight to my contacts. I found Dmitri's number and made the call.

"Comrade Zack, I did not expect you to call me," said Dmitri in his usual cheerful voice.

"I didn't expect it either, Dmitri. If you are tracing this call, don't bother. I'm in northern Alberta in the middle of bum-fuck nowhere and once this call is over, we are gone."

"*Da*, I see that. Why are you calling? Do you wish to turn self in?"

"Not quite," I said, "but I will do soon. We only hit the Mint because the Acolytes have Bree and threatened to kill her unless we stole the gold for them."

"*Da*, I figured something like that."

"Thanks for believing in me. The Acolytes changed the deal and still have her. We just pulled off another small job, and they will be contacting us tomorrow at 9:00 p.m. Eastern to make the swap. I suspect they are going to screw us again, but we are taking steps to deal with them. After that exchange, there is a strong chance we will know where their hideout is. We are going to hit them and take them down. Before we attack, I will call you and give you the address. If things go well, you can arrest them and us and hopefully get the gold back too. If things don't go well, you can avenge us and finish what we started. I'd suggest you move your team to EIRT Headquarters, as we suspect the base in nearer to Toronto than Ottawa."

"Sounds like plan, but you could be under duress. This could be a ploy to move us away from capital…"

"I swear it's not. You have two teams, leave one in Ottawa then. Either one of your teams is more than a match for us anyways. I'm giving you a chance to take down two wanted groups of criminals in one shot. Do you really want to pass on that?" I said.

"I will talk to captain."

I smiled at his answer and said, "Good, I will call you tomorrow. Take care, my friend, and Blue says hello."

"You too, and tell Blue, I say hi too."

I ended the call, and we disappeared into the shadows.

***

I was in bed just after midnight Eastern Time and there was a soft knock at my door.

"Come in," I said.

The door opened, and Liv's lovely silhouette was outlined in the lights from the hall for a moment before she quietly entered my room and closed the door. The light had messed up my night vision, but I heard her soft steps approach my bed. She stopped in front of the bed and I strained to figure out what she was doing.

She lifted the blanket and slipped into my bed. "I thought you might like some company…"

I immediately felt her soft skin against mine and realized she was naked too. She snuggled up against me and kissed me. The kiss was tentative at first but quickly deepened. She shifted deftly on top of me and whispered into my ear, "This wasn't how I pictured our first time, but if we are going to prison tomorrow, then I thought remembering this might make your butt raping in jail easier to take…" She giggled as she nibbled on my ear lobe.

I sort of found that funny. It would have been more amusing if that wasn't one of my fears for my future. She kissed her way down my neck, and I then I felt her two fangs gently pierce my skin. I was about to protest about her feeding on me, but then she shifted back, and I entered her; suddenly I didn't care about her using me as a snack. I also stopped worrying about tomorrow and just lost myself in the here and now.

A couple of hours later, which had flown by, Liv said, "The sun is rising soon…"

I nodded, and she kissed me one last time. She broke the kiss and got out of bed. I admired the sight of her shapely bare bum as she picked up her clothes from the floor.

"Liv…" I started to say when she reached the door.

She simply said, "I know. I do too," and left me in the darkness. I smiled and drifted off to sleep. I slept better that night than I had in a long time.

Chapter 31

Friday, May 9

Stella had the ten receivers and two trackers assembled by noon Eastern the next day. She and Blue put two each in London, Kitchener, St. Catharines, Barrie, and Ottawa. They also put fresh batteries in the six we already had in place. With the sixteen receivers distributed, we now covered a good part of the province; I just hoped it was enough. It would really suck if their hideout was in a location we didn't have coverage for.

I was still half-asleep and waiting for my coffee to do its magic when Stella pointed to the briefcases of cash and asked, "If we are going to jail, what should we do with these?"

I pondered that; it wasn't like we could take them into battle with us. Also, if we were arrested, the money being stuck here in an underground lair that only a shadow-traveler could access would mean it would effectively be out of reach.

Stella was quicker than I was and asked, "What if we left them with Sarah for safe-keeping?"

That would work. If we were arrested, then Sarah could use the money to get us good legal counsel, and if by some miracle we weren't arrested, we could collect them back from her easily enough. "Yeah, once the sun is up, give her a call and go drop them off."

Stella nodded and went back to tinkering with the freeze ray. I was tempted to warn her to be careful but just left her to it. The pending jail time tonight had me thinking that I needed to get my affairs in order. It dawned on me that I really didn't have much to do. I had no living blood relatives that I knew of. My family was pretty much this team, and we were all looking at the same fate, except Bree, who by being a hostage, wasn't involved in our mini crime spree.

The only close friends I had outside of here were Marion, Rob, and Annette. I'd have loved to go visit Rob in hospital one last time, but there was no way the authorities wouldn't have him under observation.

Even if they didn't, there would be Hamilton cops visiting him at all hours, and too many of them knew me. I didn't want to get in a confrontation and risk injuring them. The best I could do was say a silent prayer for his recovery and mentally wish him, Annette, and their unborn baby the best for the future.

Olivia rose at three and Stella and Blue left with the money for the English vampire court shortly after that. Once Liv and Alteea had their glass of wake-up juice, the three of us retired to the library.

"Mistress, if everyone but Bree is going to prison, who's going to stop Bree from eating me?" asked Alteea with a nervous flutter of her gossamer wings.

Olivia laughed and shook her head. "Bree won't eat you—she loves you just as much as I do."

Alteea gave Liv a doubtful look. When I thought back on the multitude of pixie recipes Bree claimed she had at various times over the last few weeks, I couldn't blame Alteea for being a little skeptical. Bree was joking, of course, and usually only brought them up when Alteea was eying one of her desserts. It didn't help that from the beginning Alteea had been wary of our angry Were. Weres were a natural predator of pixies, and I'm sure Alteea thought we were a bit nuts for living with one.

Liv got serious and said, "I swear she won't eat you, and I need you to keep an eye on Bree for me. If we are in jail, she is going to be on her own. Take care of her for me, okay?"

Alteea nodded her little chin reluctantly, and said, "As you wish, Mistress."

I decided the mood was getting a bit somber and brought up one of the amusing mishaps from one of Blue's training sessions. They giggled and soon we were telling one silly story after another and that was how we spent the rest of the afternoon.

Blue and Stella didn't get back until just before dinner. It sounded like they too had a relaxing afternoon with Sarah, and it was good to see the whole team in good spirits. We picked our favorites from the Food-O-Tron, sat down, and enjoyed our last meal together.

***

200

Just before nine, Blue shadow-traveled us to another coffee shop with Wi-Fi. This time we were in Lexington, Kentucky. We took our beverages outside behind the building. I fired up the laptop and connected to the wireless Internet.

The sun had just set and the alleyway we were in was quiet and deserted as the darkness settled in around us. The e-mail arrived right at nine and soon I had Melvin's smug face on my screen.

"Do you have the freeze ray?" asked Melvin.

"What? No foreplay, just right to business? It's like you are taking me for granted…"

Terror-Byte stared back blankly at me for a moment and with an annoyed look said, "Freeze ray, now!" I nodded and held up a picture of me holding the Arctic Avenger's gun that I'd printed out earlier. "What is this? Another picture? Show me the gun!"

I sighed, pulled the picture away, and said, "We've been over this. We have no Internet where we are hiding…"

"So? You could have brought it with you," argued Terror-Byte, his voice shrill.

"Mel—" I started to reply, and as much as I enjoyed tweaking him, he still had Bree, so I said, "Terror-Byte, we are using Wi-Fi outside a coffee house in a major city. We are wanted criminals, thanks to you, and a three-foot silver assault rifle looking thing isn't exactly inconspicuous."

He frowned and said, "I didn't see anything on the news about the Hall of Heroes being hit, so how do I know you really have it?"

"We got lucky and snatched it right under their noses. They don't even know it is gone; that's why there has been no news about it." He stayed silent, so I added, "Look, why would I lie about it? You are probably going to make us drop the gun off somewhere like the last time. If the gun isn't there or if it's a fake, you'll kill Bree."

He cheered up at that and said, "Very well, same warehouse as before. You have ten minutes. If there are no tricks and you deliver the gun, I will e-mail you at ten and tell you how to get your panther."

He cut the connection and my screen went black. I closed the laptop and Blue, without a word, opened another shadow portal and we disappeared.

Stella and the rest were waiting for us when we stepped out of the shadows.

"Same deal as before; we drop off the gun and he'll contact us at ten. Set the timer for thirty minutes."

Stella nodded and started adjusting the timing gear on the clamp.

"The timer isn't exact, so it will be close to thirty minutes," she said, looking up.

"How close?" I asked.

"Plus or minus a couple of minutes," answered Stella.

I glanced at my watch. It was 9:05 p.m. now, so that meant it would go off between 9:32 p.m. and 9:38 p.m. It would take Blue and Stella less than five minutes to check the receivers and another minute or two to get a rough location on where the hideout was. Blue could use the shadows to search inside the buildings in the area to find their exact location, and then it would take another couple of minutes for her to scope the place out and then we'd rescue Bree. I quickly did the math in my head, and we'd be able to strike about five minutes before Terror-Byte e-mailed us at ten. I wanted to hit Melvin as quickly as possible after the drop in the hopes that they wouldn't be expecting us. If this turned out to be the last job he wanted us to complete, he would kill Bree—another reason to go after them sooner rather than later.

"That should be okay. Are the tracker and clamp both secure in there? I'd hate for them to start rattling around and be detected or worse—come apart."

Stella bobbed her head and said, "There is enough double-sided tape in there to hold down an elephant; they'll be fine."

***

I emerged out of the shadows into the familiar warehouse. Not much had changed since the last time. There were two new burn marks on the floor where they'd teleported in and out. There was another circle set up a few feet away from where the first one had been. I walked to the center of the warehouse and carefully put down the freeze ray. I said a silent prayer to Odin and headed back to the shadow portal.

I stepped into the shadows and cursed as I collided with the back wall of the warehouse instead. I rubbed my head, took a few steps back and wondered what the hell was going on. Why would Blue close the portal? I instantly worried that the Acolytes had somehow blocked the shadow portal and that this was a trap. Sparks dripped off my hands as I went on alert, but the warehouse was dead quiet; nothing seemed out of place.

Blue's head and arm popped out of the shadows and she waved to me. I hurried over and this time reappeared in the lab when I stepped in and out of the shadows.

"What the heck, Blue?" I asked while feeling the goose egg that was starting to form on my forehead.

"Sorry, Liv insisted that I open a new one for her."

I looked around and realized that Liv wasn't here. "What is she doing?" Dread filled me. I worried she was going to do something stupid like attack the Acolytes during the drop or try and sneak into the circle when they teleported back to their base.

When Blue answered, "Going to get pizza," I was stunned silent. *The girl can't even eat pizza, why the hell would she risk her neck to go out in public?* And then it hit me—she went to get some for Bree. Bree had been a guest of the Acolytes now for days and there was a good chance they weren't feeding her enough. If she was hungry, she'd be weak and her control over the beast would be poor too. This was something I should have thought of. I also wondered why she hadn't just used the Food-O-Tron, but then realized that the heavy cast-iron pans that it used weren't practical for easy transport and that boxes of pizza would be much easier to take with us.

"And that couldn't have waited a minute until I returned?"

Blue shrugged and said, "You know how she gets…"

Yeah, once Liv had her mind made up, it was easier to move mountains than to change her mind. Most times it was just easier to give in than to fight her on something. I nodded.

I glanced at my watch. It was just past nine p.m. Melvin and his crew should be picking up the freeze ray in the next five minutes. Blue turned away from me and focused on the shadows to spy on the warehouse and we waited.

The minutes slowly ticked by and as each one passed, I grew more and more anxious. The timer on the tracker could go off at 9:32 p.m.

if the Acolytes stalled long enough and it went off in the warehouse, we were done.

At 9:18 p.m., Blue said, "The circle is flaring; Terror-Byte, Hexadecimal, and Meat-Shield have just teleported in."

I breathed a sigh of relief. They had at least fourteen minutes to grab the freeze ray and teleport back out, which should be plenty of time.

Blue continued her running commentary, "Hexadecimal cloned herself and the clones are spreading out in a protective circle. They are walking over to the freeze ray. Terror-Byte is talking non-stop over his communicator to someone at base."

So far this was going just as it had before.

"They have stopped at the freeze ray. Terror-Byte is moving behind Meat-Shield with Hexadecimal and he ordered her to use one of the clones to pick-up the gun."

He must be worried that we booby-trapped it or something.

"A clone has picked it up and handed it to Terror-Byte. He is studying it intently, turning it over and looking at it from different angles. He is smiling and just ordered Meat-Shield to start building the teleport circle."

I pumped my fist and Stella and Alteea cheered out loud behind me.

Blue went quiet for almost a minute and then said, "The circle is built. It is activating, and they are gone!"

I looked at my watch and smiled; 9:24 p.m. The tracker was in place, and now we just had to hope that when it went off it was in range of the receivers.

Blue stepped forward and disappeared into the shadows. She reappeared thirty seconds later with Olivia in tow.

"Jeez, Blue, I was standing there for like five minutes..." said Liv.

Liv was carrying four large pizza boxes, and they smelled great. As she walked by me, I reached for one of the boxes and got my hand smacked by Liv for my efforts. "That is for Bree!"

"Really? She is going to miss one slice from that pile?" I asked.

"Maybe, she could be starving, and that one piece could make all the difference!"

I rolled my eyes; even Bree's amazing appetite couldn't best four large pizzas in one sitting. I was pretty sure her record was two and a half. It wasn't worth fighting about so I let the matter drop.

***

At 9:40 p.m., Stella and Blue disappeared into the shadows to check the receivers. I started pacing across the hangar nervously the moment they left. We'd know in a couple of minutes if we were good or not. I worried that I should have had Stella build more receivers to give us even better coverage, or that the signal from the tracker was blocked, or that Terror-Byte had found the tracker before it went off.

The plan, when we came up with it, seemed solid, but as the seconds ticked by, it felt like less of a plan and more like a crapshoot.

Stella and Blue came out of the shadows, and Stella was smiling. "They are somewhere near Pearson Airport."

Pearson was Toronto Pearson International Airport. It was the largest airport in Canada. The area around it was heavily built up and had plenty of places for them to hide.

Blue immediately turned and stared off into the shadows. In less than thirty seconds she said, "Found them. They are in an old warehouse. It is the last one at the end of a row. Bree is in the basement and the Beast Whisperer is standing guard nearby. Other than the cell, a cot outside the cell, and a large target range, the basement in empty."

She paused and said, "The rest of the Acolytes are on the main level of the warehouse. Terror-Byte is using the freeze ray and zapping random small things. All of them are watching him and laughing. The only one missing is the Bartender."

She went quiet and I assumed she was looking for him. "He is sleeping and has a large bandage on his head."

The Bartender obviously hadn't recovered from the hit I gave him the other night. I wondered how hurt he was and if he'd be a factor in the upcoming fight or not.

Blue went over the layout of the warehouse. I perked up when she described a platform at the back that had a large archway with lights around it. We guessed that must be the main teleport gate, and the gold was sitting on a cart right beside the platform.

I was buoyed at the mention of the gold still being there. If we could recover it, that would go a long way in reducing our sentences.

Further down the west wall was a large TV screen with a conference table in front of it. Blue noted there was a camera mounted on top of the TV. In the southwest corner was a door and a stairway that led up from the basement. There was a fire exit on the center of the south wall. There were wooden structures they'd built along the entire east wall. In the southeast corner were bathrooms and communal showers. Beside it was a kitchen and dining area, and then there were ten small living units that ran all the way down to the north wall.

I got worried when Blue mentioned ten rooms, as we'd only encountered eight Acolytes so far. Another two unknown Enhanced Acolytes would be a complication we didn't need. Thankfully, Blue said the first two units beside the dining room and kitchen were empty.

"The center of the warehouse is mostly open space. The Acolytes are currently there in front of the kitchen," finished Blue.

"Anything outside the warehouse we need to be careful of?" I asked.

Blue zoned out for a few seconds while she checked the shadows. "There is another warehouse to the right of it, but there are no people in it. Behind the warehouse, there is empty space that runs back about fifty feet, then there is a fence which is part of Pearson's boundaries, but just beyond the fence there are large tanks of aviation fuel. The left side is another fence that belongs to a courier company. In that yard there are just empty shipping pallets and older delivery vehicles."

Other than the fuel tanks, it looked like we were okay if the battle spilled out from the Acolytes' warehouse.

"Okay, time is ticking, folks," I said. "We need to hit them soon, and I still have to call Dmitri. Our priority is to get Bree. After that, we need to get the gold and take down the Acolytes."

Blue said, "I will handle the Beast Whisperer. I can emerge from the shadows and take him out without anyone being aware."

"Try for a non-lethal take down. The suits may have heartrate monitors on them and if you kill him, it could alert the others." Blue nodded and I continued, "Once you have him down, open another portal for us and we'll get Bree."

I thought about the gold and the Acolytes and a plan started forming in my mind. I asked, "Are there shadows near the ceiling of the warehouse?"

Blue nodded and I said, "Here's is what we are going to do ..."

***

At ten minutes to ten, we were standing in Sam Lawrence Park on Hamilton Mountain overlooking the lights of downtown Hamilton. It felt good to be back in the city. I fired up my iPhone and waited for it to power up.

I scratched my chin; it was weird going into battle without wearing my usual balaclava. I had decided to forgo wearing it as there wasn't any point in hiding my identity when I'd been outed by the national media, but I still felt kind of naked without it.

The phone came to life and texts and e-mail messages streamed in. All my focus on getting Bree back and taking down the Acolytes was shattered in an instant by a single text: "Turn yourself in, Airhead!" It was from Rob. He was awake and out of his coma. I wondered if this might be some sort of trick, but Annette sent me a bunch of messages saying he was awake and doing fine. Also, the fact that the only person who called me Airhead was Rob, convinced me it wasn't a trick.

My fear about how tonight would go almost melted away instantly. Rob being injured was what started this whole ordeal in the first place. Rob emerging from his coma felt like a good omen for us tonight.

"Zack?" asked Liv.

"Sorry, there were texts from Rob and Annette; he's out of his coma."

"That awesome!" said Liv and she gave me a hug.

Stella said, "That's great, but we need to get Bree."

I nodded and found Dmitri's number and called him.

"We found them. Their hideout is in a warehouse near Pearson Airport," I said.

"That is good, give address and we take them down," said Dmitri in his usual heavily accented Russian accent.

I gave him the address and said, "We, not you, are going to finish this, my friend. They kidnapped our teammate and used her as leverage to make us steal for them, and they injured my friend and killed a Hamilton police officer; we owe them for that. If we fail, then you can finish what we started, but we are not sitting on the sidelines for this one."

Blue disappeared into the shadows at that point and we were a go.

Dmitri said, "*Da*, I understand… See you soon, my friend."

We ended the call and I waited for Blue to reappear. One way or another, everything ended tonight.

Chapter 32

Friday, May 9

Blue popped out of the shadows not thirty seconds later and said, "The Beast Whisperer is down."

I went through the open portal with the rest of my team hard on my heels. William Sidney's small, nerdy form was lying on the ground to my left. His chest moved as he breathed, so he was still alive, but unconscious.

I looked up and Bree was staring intently at William and her icy blue eyes glowed. Blue stepped around me and ignited her sword. She cut silently through the lock on the cell in one quick swipe. Blue opened the door so Bree didn't have to touch the silver bars.

"Bree!" called out Liv in excitement, but Bree ignored her.

She stormed out of the cell and made a beeline for the Beast Whisperer's unconscious form. She reared back and kicked his armored chest hard enough that his body lifted from the ground and said, "That is for ogling me when I was naked and for your crude comments." He hit the ground and she kicked him again and said, "And that is for messing with me and my beast!"

His body hit the ground again, and Bree started winding up for another kick, but suddenly stopped and asked, "Do I smell pizza?"

Bree turned and saw Liv holding the boxes of pizza and ran over to her. She hugged Liv and in the same motion took the pizza from her.

Bree had one of the boxes open and was stuffing two large slices into her mouth and said, "So good... missed you..."

Liv glowed happily at the 'missed you' part, but I wasn't entirely convinced Bree wasn't talking about the pizza.

Like Rob's text, seeing Bree alive and unharmed lifted another weight from my shoulders. She looked a little thin and worn but seeing the energy with which she attacked William and the pizza, reassured me that with a bit of time and lots of food, she'd be back to her normal self soon enough. A part of me just wanted to have Blue open a portal and go home. Sitting around the kitchen table and watching Bree consuming a mountain of food sounded pretty good right now. But the job wasn't done.

I cleared my throat and said, "I hate to interrupt, but we still have a job to do. Bree, stay here, fuel up, and then change. Join us upstairs when you are ready." I turned my attention to the whole team, "Remember the plan—wait for twenty seconds once I go through the shadow portal, okay?"

Everyone nodded, and I started calling on my power. Once I had a huge charge built up, I nodded at Blue and she opened another portal. I stepped through and immediately started plummeting towards the floor of the warehouse.

I used my Air power to slow my descent and ended up hovering just over the cart of gold. A cry of alarm went up from the Acolytes and I yelled, "Evening, Melvin, you have three seconds to surrender. One..."

Melvin immediately went for the freeze ray, which was propped up against the wall beside him.

"So be it..." I said, and with a motion of my arms released a large blast of hurricane force winds in all directions around me.

Melvin's hand had just touched the freeze ray when the winds slammed into him. He and the gun were both flung hard against the far wall. The freeze ray bent at an odd angle when it crashed off the concrete wall, and I knew it was no use to anyone anymore. The other Acolytes were tossed into the air like ragdolls. They tumbled and smashed into the outer walls. The wooden structures they'd built to live in shattered like toothpicks and disappeared in a cloud of debris. Water streamed out of the ground from where the toilets and showers used to be. A loud crash behind me caught my attention, and I saw that their delivery truck was now over on its side. The building itself shuddered, and I feared that it too was coming down and immediately halted the flow of air.

I had put more than half my power reserves into that first attack and the effects were devastating. I'd also never released that type of power inside a small space before. All around me it looked like a bomb had gone off. The only thing spared was the gold directly beneath me. Everything else was damaged or destroyed.

This was only the second time in my life that I had used this type of attack and the first time I'd ever used it in combat. The first time I did this was in my teenage years when my mother was training me. That time though it had been outdoors in a lightly wooded area, so other than knocking over a few small saplings and kicking up a lot of dirt, it hadn't been this impressive. My power had grown since then. This amount of power usually took too long to summon and caused too much destruction.

Today, however, it felt good to let that fury out. The Acolytes had bested us twice, and it had been time to take off the kid gloves. I also had given them a chance to surrender, so it wasn't my fault if Terror-Byte had been too arrogant to heed that warning.

The whole warehouse was eerily still and silent. A car alarm echoed off in the distance. The silence was broken when some boards shifted, and a mattress was tossed aside. Meat-Shield lifted himself out of the debris with a dazed look on his wide face. The fact that he was still conscious was a tribute to his ability to soak up damage.

A pained cry pulled my attention to a corner of the warehouse. Melvin was still conscious too, but his right arm hung limply from his body as he tried to get to his feet. He slipped in the pool of water growing around his feet and screamed as he fell on his injured right side. He also had a nasty gash in his forehead that streamed blood. As an expert in broken shoulders with having wrecked mine twice this year already, I had some sympathy for the pain Melvin was currently experiencing, but not that much.

I spotted a black armored leg sticking out of a pile of debris and twenty feet down, nearer to the entrance, there was a limp arm under some smashed wood. Both were still attached to their owners but were unmoving. I spotted Carla's dark spiky hair as she lay unmoving and face down against what used to be their kitchen sink.

I turned at the sound of steps behind me and smiled as my team popped out of the shadows. Stella's Hyde form roared and charged at Meat-Shield. His eyes went wide, and he said, "I surrender, please, I surrender!" He got down on the ground and put his hands on his head.

Liv blurred by me, and Melvin cried out as she yanked him to his feet. She twisted his good left arm behind his back and gripped his neck with her other hand to keep him in place. Melvin went white when Liv flashed her fangs and snarled, "You took my friend!"

Melvin stammered, "Please... I'm sorry... please don't eat me..."

Liv laughed and said, "I don't even like touching you, so I'm not going to put my mouth anywhere near you." Melvin calmed a bit at that, and Liv added, "But make the slightest wrong move and I'll snap your useless neck."

I heard the whistle of a blade and sensed sparks behind me. I turned to see Blue sheathing her sword. She'd cut the power lines to the teleportation gate as planned so it couldn't be used to send through reinforcements. Judging by the half-shattered archway, cutting the power was probably overkill.

The sound of a helicopter coming in low and fast over the warehouse filled the air. The cavalry had arrived. Thankfully, their role was just as a clean-up crew now and not to rescue us.

The large conference table that had been blocking the door to the basement stairs suddenly flew through the air and crashed down on the concrete floor. Bree in her hybrid Werepanther form appeared in the doorway and roared loud enough that it shook the building. Her glowing blue eyes looked around looking for a challenger and seemed disappointed when no one presented themselves.

"Welcome to the party, Bree," I said with a smile as I lowered myself out of the air. "You missed last call by about a minute. The party is wrapping up and any second the cops are going to shut it down for good. You and Blue can check on some of the party goers; it seems that some of them have had a few too many..."

She tilted her furry dark head at me and gave a low growl, which was panther for 'huh?'

"Check the debris and see if any of the Acolytes buried among it are still alive, okay? Also, GRC13 is going to be coming in here with guns blazing in the next minute or so. Don't attack them and try and look as unthreatening as possible."

Bree and Blue headed over to the far side of the warehouse and started digging out Acolytes. I sat my tired ass down on the edge of the gold cart; releasing that much power had been draining.

The sound of the helicopter's rotors powering down in the distance meant GRC13 was on the ground. They'd be here shortly, and part of me was nervous, as that meant we were going to jail soon. I just hoped we weren't in for a long stay. We'd probably be okay. After all, our crimes were done under duress, we just caught the Acolytes, and we recovered all the gold we stole.

On the other hand, we were Enhanced and just for that reason alone a lot of people would be happier to have us in prison than free and wandering about. With my luck, we'd pull a judge who was a closet Humans First member and we'd get the book thrown at us.

My head perk up as I sensed two powerful Air and Ice elementals nearby. Thankfully both were my type of powers, so it was more a warm fuzzy feeling than it would have been if they'd been Fire or Earth.

"Heads-up people, GRC13 is here," I yelled.

Liv nodded as she dragged Melvin over to me. Stella's Hyde form just shrugged her misshapen muscled shoulders as she continued sitting on Meat-Shield. Bree and Blue didn't pause in their work of rescuing Acolytes from the rubble. I only spotted Alteea's aura buzzing around in the rafters as she had her glamor fully up. I hoped she was high enough up that Dmitri's Were senses wouldn't notice her.

A large brown furry leg kicked the front door off its hinges and Dmitri's massive hybrid Werebear form came through a moment later. My eyes widened as Captain Cooper came flying in behind him. That explained the Air elemental I'd sensed. Ben Cooper was in his sixties and had a prosthetic right leg and left arm. I thought he was now spending his time behind a desk and not in the field.

"Police—" he started to yell, but as he flew up and surveyed the damage, whatever he was going to say died on his lips. He spotted me sitting on the gold and flew towards me.

Ariel's trim form entered the warehouse next. Ariel was a powerful Ice elemental that had been on the other GRC13 team when we worked to take down the demon together. I guessed she'd moved over to Dmitri's team to help balance out the two teams with her veteran experience.

Right behind her, a younger guy in tactical gear came in. He was Enhanced and had an orange, yellow, and silver aura that was about four inches in diameter. The orange core meant Super class, but I didn't have the foggiest on what the yellow and silver meant. The four-inch aura meant he was powerful but not overly so.

As soon as he cleared the doorway, another Enhanced came in. Her aura was an orange, gray, and gold one that I recognized. Her name escaped me for a second—it was something with an 'M.' Maggie, no, Magda; that was it. We'd only briefly met, as she'd been injured on GRC13's first meeting with a demon. She had the ability to manipulate metal; she could call it to her and reshape it on the fly. Her aura was close to six inches in size.

On the deployment where she got injured, she had been in a cabin in the middle of the woods, which meant they couldn't fully utilize her powers due to the lack of metal around her. Here in the middle of an urban environment, I'd bet she was easily the most dangerous member of this team.

Once Magda cleared the doorway, more GRC13 officers poured in, but none of them had auras. While they weren't Enhanced, that didn't mean they could be ignored either. They were skilled and highly trained.

"Stand down, but stay alert," said Captain Cooper in a commanding voice as he hovered in the air just above me.

I was relieved to see that all the officers lowered their weapons after that. Ben descended in front of me and said, "You have a lot of explaining to do, Hurricane, but it's good to see you again."

He held out his good hand and I shook it warmly. "Yeah, but I have gifts. First and foremost, the gold I'm sitting on, and allow me to introduce Melvin, aka Terror-Byte, leader of the Acolytes."

He turned his steely gaze on Melvin and coldly said, "You, son, have even more to answer for…"

Melvin shrunk under his gaze, and moments later, was taken from Liv by two GRC13 officers. He cried out as they cuffed him due to his injured shoulder. They attached a power blocking collar and cuffs to him.

Four officers approached Stella with caution. She grunted at them and they stopped dead in their tracks and raised their weapons.

"Stella!" I yelled. "Get up and let the nice officers take Meat-Shield into custody, okay?"

She grunted at me too but got up and changed back into her harmless little girl form once she'd moved far enough away. The officers swarmed Meat-Shield's prone form and started restraining him with another set of power blocking cuffs and a collar.

Dmitri's big furry form lifted Blue off her feet as he embraced her. I almost giggled when 'bear hug' popped into my mind but managed to suppress it.

Magda raised her arms and all the metal in the debris lifted and hovered off the floor as if by magic. She flicked her hands, and it all shot off and crashed down loudly in the empty, water-soaked corner. Officers started pulling bodies from the remaining debris.

One of them checked Carla's unconscious form and said, "She's alive but may have a back injury. Get the support board from the chopper."

Another officer nodded and jogged for the door.

I was pleased that Carla was still alive for her mother's sake. I'd promised that I would try to bring her in safely and was glad that I had managed to keep that promise. Being an accessory to murder did mean that she was looking at a long jail sentence, but at least Paula could visit her in jail; it was better than the alternative.

Melvin was being led away when a crisp English accented male voice filled the warehouse. "You have failed me, Terror-Byte!"

Melvin flinched like he had been hit and started to shake in fear. "I'm sorry, Master."

Melvin's attention was on the TV in the far corner of the room. The flat screen had a large crack but amazingly enough still worked. There was an outline of a man in a dark robe in the shadows. I couldn't make out any of the details of his face.

The man raised his hand and pointed at Melvin and said, "You know the penalty for failure."

Tears ran down Melvin's young face and he said, "Please, Master, no. I swear I won't tell them anything…"

The voice didn't answer but reached down and hit a button. Seconds later, Melvin and Meat-Shield screamed and started to convulse. Melvin's face started to waver, and I blanched as it and the rest of him began to melt like someone had poured acid on him. The other Acolytes were shuddering, and they too started to melt.

"What the hell is happening?" yelled Captain Cooper as he looked at horror at Melvin's decomposing form on the floor.

I thought back to the corpses of the European Acolyte team. I'd assumed that it was Doctor Bubbles who had mutilated them when they had been trapped in his bubbles but realized that he just took credit for it. It was actually whoever was behind the Acolytes that had done it. He must have built safeguards into the suits so that if a team was captured, he could activate it and kill them all before they gave away anything.

In my anger, I used my powers to fly over to the screen and yelled, "They were just kids, you monster!"

"They were foot soldiers who failed me; they brought this on themselves," answered the cloaked man.

There wasn't an ounce of remorse in that cultured British accent; he sounded as though he had just taken out the trash. That lack of emotion unnerved me a bit, but I was too mad to care.

He turned towards me but remained veiled in the shadows. The light on the camera was on, and I realized he could see me, and he said, "You must be Zack Stevens, the Hamilton Hurricane."

I nodded. "James Niven, I presume?"

"That is just an alias I used; you may call me The Master!"

Instantly I answered, "Only if I add 'bater' to the end of it."

He paused and then said, "Oh, how droll. I, too, can be quite witty. I think you will find this a real blast…" He chuckled and hit a button.

"SELF-DESTRUCT IN ONE MINUTE," echoed throughout the warehouse.

"Farewell, Hurricane," he said, and the damaged screen went black.

Chapter 33

Friday, May 9

"Fifty-seven seconds until self-destruct..."

Liv blurred up to me and said, "You just had to piss off the evil super villain, didn't you?"

I shrugged and said, "C'mon, Master-bater was funny."

Liv grinned as we ran back over to the captain.

"Everyone clear out of here. Grab a few of the bodies for evidence," ordered the captain. He looked around and turned to the one Enhanced officer I didn't know and added, "Ahmed, shield the helicopter; it won't be able to take off in time. And someone contact Pearson and get them to reroute the planes away from this area!"

"Forty-six seconds until self-destruct..."

"Blue, open a portal, get the team and this gold out of here," I said.

"Hold on, you aren't taking this anywhere," said Captain Cooper, looking pointedly at the gold.

"Look we don't have time to argue. Do you really want eighty million in gold sitting anywhere near here when this place explodes?"

He sighed but nodded. Blue sprinted over to the teleportation platform and opened a portal in the shadows. Liv immediately pushed the cart of gold towards it.

"We also have another problem," I said.

"The fuel tanks out back?" he guessed.

I nodded and watched Liv disappear into the shadows. Stella, Alteea, and Bree disappeared after her. Blue turned to me and raised a questioning purple eyebrow at me.

"Go," I said. "I have something I need to do here first. I'll call you when it is done."

She nodded and then vanished into the shadows.

I turned to Captain Cooper and asked, "You still have a bit of wind left in you?"

He smiled and said, "Yeah, what do you have in mind?"

"The two of us go out back between the tanks and building and just before this building blows, we hit it with everything we have."

He scratched his chin and said, "If we throw enough wind at it, it may be enough to push the blast away in other direction! This is going be dangerous as hell, but we don't have a choice."

"Twenty-eight seconds until self-destruct..."

I looked at my watch to get it in sync with the timer, and the two of us flew to the back door. It was warped but thankfully opened without an issue. We cleared the overgrown field and reached the back fence in seconds. We braced ourselves against the chain-link fences and started gathering our powers.

If this didn't work, then we were in deep shit as I knew this was going to drain the rest of my power completely. If those tanks behind us went up, we wouldn't be able to get clear of the blast.

I watched the seconds tick by on my watch and said, "I will count down from five. On 'two' hit it with everything you have, okay?"

He nodded, and I said, "Five."

"Four."

"Three."

At two, we released an awesome amount of wind towards the building. The overgrown field in front of us flattened like a giant had stepped on it. The warehouse shook for a moment as the winds hit it and then there was a blinding flash and it exploded. The concussion from the blast slammed us both hard into the fence, but it wasn't followed by a searing wave of heat. We bounced off the fences and fell into the long grass in front of us.

Small pieces of debris rained down on us, but the tanks were intact. We were battered but alive.

Captain Cooper moaned beside me and said, "I'm getting too old for this shit..." I just laughed, and he added, "Not sure what you are laughing at, and by the way, you are under arrest."

I nodded, and his radio went off. "Captain Cooper, Captain Cooper, are you there?" asked a concerned voice.

He rolled over, unclipped his radio from his vest, and said, "Barely, but I'm here. The Hurricane and I are behind the warehouse. The tanks are intact but both of us need assistance to get out of here."

"Roger that, sir, we'll be there shortly."

Captain Cooper clipped up his radio, and I said, "I have a favor to ask..."

His officers found us a few minutes later and as soon as they saw him, he said, "This man is resisting arrest, taser him!"

The lead officer looked down at my splayed-out form and frowned in confusion. I barely was able to wave my arms at him and I weakly said, "I'm resisting..."

He reached for the Taser on his belt, but didn't draw it, and asked, "Sir?"

A female voice that I recognized said, "Get out of the way, Kowalski, let me through."

Kowalski stepped to the side, and the moment he was out of the way, Officer Barclay fired her Taser. The barb hit me in the upper thigh less than an inch from my left nut. The juice started and my concern for the family jewels disappeared as my body tingled in pleasure as the electricity flowed through me. I let out a soft moan and Officer Barclay laughed.

I heard the captain chuckle beside me and then we all lost it at Officer Kowalski's dumbfounded expression.

Once I stopped laughing, I pulled the barb from my pants, used my Air power to lift me off the ground, and said, "Thank you, Officer Barclay."

"You're welcome, but this is starting to become a habit."

I nodded. After using up all my power fighting the demon last month, Officer Barclay had tasered me then too.

"Hurricane, some assistance here," barked the Captain.

I nodded and used my Air power to lift him off the ground. I turned him so he was upright and floating beside me.

"You drop me, son, I will make sure they add time to your sentence," warned Captain Cooper.

"But what? How?" stammered Kowalski.

The captain sighed and said, "Close your mouth, Kowalski; he is an Air elemental, and Electricity is also his element. Officer Barclay tasering him is like you drinking Red Bull—it gives him a boost."

"Oh," said Kowalski, his eyes widening. He put his hand on his Taser and said, "You're an Air elemental, do you want a boost too?"

"Taser me, son, and I will put my one good foot up your ass, and you will be on shit detail until you retire," said the captain. Kowalski looked like a kicked puppy, and the captain added in a softer tone, "I am an Air elemental, but unlike the Hurricane, I can only control Air and not Electricity. If you shocked me, it wouldn't recharge my power and it probably would just make me piss myself, clear?"

"Crystal, sir," said Kowalski.

Sirens started up in the distance as first responders reacted to the blast.

Ben Cooper turned his attention to Officer Barclay and asked, "Any casualties?"

"No. Ahmed's energy bubble protected us and the chopper, sir. Ariel is currently using her ice to contain and put out the fires."

Ahmed was the Enhanced with the orange, yellow, and silver aura and I figured that his power was to use the energy around him as a shield. It was more of a defensive type of power, but in GRC13's line of work, it was probably one that would be extremely useful. Of course, he might have a way of using that same energy offensively as well, which would be even more valuable.

The captain gave a small, satisfied smile and said, "Good, and by the way, don't forget to fill out the paperwork for discharging that weapon." Officer Barclay grimaced but nodded. "Hurricane, get us to the chopper so I can sit my old bones down and not have you carrying me like this."

"Your wish is my command," I said and floated us at walking speed towards the helicopter.

The warehouse was completely gone, and in its place was just a pile of smoking rubble and rebar. I spotted the twisted and blackened frame of the truck among the debris. There was ash and dust in the air around us and small fires burning around the area, but Ariel was putting them out at a good pace with her ice. I doubted that there would be much for the fire department to do when they got here.

Dmitri sat on the side of the chopper wearing a pair of sweatpants in his human form. A grin flashed across his large hairy face when he saw us. I waved and smiled back but then frowned at the sight of the three tarp-covered bodies laid out on the ground beside the helicopter.

I'd wanted to take the Acolytes down and wouldn't have been shocked if my wind blast earlier had accidently killed a couple of them. Nobody deserved to die like that, though I'd strongly consider making an exception for The Master. If I had accidentally killed anyone, they were the lucky ones, as they were spared from a horrific and agonizing death by The Master a few minutes later.

I lifted the captain up and gently placed him on one of the helicopter's seats. He nodded and then patted the seat beside him and pointed at me. I turned off my power and climbed aboard.

"You want me to call my team and have them bring the gold?" I asked.

He shook his head and asked, "Are they in a secure location?" I nodded, and he added, "Good, the gold will be safer there than here. Besides, I'm not sure if we could even carry the gold in this thing. Call them and tell them you will be in touch. Once we have cleaned up this mess, I'll make some calls and we'll have them deliver the gold directly back to the Mint."

I pulled out my phone and figured this was just the start of a very long night.

Chapter 34

Saturday, May 10

We were at the site for over two hours while the captain coordinated with local law enforcement, the fire department, and Environment Canada before he left a couple of EIRT investigation teams there to finish the cleanup.

As the rotors started spinning, everyone around me went tense, like they were expecting trouble or something.

The captain turned to me. "As you are under arrest, there are certain procedures I have to follow..." He glanced over to Officer Barclay who held up a pair of power blocking cuffs.

I nodded and held out my hands. She clipped them on and said, "Sorry."

I barely heard her as I instantly couldn't feel my power anymore. It felt like a part of me was gone—like I was missing one of my senses. I sat there stunned as another officer attached the power blocking collar to my neck. The warm fuzzy feeling I had from being near another Air elemental vanished. The auras that had been around Dmitri and the captain and Ahmed had disappeared.

Captain Cooper leaned into me and said over the increasing rotor noise, "Sorry, Zack, I didn't want to do that, but the director is at EIRT headquarters, and if he saw you get off this bird without the cuffs and collar, I'd be stationed in Cold Lake, Alberta so fast it wouldn't be funny."

Oh, joy; this night just got a whole bunch shittier. Robert Smyth was the politically appointed director of GRC13 and the two of us mutually disliked each other. The smug bastard would love this. I wouldn't be surprised to find him waiting at the helipad with a big grin on his face and a large popcorn in his hand to enjoy the show.

This was my first ride in a helicopter, and I wasn't a fan. I was used to flying under my own power; being at the mercy of a pilot was unnerving. The helicopter's open side door certainly didn't help with my fears. The captain had ordered that so he could use the wind rushing in to recharge his powers.

Thankfully it was a short flight, and we touched down in downtown Toronto before I really started freaking out.

The captain used his power to lift himself out of his chair and then floated an inch or so off the ground as we all walked into the building through the rooftop entrance.

As soon as we entered the building, a guy in a suit said to the captain, "The director wants to see you and the prisoner in Conference Room D."

Captain Cooper nodded and said, "Barclay, Kowalski, you're with us. The rest of you get some chow but be ready to move out shortly."

After a short elevator ride and a slightly longer walk, or float in the captain's case, we entered Conference Room D. It was a decent sized room that was dominated by the polished dark-wood conference table in the center of it. The table could seat sixteen, but the only black leather chair that was filled was at the head of the table with Director Smyth in it.

"Director," said Captain Cooper with a slight nod of his head.

"I got reports of an explosion at the crime scene. Were any officers or civilians hurt?" asked the director, getting straight to business.

For a second, I was impressed that he cared, but then I remembered the only thing he was ever concerned about was his own ass. He wasn't asking because he was concerned. He was afraid there would be fallout if any innocent civilians or officers under his command died.

"Director, my power levels are quite low, may I sit down first?"

Smyth dismissively waved his hand at one of the chairs to his right and said, "Very well, but the prisoner will remain standing."

There was the pompous, annoying twit I remembered. I raised my cuffed hands and scratched my left eye with my middle finger, flipping him the bird. He either didn't see it or chose to ignore it.

Ben Cooper sat down and sighed tiredly, and I realized that he hadn't been kidding about being low on power. It wasn't in his nature to display weakness like that.

"No officers or civilians were killed or injured at the warehouse tonight. Unfortunately, all the Acolytes were killed at the scene."

Smyth's lips curled slightly into a half smile and he looked at me and said, "Another thing that will be added to your list of charges."

"He didn't kill any of them," replied Captain Cooper instantly. Which, to be honest, may have been generous, as I was pretty sure my initial attack may have killed one or two. "When we arrived, the Hurricane…"

The Director cut him off and said, "He no longer has hero status, please refer to him as 'the prisoner' or 'Mr. Stevens.'"

Not allowing the captain to refer to me as 'the Hurricane' was typical of the pettiness of Smyth. A man like that didn't deserve the honor of overseeing GRC13. The men and women at GRC13 were the best this country had to offer. Allowing him to lead them seemed like a huge disservice to those fine officers.

"Very well. Mr. Stevens and his team had defeated the Acolytes, and they had secured the ones that were conscious and were providing aid to the Acolytes that were injured. They did not resist us taking control of the scene and were cooperative…" He then spent the next five minutes going over everything that happened up until the point where Blue and the rest of my team left with eighty million worth of gold, at which point Smyth lost it.

"You let wanted criminals walk away with eighty million dollars in stolen gold? I should have your badge for that! What were you thinking?"

The director paused to gather his breath to continue his rant, but Captain Cooper interrupted, "With all due respect, sir, my options were limited. The warehouse was going to explode in forty-five seconds at that point. We didn't have time to get it on the chopper and for it to lift off. We also had no idea how big the blast was going to be. I'm sure the gold is safe, and I will have it back to the Mint in the next twenty-four hours."

"How can the gold be safe? It is currently with criminals."

"You and I both know that is only technically true. You read Dmitri's report; they only stole the gold because the Acolytes had their teammate. Also, if they were truly criminals, why call us and give us the location of the Acolytes' hideout?"

Smyth slowly nodded and added, "That gold better be returned, or I will have your badge. Now continue your briefing."

I almost smiled when the captain emphasized my part in preventing the blast from reaching the fuel tanks, adding that I did so at great personal risk and prevented untold damages and loss of human life. The director waved him on, and he finished up shortly after that.

The director gave a reluctant nod and said, "Write up a full report and I want that on my desk first thing Monday morning. You will call me directly the minute the gold is returned. Now I have calls to make, so I will leave you to get on with it."

Smyth got to his feet and started to leave the room but stopped in front of me. "Those cuffs suit you. I suspect that this won't be the last time I see you in them."

"So does that mean I can't count on you for a character reference for my trial?" I asked with a grin.

He didn't bother answering and just turned and left the room.

***

An hour or so later, I was on the roof of EIRT headquarters with the entire GRC13 team. Liv stepped out of the shadows with the gold cart and the rest of my team followed behind her.

Captain Cooper had made some calls, and we were expected at the Mint in Ottawa shortly. The captain wasn't coming with us. He and the non-Enhanced officers were heading back to their base in the helicopter. Dmitri, Magda, Ariel, and Ahmed were to accompany us to the Mint, which we would shadow portal to.

Ben Cooper sat on the edge of the helicopter looking every one of his sixty-some odd years at this moment. He looked at Dmitri and said, "Call me once the Mint has officially accepted the gold; the director is waiting for my call."

He turned to me, held out his hand, and said, "Zack, it's been fun, but let's not do this again, okay?"

I raised my cuffed hands, awkwardly shook his hand, and wished him well.

I turned back to Blue and said, "Alright, let's get this over with."

She nodded and opened a portal. They had put Stella and Liv in handcuffs and collars like I was, but Blue and Bree were still free. Alteea wasn't here, and I assumed she was either at the house or at the secret lab. Magda pushed the cart and went through the portal first, Ahmed went next, and my team followed them.

I spotted Captain Cooper making a spinning motion with his hand and the blacked-out helicopter started coming to life as the rotors began turning. I threw him a wave and stepped through the portal with Dmitri and Ariel right behind me.

We came out of the shadows directly in front of the vault. The room was a full house. There were close to a dozen officers in full tactical gear, a man and a woman both in business suits, two people in lab coats, plus all of us and the four from GRC13.

The two lab coats had a table set up in the corner with gold on one side of it and an empty cart on the other. There was a digital scale on the table, and they were weighing one of the gold bars. They had already placed two gold bars on the new cart.

The lady in the suit stepped forward and said, "I'm Dana Saunders, Master of the Royal Canadian Mint." She turned to her right and added, "This is Jack Cowen, he is my Director of Security." The two were a study in contrasts. Dana's demeanor was friendly, but the look Jack gave me made wish I wasn't wearing the power blocking cuffs and collar as I felt a touch vulnerable at that moment. Dana was average height but beside Jack's six-foot-something muscular frame, she seemed smaller. I put Dana in her late fifties to early sixties, and Jack was probably about a decade younger. Jack's short silver buzzcut and his rigid but alert demeanor had me betting on a military, or at least a law enforcement, background.

Dmitri stepped forward and introduced his teammates and us and when he finished, Dana said, "While they are assessing the gold, we have some questions we'd like answered, if you'll follow me."

Dana turned, and we followed on her heels. Three of the four GRC13 operatives went with us. Magda stayed behind to keep an eye on things. Four of the officers from the Mint also tagged along; the rest remained behind to guard the gold.

We reached a conference room that was almost a copy of the one I'd been in earlier at EIRT headquarters. The large conference table was cherry wood rather than the deep brown the other one had been. The black leather swivel chairs were the same style and might have even been the same model. The generic art on the wall was probably different too, but I hadn't paid that much attention to it.

Two of the four guards took up positions at the entrance to the conference room and the other two took up stations behind Dana Saunders, who sat at the head of the table. Jack took the seat to her immediate left and the rest of us filled in the empty seats.

"Talking to Ben," said Dana, and I realized that she meant Captain Cooper, "he informed me that you did the heist here under duress as the Acolytes were threatening to kill your friend, is this correct?"

"Yes, ma'am," I answered politely.

"Is your friend okay now?" she asked with concern.

"Yes, thank you. Bree is here with us now. That is why she isn't in handcuffs."

She turned to Bree and said, "I'm glad you are unharmed." Bree gave a small nod and Dana turned her attention back to me and said, "Since it was under duress, I'm sure you wouldn't mind answering a few questions for us. The Mint hadn't been successfully broken into since the late eighties until you did it. Security is our primary goal here. We have studied the tapes from the vault and one thing is puzzling us. How did you float that umbrella across the vault, and have it open itself inside the cage? A spell or something?"

With Alteea's glamor making her invisible, that is what it must have seemed like when watching the recording, as she wouldn't have been caught on film.

I explained Alteea's role in the heist and exactly how we pulled everything off. The moment I finished, Blue offered Jack a few suggestions for improving security.

Blue got on a roll and made another ten or so suggestions. To my surprise, Jack's unhappy demeanor lessened with every suggestion and he was almost smiling by the time Blue wrapped up.

He spoke for the first time and in a deep voice said, "Thank you, Blue, those suggestions are all very helpful. When the meeting is over, I will give you my card and I wonder if you would be able to visit our Winnipeg location and give your opinion?"

Blue smiled and said, "There is no need for me to physically visit it. I can spy on it from the shadows and e-mail you my findings."

"I look forward to getting that e-mail."

There was a knock at the door and one of the officers on guard opened it up. One of the lab coats entered.

Dana asked, "What is it, Mike?"

"Ma'am, all the gold is there, and nothing is missing. Aside from a few dents and scratches, everything is okay. The gold has been secured again in the vault."

"Very good. You can go home once the logs are updated."

Mike, the lab coat, scurried away, and Dana turned her attention back to the table. "Well in that case, you're all free to go."

Chapter 35

Saturday, May 10

We returned to EIRT headquarters. Liv, Blue, and I were formally charged and taken into custody. Due to the lack of evidence against Stella, they uncuffed her and said she was free to go. A deal was made that Blue could take Stella and Bree home before being taken into custody on the condition that she also gave the GRC13 officers a portal back to their base as well. Blue also agreed to leave her sword with Stella, which surprised me as I thought she wouldn't give that up without a fight.

We were processed. I decided when looking at my new jumpsuit that orange wasn't my color; it also chaffed a bit in places. We ended up in the high security cells in the basement.

As I entered the cell, they removed the cuffs but left the power blocking collar in place. The heavy steel door closed with a solid thud behind the officers as they left. My new home was an eight-by-ten cell with a toilet, sink, and small steel bed that was bolted to the wall and the floor. I sat on the bed and the light went out in the cell. I shrugged, lay down, and went to sleep.

I awoke the next day to someone sliding a metal tray of food through the slot in the bottom of the door. I picked up the tray. The meal was a tuna fish sandwich on whole wheat with mustard, a pickle on the side, and an apple that had seen better days. I hated mustard, and the sandwich tasted like sawdust, but I was too hungry to care and finished it all.

With the cell being underground and having no windows, I had no idea what time it was. Not knowing the time started to eat at me. There was also nothing to do. I sat back on the bed and just passed the time thinking about what had happened and about life in general.

The Acolytes were done, but the Master was still out there. I hoped that losing two of his three teams would put a serious crimp in his plans. It hit me that for taking down Melvin and his crew, we were entitled to the one-point-five-million dollar bounty and then frowned. Having a criminal record meant my hero status would be revoked, but I wasn't sure if the same was true for my bounty hunting license. I suspected it too might be taken away. The same would be true for Blue and Liv, but Stella and Bree would still have theirs. Stella could claim the bounty and split it with us. If we got out of here, we probably could still bounty hunt, but we'd have to put the claims through in Bree and Stella's names.

The big question was what sort of time we'd be looking at. We returned the gold and took down the group ultimately responsible for it being stolen in the first place. Our crimes were also done under duress, and I hoped those factors would help in reducing the sentence. The other thing that concerned me was that any time I got might mean a death sentence. Being Enhanced, we'd probably be shipped to the Super-max in the Arctic. I was sure there were a few people there that I'd put away, and they wouldn't be happy to see me. The idea of being in a place like that without my powers wasn't a comforting thought.

***

My cell door opened after what felt like forever but could have been hours or even minutes. I smiled at the sight of Sergeant Ray Dunham as I looked up.

"Hey, Hurricane, I heard you were here and thought I'd stop by."

It was odd seeing Ray without his familiar purple, brown, and silver Werewolf aura surrounding him, but I was glad to see him. That lack of aura really brought home how much I missed having my powers.

He handed me a thick, slightly worn paperback and said, "A little something to help you pass the time."

I glanced at the cover and smiled; it was the first book in the *Game of Thrones* series. I'd read it before, but it had been years since then. I'd kept meaning to reread the books but never found the time.

"Thank you. Odd question, but can you tell me what the time is?"

He checked his watch and said, "Just past two p.m. Stop thinking about the time or you'll drive yourself crazy."

"Any idea when visiting hours are?" I asked.

Ray shook his head and said, "These are maximum security cells; the only people allowed down here are EIRT officers. There are no visitations while you are being held here."

That sucked. It was even worse knowing that Blue was in here and couldn't use the shadows; I had no doubt that if she was out, she and the rest of them would be sneaking in visits.

We chatted for a bit until he announced that he had to start his shift. I started reading.

I had only gotten in a couple of chapters when a voice said, "The prisoner will stand and face the wall!"

I got up and did as I was told. The cell door swung open and six EIRT officers entered the cell. They attached power blocking cuffs and regular leg shackles to me. "Can I ask what is going on?"

"Your legal counsel is here," answered one of the officers.

I shuffled out of the cell and down the hallway. We took an elevator up one floor and entered a dimly lit interrogation room. It was empty other than two plain chairs and a metal table that was bolted to the floor. They sat me down in the one of the chairs and connected the leg shackles to a steel bracket in the floor. The EIRT officers left without a word.

The door opened a short time later and in walked a lady in a slightly ruffled navy suit carrying a briefcase. If this was my lawyer, then by my first look at her, I was going to jail for longer than the Manson family. The first thing I noticed was her brown hair; it was in a perm that stuck out eight or so inches in all directions. It almost looked cartoonish, like she'd stuck her finger in an electrical outlet. She also wore oversize round glasses that made her brown eyes look twice as big as normal.

She said, "I'm Claire Fontaine. I'm with McFadden and Associates. I am your legal counsel."

I perked up a McFadden and Associates. They were one of the top criminal law firms in the country. They had represented several high-profile criminals in the last few years and had a good record for getting their clients off, or at least getting them reduced sentences.

"Sarah says 'hi' and has covered our retainer. I have handled a number of cases for the English vampire court over the years."

I was starting to feel a whole lot better with each passing second. The English vampire court only used the best; if Claire had worked for them in the past, then I was in good hands.

She opened her briefcase and pulled out a file and a legal pad and said, "I have briefly reviewed your case and feel that I should be able to get the case dismissed in short order. The crimes were committed under duress. You recovered the gold and captured the Acolytes. These factors are in our favor and don't leave the Crown with much to work with. Once I leave here, I will make some calls and will hopefully convince the Crown to drop the charges."

I smiled at that. If the charges were dropped, then my hero status would be returned, and my bounty license would also be intact.

***

The next day, I got two more visitors. The first was Claire in the early afternoon. We once again ended up in the same interrogation room and she didn't have good news for me.

"I have spoken to the Crown. They are digging their heels in and are reluctant to drop the charges. I got the feeling someone is pushing them to do this, as this isn't a winnable case for them."

Director Smyth's name immediately popped into my head. The inquiry into the deaths of GRC13 officers at the hands of the demon had yet to be called. I suspected Smyth was using all his political capital to get it delayed or squashed. He knew I held him directly responsible for those deaths, and I would happily testify to that as well. If he could get a criminal conviction against me before the inquiry, then that would go a long way to neutralizing my testimony.

It could also be something as simple as someone at the Crown that had a Humans First agenda or just didn't like Enhanceds in general. In the end, it really didn't matter who was behind it, we just needed to get this resolved.

"We are scheduled for a preliminary hearing Tuesday afternoon, here at EIRT. If the Crown continues to drag its feet and not drop the charges, there is a good chance the judge might at the hearing."

I was buoyed by Claire's confidence and hoped that this could all be wrapped up in the next couple of days.

***

My cell door opened just after dinner and Bobby Knight's smiling face walked into my cell.

"About time you got here; I have been calling for room service for hours. I was just about to give this establishment a bad Yelp review."

He laughed at that. I sat up and he grabbed a seat on the bed beside me and said, "I bring news; the Acolyte team in Asia was taken down by the Chinese government's Anti-Monster squads."

I smiled a bit at 'Anti-Monster' squads. Western governments had all changed from Anti-Monster squads to Enhanced Response Units. Communist China didn't give a rat's ass about being politically correct and still used the Anti-Monster squad name.

"When?" I asked.

"A couple of hours ago. They laid a trap for them. Did you see that announcement a few days ago about a professor in China claiming he had invented a successfully working anti-gravity device?"

I shook my head and said, "Where we were hiding out didn't have Internet."

"There was a press release and a short clip showing a student floating on a hover board. It went viral on social media. People were talking about how this could revolutionize travel. Auto and aircraft manufacturing stocks were down on the news by almost 10 percent. There was going to be a full demonstration of the technology on Monday at the university for the media."

I smiled. "Let me guess, it was a hoax to draw out the Acolytes?"

Bobby nodded and said, "Yup, the professor was replaced by a Super with shape changing abilities and the lab and the professor's house were covered by the Anti-Monster squads. The Acolytes hit the lab last night and were taken down in the less than a minute. They were mostly taken alive but then suffered the same fate as the other two squads and were remotely killed."

I cursed at that as it meant there was no way to track down the Master. On the upside, all three of the Acolyte teams were done, so at least the Master's wave of crime was over for now.

"Also," said Bobby, "in the good news department, I talked to Rob this afternoon and he seems to be back to his usual chipper self. The tests have come back, and it looks like he will suffer no long-term memory or side effects from the coma. He says 'hi,' and will visit you once you are out of here."

I smiled at that but then frowned. "Even Rob as a Hamilton police officer can't get in here to visit?"

Bobby shook his head. "This area is strictly EIRT and GRC13 only. Rumor has it you won't be here much longer anyway. After your hearing on Tuesday, you will either be released on bail, have the charges dismissed, or be moved to a long-term holding facility."

We chatted for a good while and then Bobby said, "I need to get going; hanging out with hardened criminals isn't good for my career."

"Bite me."

"You'd probably like that," said Bobby with a grin.

"I'd have to be here a lot longer before you started looking good!" Bobby laughed, and I added, "Seriously though, thanks for stopping by."

He nodded and then was on his way.

***

Late Tuesday morning, I was escorted from my cell to the small conference room for what I assumed was a pre-hearing meeting with Claire to go over things one last time before we were in front of the judge.

I was surprised at how nervous I was. If this hearing went poorly, I could be transferred to a holding facility where I might end up in general population while I waited for my trial. As an ex-hero I doubted I would receive a warm welcome among the prisoners there.

Claire walked in smiling a few minutes later. To my surprise, two EIRT officers entered with her.

Claire held up a folder and said, "This is the paperwork to set you free. The Crown has dropped all charges against you and your teammates. The officers are here to remove your restraints."

They removed the cuffs around my wrists and ankles first. When the collar was removed, I staggered as my power came rushing back. Not using it for this long, I was brimming with power. My teeth grated a bit as I sensed an Earth elemental in the building somewhere but even that annoyance felt good. It felt amazing to be whole again.

An hour later, after signing a bunch of forms and getting my clothes and possessions back, we met up with Blue in the main lobby of the building.

"I shadow-traveled Olivia back home; her corpse is currently resting in the cold cellar at home."

That was good as it meant we didn't have to come back here tonight to get Liv when she woke up.

A couple of EIRT officers escorted us to the exit. I stepped out to a mild but sunny day and just enjoyed feeling the sunshine on my skin.

Blue wandered off to an area with shadows and opened a portal. Her purple eyes gazed at me and she asked, "Are you coming?"

I shook my head and said, "I'll meet you at home. I'm going to fly home and burn off some of this excess power I have flowing through me."

Blue nodded and disappeared into the shadows. I smiled, gathered my power, and took to the sky.

Chapter 36

Tuesday, May 13

“**O**h my God! I'm home!” yelled Olivia from the basement. The sun had just set, and our vampire was now wide awake. There was a crash not even a second later as Liv came through the basement door so fast that it almost came off its hinges. Alteea fluttered in the air behind her.

Stella was the closest to the door and the first in the path of Hurricane Liv. She was snatched off her feet and wrapped up in a hug in less than a second.

“Stella! I missed your sweet little face!” gushed Liv.

Blue stepped back behind Bree. After finishing with Stella, Bree was next.

“There's my bestie! Prison life was hard; I was so bored. I want to go hunting, watch movies, do each other's nails, go driving… Oh, and go shopping, especially shopping.”

Blue tried to move behind me, but I blocked her path and Liv got her next. “I was so bored, I even wanted to go training. Can we train, but not tonight, maybe tomorrow night?”

Liv released Blue and her green eyes locked on me. Before I could blink, I suddenly had Liv pressed up against me and her lips on mine.

“There's my tasty Elemental…” she said without breaking the kiss.

I was trying to behave myself, but Liv felt really good at this moment and the kiss deepened.

Liv moved from my lips and her warm breath was on my right ear and in a loud lusty voice, she said, “Damn, prison life wasn't the only thing hard around here…” and she ground herself into me to prove her point.

I felt heat fill my cheeks.

“Liv! Not in front of the children!” said Bree.

I popped my eyes open and laughed as Bree had her hand over Stella's eyes and a teasing grin on her face.

Liv burst out laughing and said, “Sorry.”

She moved away from me and I shifted more behind the counter to hide my, um, excitement from everyone.

The doorbell rang, and now it was Bree's turned to move faster than light. She rushed for the front door and returned carrying six large pizzas and a smile.

Liv let out a deep sigh of pleasure as she opened the fridge and spotted the three brimming pint mugs of blood waiting for her there.

"Thank God," she said as she picked up one of the glasses and drained a good half of it in one long pull. "Did you know in prison, they only gave me one pint a day? Sure, I can get by on that, but I may have missed the Food-O-Tron more than anything else..."

She finished the rest of the glass and grabbed another full one. This time she also found a shot glass and poured some out for Alteea who was hovering anxiously nearby looking for her share.

They both joined us at the table as we started digging into our pizza. I'd been looking forward to a nice medium-rare steak as my first meal when I got out, but I had to admit the warm gooey pizza and the ice-cold beer were both going down nicely. When I went inside, there was a part of me that was worried that I'd never have another dinner like this with my team. As I sat there listening to excited conversation and laughter around the table, I was glad that I was getting that chance.

During dinner, we talked about how we passed the time inside. Blue shrugged and said, "Yoga and meditation," and I got the feeling she could have done this for months without an issue. I told them about the *Game of Thrones* book that Ray dropped off for me.

"You got a book?" asked Liv with an annoyed tone in her voice.

"You wouldn't have liked it—there weren't any pictures."

Liv flipped me the bird and said, "I was going crazy in there; it may have been days, but it felt like every second was an eternity." She shuddered and added, "So bored."

"Hey," I said, "at least for most of the time you were in your death-trance; it could have been December."

Liv nodded somberly at that.

After dinner, Blue and Stella announced that they were going to the English court to visit Sarah and retrieve our briefcases of cash.

"You two be sure to come back here once you have the money... No stopovers in Vegas, you hear?" I said.

Stella laughed, and Blue's tail twitched playfully as they disappeared into the shadows. Once they'd left, the rest of us retired to the living room and spent our time just talking and having a good time. Maybe too much of a good time on my part; by the time Stella and Blue returned a few hours later, I had a pretty good buzz going on.

"We're going to get some sleep," said Stella. Then she held up the two briefcases she was carrying and added, "We'll deposit these first thing tomorrow when the bank opens. Good night."

We all wished them a good night and got back to talking. Liv snuggled up to me and said, "I think we should do a little celebrating on our own now..."

"Yeah, about that..." I said. "I'm a bit concerned that Bree will hear us, um, you know."

Bree's head popped up at that and Liv frowned. "You're really worried about what she'll hear?"

I forced myself to keep a straight face and said, "Yeah, if she hears our hot lusty sex, I'm afraid she'll feel left out... I think it would be better for everyone if she just joined us..."

A couch cushion flew at me and Liv beat me a couple of times with a pillow.

Bree licked her lips and said, "Liv, maybe he has a point..."

Liv's head shot around and glared at Bree. Bree burst out laughing and said, "It probably will take both of us to drag his drunken ass to bed."

They both cracked up at that. A few minutes later, I did end up with both lovely ladies in my room, but they just dumped me on my bed, turned off the light, and left me to sleep it off.

***

The next morning when I woke up, I had two pleasant surprises. First, I wasn't anywhere near as hungover as I probably should have been. Second, my phone was buzzing, which was what had woken me.

"Hey, Airhead, glad to hear you won't be wearing orange any longer," said Rob.

"Rob! Dude, it is so good to hear your voice. You doing okay? Any odd side effects from the coma, like you're suddenly a good poker player or you now suffer from erectile dysfunction?"

"Nope, I'm back to being 100 percent me. Your healer friend did good work."

I'm embarrassed to admit it, but as we talked my eyes welled up a couple of times. Must have been springtime allergies.

We chatted for a good half an hour and then Rob got to the reason he was calling, "Annette is going to pop soon, so I thought this Friday I'd have a poker game before I have to start being a respectable father. Besides, babies are expensive, so cleaning you guys out of money will help offset that."

"Don't count your chickens so quickly. My prison time really sharpened my poker game. I had to play well enough to keep me in the lifestyle that I am accustomed to. I had to win enough cigarettes and money off the other inmates to bribe the guards to smuggle in luxuries for me..."

Rob laughed and said, "Whatever. I happen to know you were in solitary confinement the whole time..."

***

I checked the e-mail on my phone to see what I'd missed since being locked up. There was an e-mail that had been there for a few days from Captain Cooper. It had the federal claim number for the bounty on the Acolytes and all the documentation we needed to make the claim. That would be my priority after I got some breakfast.

I found Stella and Blue in the kitchen with a laptop open in front of them.

"The money is back in the bank," said Stella, "and I have just finished transferring the funds back to everyone's personal accounts. Between getting dinged on exchange rates, legal fees, and the English vampire court's fees, we are out about $250,000."

I grimaced at that, but then smiled and said, "Captain Cooper e-mailed me the Acolyte claim information, so even with those expenses we are still going to be up at least one-point-five million."

"Speaking of bounties," said Stella. "There is a new one posted; they are offering five million for capturing the Master."

That was one bounty I'd really like to get. That man had a lot of blood on his hands. Besides the three people the Acolyte teams had killed, there was also the deaths of the twenty-four Acolytes themselves he needed to pay for. I thought about Paula Priest, Bug Girl's mom, and how she would never see her daughter again. I hoped in time that she might get over it, but losing a child was something you never really got over.

As I made my breakfast, I thought about the Master. We had no idea where to find him. All we knew was an alias and that he was an older English gentleman. Blue's hologram disguise popped into my head, and if he was wearing something like that when he visited Terror-Byte and his mother, he might even be a she and the accent might have been faked too. We also had no idea what he was building with all the stolen items. I'd hoped that having all three teams taken down would halt those plans, but I got the feeling it would just be a temporary setback for him. I still worried that there were more Acolyte teams hiding and training at this moment. At least going forward, after seeing the footage of how the other teams met their grisly ends, he'd have a much harder time recruiting troubled Enhanceds in the future.

I joined Stella and Blue at the table and ate my breakfast. Stella informed me that she updated her alert system to scan for any mention of the Master as well. It would also still be monitoring for industrial break-ins, in case any new Acolyte teams did appear. Stella said that she and Blue were going to do some searches to see if there were any new leads on the Master. I didn't expect they'd find anything but wished them well.

Bree had told us about what she'd learned of the Master and the Acolytes while she was captured. This whole, 'he is preparing for the war against the humans,' shtick he was peddling didn't ring true to me. If he was so concerned about Enhanced Individuals, he wouldn't have murdered more than twenty-four of them when the Acolytes were caught. No, he was just another power-hungry asshole who used those poor kids for his own benefit.

I had no doubt that he was still out there and up to no good. There was no trace of him for now but when he did pop his head up again, we'd be there to stop him. And now we had five million more reasons to nail his ass.

Epilogue

I'd been looking forward to Rob's poker game all week, and Friday was finally here. At around two that afternoon, Rob's name came up on my phone.

"We had a boy!" Rob practically yelled from the other end.

"Holy crap, dude! That's awesome! I thought Annette wasn't due for another couple of weeks?"

"Yeah, she was early, but both she and the baby are doing fine."

"That's good to hear. Does the little guy have a name yet?" I asked.

"Ian Robert Quinn."

I smiled; Ian was Rob's grandfather's name. He and Rob had been close. He had passed away about five years ago. I loved that Rob had chosen to honor him this way.

We chatted for a few minutes and I found out that Annette was up, and they were happy to have visitors. Rob had more calls to make so I told him I'd see him soon and let him go.

I tracked down Stella and Blue and told them the good news. Blue opened a shadow portal and the three of us went to go visit. Blue turned on her old man disguise before we went through. We came out in an empty room two doors down from where Annette was.

Rob's parents were just coming out of the room with big grins on their faces. We stopped and chatted with them for a bit before popping in to see Rob, Annette, and baby Ian.

Annette looked tired and worn out but happy. She was holding this tiny little thing in her arms while Rob hovered beside them as proud as can be. They glanced up as we entered. Both smiled and then frowned at the strange old man beside Stella and me.

Blue dropped the disguise for a few seconds, waved, and then reactivated it. Rob and Annette both had looks of surprise and awe.

"That is an amazing piece of tech you have, Blue," said Rob, shaking his head.

Blue nodded. "Thank you, but not as impressive as that cute little guy Annette is holding."

Rob just grinned in agreement at that.

"You know, having Annette go into labor and deliver a baby just to get out of losing money to me tonight at poker is a new low, even for you, buddy," I teased.

Rob laughed and said, "Isn't it great that I have a wife that will do small things like that for me?"

We hung out, chatted, and admired Ian for a good ten minutes or so before a nurse came by to check on mother and son and shooed us all out of the room. We said our goodbyes to Annette and baby.

"You ready for all of this?" I asked with a grin once we were out in the hallway.

Rob shrugged and said, "I hope so. I still can't believe I'm a dad. I mean I knew I was going to be one, but now that I can actually hold him and see him…"

"You'll be a great dad," I said, clapping him on the shoulder. "Besides, even if you suck at it, I'm sure Annette will be the world's greatest mom."

"I'm still off on medical leave for the next couple of weeks, and I'm probably going to take extra time off to help Annette with the baby, so try and stay out of trouble since I won't be around to bail you out."

I nodded and said, "You just focus on that lovely family, and I'll keep my head down."

We chatted for a few minutes and I told him that when they were all home and settled that we'd come by and visit.

Blue took us home.

***

Liv was both excited and pissed about the new baby. By the time she woke, visiting hours were over at the hospital and Liv wanted to see Ian. Blue came to her rescue and said the maternity ward was quiet and she could sneak us in via the shadows to see the baby.

This is how we found ourselves a few minutes later standing in front of the window to the maternity ward, watching Ian sleeping in his clear crib.

Bree and Liv were both gushing over little Ian while Stella kept watch.

"Oh my God! He is so cute; I want one!" said Liv excitedly.

"I'm willing to try if you are," I said with a leer.

"You know as a vampire, I can't have kids," answered Liv sadly.

"Not with an attitude like that you won't!" I said and added, "C'mon, there is probably an empty supply closet around here somewhere…"

Liv shook her head. "I'm not having sex in a supply closet!"

"Hey, don't be mad at me. You were the one that wanted a baby. I was just trying to help."

Liv stepped closer to me and put her arm around me. I slipped my arm around her too. I smiled when she leaned into me, gave me a chaste kiss on the cheek, and said, "I know. Now shut up and just admire the view."

I looked down at Ian, sleeping peacefully, and took her advice.

The End.

Author's Note

I hope you have enjoyed reading the Bounty series as much as I have writing it. If you could leave an honest review from wherever you purchased this book, that would much appreciated.

In 2017, my goal was to write and publish three books. With this book finished, that goal has been accomplished. I have plans to write more books in this series but that will entirely depend on the sales of the first three novels. I have already written the drafts for books four and five, and I'm currently working on the outline for book six.

If you are a fan of series and want to keep up to date with what is going on, please visit my website at http://www.markusmatthews.com or my Facebook page at https://www.facebook.com/TheBountySeries/.

Also, if you want to give feedback or have questions, you can e-mail me at me@markusmatthews.com. I'd love to hear your thoughts on the series.

Lastly, thank you for reading and supporting the series, I can't express enough how much that means to me.

-Markus Matthews (August 2019)

Printed in Great Britain
by Amazon